# BLOOD JUSTICE

## APOCALYPSE CHRONICLES
### BOOK 2

## DARREL SPARKMAN

ROUGH
EDGES
PRESS

Rough Edges Press
An Imprint of Wolfpack Publishing
9850 S. Maryland Parkway, Suite A-5 #323
Las Vegas, Nevada 89183

roughedgespress.com

Paperback ISBN 978-1-68549-284-7
eBook ISBN 978-1-68549-283-0
LCCN 2023935174

# BLOOD JUSTICE

# ONE

LANE TILTED his head and slipped the punch that would have felled him like Thor's Hammer dropping on a box of pretzels. A testament to Dickie's oversized brute power was the hole left in the drywall behind him. He had a vision of the man's hand waving around outside the building, having gone through the wall, insulation, and outdoor metal siding. The lucky bastard had missed the stud.

It had been like this for three weeks, played out in different scenes with the same actors and similar results. The Gallows Bar and Grill was on the north side of White Rock at the junction of H Highway and MO 160. It used to be a small convenience store until Casey's General Store and the Dollar Store moved into town, once again proving there was no customer loyalty when a cheaper price was waved in front of them.

An enterprising and well-traveled woman bought the place cheap, named it The Gallows, and remodeled. Now it was a decent bar with live music and dancing on Saturday night. Weekdays, music and YouTube videos were streamed to the big screen on the wall. If any alter-cations broke out, Ruby turned up the volume. There was a karaoke setup if anyone felt the urge to humiliate them-selves. The last three Fridays, Jim made it his favorite place to stop in the early afternoon to grab a beer and take a chunk out of Dickie.

The Good Old Boys were a local group of rednecks and junior high dropouts that fancied themselves a gang. Hence the GOB gang tags painted on a few buildings around town. Railroad trestles and overpasses were the next-best favorites. What they didn't have in planning and sophistication, were compensated with pure mean-ness and dedication to their craft. Depending on the amount of meth and alcohol consumed, they got into a fair amount of trouble. The gang's leader held court at a table in the corner, surrounded by lackeys and wannabes. He and Dickie could have been twins in size and muscle.

"Hey, Dickie." Sidestepping away from the man, Jim's voice lashed out. "Why in God's name would someone with the last name of Johnson name their boy Dick?"

With a roar, Dickie splintered the wall while pulling his arm out and swung at him again with a bleeding hand. At least some of the razor-sharp drywall screws had tagged him. Ducking the clumsy move, Jim hooked a jab into the man's short ribs, right under his heart. Gasping for breath, Dickie's face blanched as he went to one knee, clutching his left side. His pained glance went to his boss, sitting at the corner table.

Following his gaze, Jim spoke to the man sitting there. "Roman, tell your boy to give it up. He's not looking so good."

Roman Fielding laughed. "Nah. This amuses me. There's not much entertainment on Fridays, at least not this early. I'll keep him going until you decide to stop coming into our bar."

Jim grinned at the man. "You don't like me?"

"Like you?" Roman snorted. "This ain't high school. But you're right. I don't. You have pig written all over you and you're cozied up with that lady sheriff. You got no reason to be here."

"Now, see? That's a problem. It's still a semi-free country, and I don't like to be told what to do." He gestured toward the bartender, a large woman with sleeve tats and unmanageable bottle-blond hair. "I'll leave when the owner says I have to."

The silence was so complete he looked around to see if the electricity was still on. It was broken only by Dickie's labored wheezing and the thunk of the minute hand on the clock as it hit three thirty. It was too early in the afternoon to be drinking, so the place was mostly deserted.

"Sorry, Jim," Ruby spoke up from behind the bar and he thought he saw genuine regret. "I've sold out."

"Sold out?" He stared at her a moment. Property or loyalty? "Who to?" He shook his head. Trying to be a writer was ruining his speech. "To whom?"

"Hey." Roman waved a piece of paper and grinned at him. "I think these are your walking papers."

Jim took a deep breath and nearly choked on someone's cigar smoke before meeting Ruby's gaze. "Are you safe working here? The sale wasn't forced?"

She chuckled and shook her head. "You mean am I afraid of these boys? Not a bit. I've got more family than they have gang members and we know where they live." She made a point of looking at Roman. "All of them. Besides," she continued, "I turned a tidy profit. I just may retire. My back's been acting up and I don't get around like I used to."

Jim glanced around the bar, finally landing his gaze on the new owner. "Well, shit."

Roman gave him a smile that didn't reach his eyes. "Sorry. See the sign behind the bar? We reserve the right to refuse service."

Jim shrugged. It was time to end this. He had plenty of work at home for exercise. Turning back to his assailant, he smiled. "Do women call you Little Dickie for a reason?"

After a quick glance at his boss, Dickie whined and came at him again. Jim backed him up with a straight jab to the throat. When the man lifted his hands to his neck with a strangled groan, Jim kicked him in the balls. Dickie dropped like a sack of potatoes. Watching him for a moment, curled on the floor in his own vomit, he glanced at Roman.

"Since you're the boss, you clean this mess up. Don't bother Ruby with it. See you around, big man."

He turned to the door and then stopped. "One more thing. Three weeks ago, you turned your dog loose on Dan Hyatt. Remember him?"

Roman's gaze was flat; his face showed no expression. "No. Should I?"

Jim nodded. "You should because he might be the death of you. He's a man about half my size. Just a simple farmer living hardscrabble west of here. Probably didn't have an enemy in the world. Got a wife and little girl, trying to make a living row-cropping against the big corporate farms. On the way back from Springfield, he got the crazy urge for a beer and stopped in here. You turned Dickie loose on him."

He paused long enough to kick Dickie in the ribs. "Your dog beat him to within an inch of his life and then tried to kick that inch out from under him. I assume for your amusement. Right now, Hyatt is fighting for his life in the ICU at Mercy in Springfield."

The big man looked away. "I seem to recall something about that. No arrests were made. No witnesses. It's all hearsay. I believe it went down as a fight gone bad with unknown participants. Correct?"

He stared at Roman a moment, sidestepping Dickie as the man tried to get up from his own mess, slipped and fell. "Know this. If that young farmer dies, there's going to be a lot of hurt going on before he's buried. And it won't happen to Dickie."

When he turned to walk out, he came face to face with Sheriff Rita Morris. All six foot of her, with raven-black hair, deep-blue eyes and filling out her uniform like a cartoonist's fantasy. Studying him with a frown, she slowly folded her aviator sunglasses and hung them over the top button of her shirt. His gaze followed, getting hung up on the freckles showing on her chest, and then swept up to her eyes. He thought some softness lingered in her gaze but could have been mistaken.

He touched a finger to the brim of his used-to-be white Stetson Cruiser. "Good afternoon, Sheriff."

She stood blinking against the darkness of the bar's interior. After a quick look around, her gaze centered on Jim. If she were a singer, fans would say she had a whiskey voice—low and throaty, always with emotion. Country music fans would flash to Lorrie Morgan if they were old enough.

If he were a bomb wrapped in a cardboard box and

tied with a big red bow, her stare couldn't have been more intense.

"Guess what? An anonymous caller reported someone disturbing the peace at The Gallows. And wouldn't you know, as I walk in, you threaten a man in front of witnesses." She glanced at Dickie with raised eyebrows. "And you're standing by a man on the floor who is holding his balls. My guess is you're the disturbance. Imagine my surprise."

He shrugged and smiled. "What are you doing here? I didn't think you rolled on bar fights. Where's White Rock PD's finest?"

"Not that it's your concern, but Russell is out sick today. The flu season is early this year. So, what's going on? Are bar fights on the MMA circuit now? You taking up cage fighting?"

He tried to find humor in her expression—didn't. His glance cut to Ruby innocently polishing a shot glass. His scowl at her didn't get any reaction. If she wasn't intimidated by Roman Fielding, she sure wouldn't be bothered by him.

"Sorry. Just having a discussion with that bag of shit sitting in the corner. Dickie kept getting in the way and falling. He might have an inner ear problem that should be checked out. I've heard that's a miserable existence." He glanced at Dickie. "And that's one miserable person."

"Dammit, Jim. I heard what you said. As much as I hate to admit it, Roman is right. There were no witnesses concerning Hyatt. You don't even know where he was assaulted or by whom. He was found on the square in front of the courthouse steps. For all we know, it could have been a gang of chimpanzees, at least until he wakes up to talk."

"He was dumped like a piece of garbage on the square." He glanced back at Roman. "It doesn't matter. I got all the information I need, Sheriff."

She grabbed him by the arm. "Let's go outside."

"Is this official?"

She didn't answer as they banged through the reinforced wooden door. He let himself be shoved against her patrol SUV, parked with the motor still running and the strobes on.

"I thought you were supposed to take your keys out. Aren't you afraid someone will steal your ride?" He grunted as she pushed him again. "Gonna frisk me?"

Rita stood with her hand on her duty belt. "You idiot. You're not helping. We both know what *may have* happened to Hyatt, but my hands are tied. Besides, I don't need to frisk you. I know what you're carrying and where both are, plus the knife. If you were going to shoot me, you'd have done it a long time ago. I have one warning for you. Stay out of this. You are not an officer of the law. You have no standing, no authority. No nothing. Stay. Out. Of. County. Business." Her finger punctuated the last few words into his chest.

"Jesus, Rita. Lay off with the kung fu finger fighting. I'm going to be bruised." His glance wandered toward the bar while he rubbed his chest. "Not sure I can stay out of this."

"Why? I know it's a bad deal, but what's this guy to you? There are tragedies all over the world. I don't see you selling everything and sending them money, or trying to fight their windmills."

"Windmills? That's good." He stared at her a moment, finally deciding to confide in her. "If you really want to know, I was in the Hot Spot the other day picking up my daily dose of Twinkies. I may change, though. They've cut down the amount of filling."

He smiled as she rolled her eyes. "Anyway, there was this jar on the counter asking for donations for the Hyatt family. It was the usual—no insurance, running behind on bills, need help, pray for us...all that. While I was standing there, a little girl came in the door, about nine or ten years old and from her looks, she'd been missing meals. All bones and big eyes, she could barely reach the jar to see if anyone had left anything. Damn near broke my heart."

Rita nodded. "She's Janie. Her mom's Jana. They're stuck on the letter J. See? I do know them. Is that it? I'm still not getting the point."

"Will you let me finish?" He combed his fingers through his hair, dislodging his hat. With a deft catch, he stood rolling the brim. "I could see the mother outside in a junker of a car, waiting on the girl. She was crying and looked like ten miles of bad road. Anyway, I contributed."

"What did you do?" Her eyes softened as she shook her head. "How much?"

"I'd just made a withdrawal." He shrugged and smiled. "Thought I'd go over to Trader Jack's and buy a new AR—he has some new ones with an IR scope. Those infra reds are sweet. Anyway, I gave the money to her."

For a moment, her face took on a cartoon look with round eyes and mouth. "Jim, that's over a thousand dollars! I'm sure they can use it, but..."

"A thousand?" He rolled his eyes. "I wish. Try two thousand. Prices are going through the roof right now."

"Two...?"

"She looked hungry." He shrugged. "All that heartache, Rita. All that hardship. Just because that animal Dickie likes to hurt people and Roman likes to watch. I figure before I'm done, Roman is going to volunteer to support that family. I think I'll suggest he take out a life insurance policy and make them the beneficiary. A big one."

She was shaking her head, trying to hold eye contact. "It'd be drug money and I'm going to pretend I didn't hear that last part."

"Like a hungry belly cares about where the money for food comes from?" He clapped his hat on his head and turned toward his truck. "It ain't right, Rita. And you know it."

"Of course I know it." Her shoulders slumped, expelling a long sigh. "Still, it's county business. Please stay out of it." Her voice hardened. "That's an order, Jim."

His laugh was a short bark as he held his hands up, palms out. "Sure. Whatever you say, Rita. Life goes on. Nothing to see here. Move along. Right?"

She continued in a softer voice. "Look, we're bumping heads and shouldn't be. Will you be home tonight? Maybe I can come by later. I can't stay, but we need to talk."

He gave her a startled look. "You do realize that nothing good ever happens when a woman tells a man they need to talk?"

Her gaze saddened as it raked across him, and he felt the razor's edge of it. "Jim, think about it. You're starting down the same road as last year. I don't know if I can go with you. It's like violence is a cloud that follows you around. You stay clean for a while and then boom—there you go again. If you keep getting into trouble, I can't protect you. No one can."

"So, from that comment, you think I'm addicted to

violence? Like some adrenaline junkie? Sweet, Rita. Thanks for the support."

He tried to see the similarities but couldn't. Last year he'd caught his girlfriend in bed with another man and had inflicted some damage on him. Hindsight? He shouldn't have done it. But doing that, he'd stepped into a world of payback by a lower-level Russian operator who took umbrage to the ass-kicking he got. When the Russian sent someone to kill him, the war started. He often thought he should have just disappeared. The loss of friends and heartache wasn't worth the vindication.

"So, last year." He stared at her until she met his gaze. "I should have let them kill me. That would have made things simpler for you?"

Color drained from her face, leaving red spots where her jaw was clenched. Her angry reply was interrupted when the radio in her SUV squawked in unison with her belt unit with some incomprehensible babble. With a despairing look, she left him standing there as she peeled out of the parking lot in her police interceptor, the blue and white strobes making him wince.

He waved at the receding vehicle. "Nice talking to you. We'll do it again sometime."

His voice sounded pathetic as he shouted after her. Shit. They'd had a passably good year, but she'd been pulling away for months. Maybe that was his record. Maybe that's the length of time it takes for a woman to get tired of him. One thing he knew—both were too old to be playing games, especially when he wasn't sure of the rules.

And Rita? Lately he felt like an oil slick on her pond water.

# TWO

RITA KEYED HER SHOULDER MIC. "Three twenty-five responding. Two minutes."

The bored dispatcher responded, "Three twenty-five. Fourteen forty."

She violently shook her head to dislodge the tears threatening to blur her sight as she tried to take her mind off her conversation with Jim. Pounding on the steering wheel didn't seem to help. "Dammit. Dammit. Dammit!"

At forty-one, they were both the same age. Part of their backgrounds were similar—military police, although Jim's last ten years had been with an organization called the Shepherds that specialized in high-risk rescue. He was the bad-boy-needing-nurture hunk that women dreamed of. Good looking in a way that left young girls breathless and older women with speculation in their eyes.

Why was she so conflicted, pushing him away? They fit together well. Very well. They'd crossed that sweaty bridge a long time ago. But dark water was flowing beneath the bridge. Both had their skeletons that left them staring into the darkness. Both held sadness that the other could not make go away. Hers was her late husband, a sheriff killed while conducting a traffic stop, catapulting her into the county sheriff's position by default as the senior deputy.

Jim's unrelenting memory was a rescue gone bad, leaving him haunted with the death of a woman and child he was supposed to save. Why was nothing simple?

Time for introspection ran out as she focused on the call. A mile away and just around the curve, her youngest deputy, Allison Crewes, had a car stopped for speeding on Highway 160. The car had pulled into a parking lot, points to the driver for thinking of the safety of both officer and civilians and had stopped with the vehicle's flashers on. More points.

But since the dark tinted windows wouldn't allow her to see inside the vehicle, the deputy called for backup while running the plates. It was a late model Chevy Equinox and could be holding any number of people. It was a nightmare for traffic enforcement.

Rita pulled in behind the deputy's patrol car, seeing her standing behind the open driver's door. Leaving her own vehicle's strobes on, she walked up to Allison and put a hand on her shoulder. The girl flinched, although she had to know Rita had stopped.

"A little tense, are we?" Rita chuckled.

A beat-up old Ford pickup drove by. The driver beeped the horn, kids waving—curious to see what was going on. The girls were sitting four across on the bench seat, which meant no seat belts. With the small-town advantage, she knew their parents and would be speaking to them when time allowed.

Allison gave her a grim smile. "Yeah, I guess. I started

to walk up to the driver's side, but my gut told me no. I backed off because I couldn't see inside. Am I a wimp for doing that?"

Shaking her head, Rita patted her shoulder again. "Always trust your gut, Allison. Always. Every time. This isn't a matter of being brave and disregarding safety. You did the right thing."

The van was dark red with deep-tinted windows. Missouri law said a thirty-five percent tint was the maximum, but every state differed. These windows had to be at least fifty percent. She had a fleeting thought, wondering how many officer's lives would be saved if tinted windows were outlawed. As it was, LEOs, law enforcement officers, risked their lives every day walking up to vehicles that they couldn't see into. She knew two patrolmen had died in Oklahoma last week, pulled into an ambush by a vehicle similar to this.

The deputy continued. "The plates came back registered to Roberts Farm. That's on the west edge of Limestone County, out on the prairie. I think that's Grant township. So, I guess it's legit."

She nodded to her deputy, knowing Limestone County was topographically cut in half. The western part was all prairie farmland and row crops, mostly with large family farms. The fertile prairie was nurtured well and produced record crops. The eastern half of the county was hill country, populated by the bottom half of Stockton Lake to the north. Cattle and horse farms dotted the rolling hills, at least the parts the government didn't own. It was beautiful country.

"Okay," Rita acknowledged, drawn back to the matter at hand. "Let's do this a little different. People with windows tinted this deep should expect a little extra inconvenience."

She reached in and switched on the PA in Allison's cruiser, keying the microphone hanging on the dash. "In the vehicle. I need the driver to drop the keys out the window." Seeing the window lower and the keys drop, she continued. "Driver, please exit and come around to the back of the vehicle."

The driver's side door opened and a dark-complexioned man moved out of the van, showing his hands first. Experienced at this? He walked around and stood by the back hatch. Wearing a tucked-in T-shirt and jeans, she could tell he wasn't armed—unless he had an ankle gun. The man still had an indent from wearing a hat tight on his head.

"Good job and thank you, sir. Now, everyone in the van, please come out and stand by the van."

The driver turned his head and spoke in rapid-fire Spanish. The side door slid open, and people came piling out. The total for the vehicle was two males, two females, and four small children. Her first thought was the clown car in a circus.

She spoke to Allison as she moved around to face the occupants of the SUV. "I'll cover you while you make sure they don't have weapons. I know they look innocent but always check. No matter what. You might say your life depends on it."

"There are no weapons," the driver spoke quickly.

"I understand, sir. Once we have someone exit a vehicle, we have to check. I'm sure you understand." Rita nodded to him as she stood with her hand on her service weapon while her deputy did a quick once-over. Once that was done and she stepped back, Rita opened the back hatch of the van to make sure no one else was hiding inside. Satisfied it was empty, she came around and spoke to the driver.

"Are you the only English speaker here?"

The man shrugged, handing her his license and insurance card.

Very well versed. Glancing at the back of the license for any restrictions, she saw he was a veteran. "Thank you for your service, sir." She looked him over. While not large, he looked solid as a rock. "Marines?"

The man shrugged and nodded. When he didn't speak, she asked. "Who do you work for, Mr. Estevez?"

"We work for Roberts Farms, me and my brother and our families, although I'm looking for other work now. I sometimes work for Donny Ray and Jacy Mane—helping with the horses."

She studied the man as he returned her gaze. None of the tells, like rapid blinking, swallowing, sweating, or plain nervousness, were showing. He seemed almost too calm.

"What kind of work do you do at Roberts Farm?" She handed back the license and insurance paper while she studied the group. The other man watched with a curious expression and small smile. The women were a little apprehensive, while the children openly grinned at her as they squirmed around their mothers' restraining hands, trying to get away. Rita smiled back—couldn't help it.

"Well, we were harvesting and sorting cucumbers, but that season is over. Now it's mostly cleanup and repair. The work has slowed, pretty much."

Rita nodded. She'd seen it before. Many farms used the cheaper labor the Mexicans provided. She knew most local farms paid minimum wage, or better. If they worked and paid their own way, mainly not on the government dole, she didn't care. It was obvious where they'd been. The back of the van was full of groceries.

"Do you know why you were stopped and told to exit the vehicle?"

Estevez shrugged. "I assume I was speeding?"

"You were." She glanced at Allison. "I don't know how fast you were going. The reason I asked you to leave the vehicle was the dark tint on the windows. Officers get nervous when we can't see inside. I'm sure you've heard about police being shot while approaching a vehicle? I lost my husband that way, so it's a real problem. That's the only reason you were treated differently than a normal traffic stop."

He nodded, glancing at his family. "I have heard of these things, in this country and worse in Mexico. We're supplied the van by Roberts Farm, so there is not much we can do about the windows. Thanks for being honest about it and my condolences." He grinned at her, teeth flashing under an impressive mustache. "I promise no harassment suits."

Her husband was the county sheriff when he was killed, while she was a deputy. He'd stopped a pickup for speeding and when he walked up, the driver fired through the door. It was always on her mind.

"Well, not that it would go anywhere, but I appreciate that. Okay, Mr. Estevez, y'all can go on home. Next time you come through town, be sure and check the speed limit signs." She smiled at him. "They're not just a suggestion, as some people think."

Estevez grinned and nodded as the family piled back into the van. She smiled back at him, his family's actions proving they understood English. The saying, salt of the earth, occurred to her. These were good people. He was a veteran, so obviously legal. Who knew about the others? She didn't mind them coming across the border looking for a better life, knowing what kind of shithole was behind them.

According to the Border Patrol, the Hispanics were a small percentage of that illegal traffic. It was the jihadis, gang bangers and other criminals she objected to—not that it did any good. No one was going to ask for her opinion. The subject was a political football being kicked around constantly, with little thought to the people concerned.

As the family drove off, Deputy Crewes spoke, puzzlement clouding her voice. "Why'd you let them go? I'm betting there wasn't a green card among them."

"What's the point? The driver had a valid license. Anyone else would have gotten a warning, too, just like them. If we contact ICE, they wouldn't come. If we hold them, the county has to feed them. And then we'll probably let them go anyway. And deportation? Another group would take their place by the next day. Better to let them go. They're just trying to make a living and survive the best they can."

The deputy was adamant. "Doesn't seem right to let them go without a ticket. They're breaking the law."

Rita stared at her deputy. "Well, here's the straight scoop. We'll call this a teachable moment. There are enough laws written to paper mâché the whole United States and Congress passes more every day—often laws that are already on the books. Not all of them are good ones. There's a lot of judgment that goes with this job, Deputy Crewes. We often need to decide what to enforce and how to do it. You should decide early what you'll tolerate and where to draw the line. Then, be consistent. Learn to pick your battles. You can't fight all the time."

———————

RITA SAT in the empty parking lot after the family of Mexicans and Officer Crewes had left. Her mind returned to Jim Lane. What had she told Allison? Pick your battles? Could she take her own advice? What were they to each other? Lovers? Infrequent...at least, now. Confidants? Not anymore. Too many roadblocks between them. It had been a long time since they discussed anything over breakfast. Both still held secrets from the other. Friends with benefits? Maybe, but the benefits had dwindled. That was her fault. She knew he wanted more and didn't know how to tell him she wasn't ready.

The biggest question was...what did she want? Was her desire to keep the sheriff's job still tied to her late husband, trying to please his memory? That was a fair assessment. She would admit to that. He'd loved the job and died in the line of duty. Was she honoring his memory by staying on with the job?

The truth was, by keeping on with the responsibility of being a county sheriff, she was shutting Jim out. Limestone was the smallest county in Missouri and she was understaffed. She had to do patrols and answer calls like everyone else. And the paperwork. Oh god, the paperwork.

All she had for deputies were Frank Tucker, an aging policeman who held down the office and doubled as the jailer for their holding cell before prisoners were shipped off to Springfield, or an adjoining county with better facilities. The man wasn't physically in shape to do anything else.

Next senior was PJ Rails, a steroid-laced bodybuilder who, by his own admission, wanted experience so he could move up to a more exciting job. He was a slow learner, self-limiting with an overblown opinion of himself and would be lucky someone didn't shoot him. Her junior deputy was Allison Crewes, a petite ex-gymnast who was their Energizer Bunny. It wasn't enough manpower to police a county that took in half of Stockton Lake with a good number of tourists. The bottom southwest quarter of the county was usually peaceful, leaning mostly to row crops on the prairie.

The rest of her county? It may as well have been in the mountains of Kentucky. There were a few beef ranches, fescue was about all the rocky ground would grow, but the rest was hardscrabble small farms. A good part of production coming out of places set back in the timber and brush wasn't legal.

She filled her lungs and expelled a long sigh. She and Jim needed to have a sit-down and talk things through. It was overdue. One thing she knew—he wanted more of a commitment than an occasional bed warmer, and she didn't have any more to offer. The perverse gut-wrenching realization was that she didn't want to lose him and didn't know how to keep him.

# THREE

THE LOW RUMBLE of dual exhaust brought Rita's attention to her window as she sat shuffling papers into neat piles on her desk. Her in-box was full, the out-box empty. Roman Fielding stepped out of his deep-red Dodge Challenger SRT. She marveled that a man his size could squeeze into such a vehicle. He was at least six foot six inches tall, maybe taller, with bulging muscles. One arm was inked with an ugly arm sleeve. Of course, he always wore sleeveless shirts. She snorted at the sight and shook her head. Limestone County's self-proclaimed God's gift to women was heading her way.

In a few moments Fielding's form filled her doorway. "Rita? May I have a word, please?"

Well, how polite. She kept her head down, staring at the latest report about an overnight smash-and-grab in businesses around the square. As a deterrent, she was giving serious thought to turning loose a pack of German Shepherds to patrol the area. With a sigh, she finally looked at him and gestured toward a chair in front of her desk—smirked when he wedged into it. If he stood in a hurry, the chair would go with him. While he watched, she opened a drawer and pulled out a pistol and laid it on the desktop.

"What can I do for you, Mr. Fielding?"

"Whoa." He eyed the gun. "That ain't very friendly. Is that a Judge?"

She shook her head. "No, although it could be a judge and jury. Actually, it's a Smith and Wesson Governor. Hold six shots instead of five, like the Judge. You might be interested to know that I alternate rounds in this wheel gun. It has both .410 shot shells and .45 ACP."

Fielding looked startled for a moment and then grinned at her. "That's so heavy, I could grab it before you can lift it and fire. Kind of useless. I'm thinking it's all for show." He paused. "I ain't scared."

"It is damned heavy." Rita nodded. "That might be a problem if I needed to pick it up. But all I have to do is pull the trigger right where it's sitting—which would be dicey—and let the gun move." She reached out and cocked the hammer. "I wouldn't bet your life on how quick I can do that. You don't look all that fast."

His gaze shuttled between her and the pistol.

"Well?" she prompted. "Do you have business, or are you here just to admire my weaponry?"

He centered his gaze on her. "I need you to call off your dog."

She stared at him a moment, knowing where he was going long before he said it. "My dog? I don't recall seeing a dog around. We do have a canine officer, but I'm sure they were nowhere near your place this morning."

He sat leaning forward, arms flexed and veins pumped, elbows on his knees. He looked startled when she mirrored his move, leaning forward, hand resting on the gun.

"You know what I mean. The killer you hang with, Jim Lane. That kind of cat don't change his spots and he's crazy. He'll come unglued soon and kill somebody. Same as he did last year."

Everyone knew at least something about the shootings last year. Any facts they didn't have were made up and embellished to resemble comic book heroes or graphic novels as they like to be called now. She knew there were no supermen involved.

"Are you afraid he'll kill Dickie and then start on you? Don't be. If he wanted to, that would have already happened. Just so you know, he gave me his personal assurance he's done messing with your man and with you. You're not on his radar anymore. Unless, of course, Dan Hyatt dies. If that happens, I'll try to intervene. I'm not promising anything."

Fielding sat back and relaxed. "So you'll protect him if that happens?"

"Protect him? That man needs less protecting than anyone I know. He doesn't need me for that." She shook her head, leaning back and then forward again when she realized her ponytail was trapped behind her back. "Mr. Lane gets no special treatment from me, or anyone in my department. Is that clear?"

Her gaze sharpened. "Why do you think he equates you with the beating of Dan Hyatt? Does he know something?"

Fielding stood, the chair hanging a moment before dropping to the floor. "We had nothing to do with that. But if he keeps pushing, he might get the same treatment. Not from us, of course. I'm concerned that whoever did it to Hyatt might feel threatened."

Smiling, she visualized them trying to take down Jim Lane. He wasn't invincible and had the scars to prove it, but she knew he could handle Fielding and his lackey—unless they ambushed him. That gave her pause.

She finally answered. "Oh, we both know better than that. I think everyone knows you're guilty, including me. It's interesting you used the word *we*. Did both of you big muscle-bound heroes beat on that little man? He probably didn't weigh a buck-sixty soaking wet. When he wakes from his coma, we'll have the answer to that question. Then I'll come see you. Don't take any long vacations."

He pointed a crooked and scarred finger at her. A fresh scab shone dull brown on his knuckle. For the first time, she noted his pupils were constricted. Surely, he was smart enough not to use his own product. She knew he was a bad actor. Proving it in a court of law was a different story. Sometimes she wished she could turn someone like Jim Lane loose on them.

Fielding's voice was a deep rumble. "You keep your man off me and Dickie. Otherwise, he's going to get into trouble. We might have to take steps."

Her fingers tapped impatiently on the handle of the pistol, drawing his gaze to it. "With you? Or both of you at once? Sounds like a threat to me."

He shook his head, palms up and open. "No threat. I'm just saying. I got a knack for predicting things, kind of like second sight."

"Duly noted. If I need a séance, I'll know who to call. Now, unless you have some insight on the stock market and my retirement package, you'll excuse me. I have work to do. Take your knack and go. Y'all come back soon, hear?"

He stared at her a moment and then stomped from the room. She didn't know what he expected, but it surely didn't go like he thought. Watching as he pulled out and chirped his tires on the asphalt, she leaned her knee against the pressure switch under her desk to turn off the recorder. She sighed, looking at the mountain of paperwork in front of her. A confession would have been nice, but Fielding was too smart for that. Sooner or later, he'd make a mistake, and she'd be waiting. The hard part would be to keep Jim from taking a hand.

Fielding and Lane were like two bulls penned together. It was just a matter of time.

————

ROMAN FIELDING SAT at the back table of The Gallows, surrounded by four men and Dickie. Of the four, he didn't think they'd score enough IQ points to make a nickel. He remained quiet until Ruby had set them all up with beer and whiskey chasers. A basket of pretzels skidded across the table to come to rest against his arm.

Ruby was rough company, but not bad on the eyes from the right angle.

"Dickie," he began, watching her walk away. "You need to disappear a while. If that farmer dies, Lane is going to be trouble we don't need. It might be better if all of you stay out of sight." He gazed at the brain trust around his table. "Another thing. I don't know whose stupid-assed idea it was breaking into the stores around the square, but you better not get caught. If the sheriff rolls up one of you on that, then it leads back to the rest of us—we can't have that kind of scrutiny right now. Do not think for one minute you will survive that mistake. Is that understood?"

The contingent of Good Old Boys nodded like synchronized bobbleheads. Dickie spoke up. "We need to move some product into the north side of Springfield. That'll keep us busy for a couple of days. I'm thinking Lane may be out of the picture soon. I'm tired of him blindsiding me and getting lucky. He doesn't fight fair."

"Fair?" Fielding laughed. "What was it that old general said? If you find yourself in a fair fight, it just shows a lack of preparation on your part. Whatever you're thinking of doing, it better not come back on me. If it does, you'll be catfish bait. Remember that old boy we caught that couldn't pay for his product? We put him naked in waist deep water up at Truman Lake about daylight—feeding time. One of those eighty-pound catfish came up and made a eunuch of him. They got the rest of him, too, once he bled out. They're as bad as hogs. Do you understand me?"

Dickie blanched and made a show of crossing his legs. "Yeah, I got it. Don't worry, boss. I ain't stupid."

"Really? You got proof of that?" Roman shook his head. "What about the labs and cookers? We can't afford any downtime on product."

"We got them moved north of Stockton Lake, into Cedar county," one of the men answered. "There's still some boys cooking around here, but they're using as much as they make. Damn meth heads are crazy."

"Yeah, but they keep the cops busy chasing them and the heat off us, so they're worth their weight in gold.

Anything else we need to talk about? Any customers holding out? Payments good?"

No one spoke, so he waved his hand and the boys left. Dickie stayed.

Roman looked around again to ensure they were still alone. "What about that Muslim fella? He still good for the product? We don't want to lose that supply. We're both making a bundle on that."

Dickie nodded. "He's got it. They're happy campers since I sent them to see Trader Jack. Jack got his hands on some of that new military-grade C-4 that's a lot more stable. Those dudes were grinning ear to ear. Somebody's going to be getting some boom-boom pretty soon and not the good kind."

Fielding looked at his second-in-command for a moment. "So, how sure are you of this solution for Lane? The one that I don't want to know anything about?"

Dickie grinned at him. "Can't miss, Boss. He won't know what hit him."

"Well, just in case your sure thing does miss, I'm going to reach out to someone I know in Springfield. We have someone on payroll that'll be perfect for this. The ladies love him, too. He comes across as a tough cop, but he's padding his retirement. I'm thinking he can harass Lane into making a mistake, like attacking a police officer who stole his girl. I don't think his lady sheriff will protect him, so they'll both be too busy to worry about us."

Dickie shrugged. "Whatever. I ain't going to miss."

# FOUR

ALINA IVANOV REMOVED her sandals before walking through the fine white sand toward her father. It was early in the day, so the sand didn't burn her feet, but she could feel the sun's heat on her body. Someone was tending a barbecue grill farther down the beach. It was a strange mixture with the fresh breeze and fishy smell of the ocean—like going into a famous steakhouse and ordering chicken.

She ran through her decision in an orderly fashion, something her precision mind was known for. It was a trait she'd inherited from her father and something that frustrated investigators. Never needing to put plans on paper, every step of past operations was safely cubby-holed and filed away in her mind. Future plans lay out in a logical manner.

Wasting away on some secluded beach was not the life for her. There were too many slick playboy types, rich jet setters, and professional vacationers. What she needed was something real. Something dangerous. She longed for a certain imperfect and unpredictable man with a temper and the strength to back it up and knew right where to find him. The fact that he might kill her on sight made the situation more desirable. And, of course, the girlfriend. A law enforcement officer who'd already threatened her life. It got her juices flowing just thinking about it.

Anton Ivanov sat under an umbrella on the beach, holding a book in his hand while staring at the azure sea off Cozumel. The retired crime boss from St. Louis, Missouri, used his thumb for a bookmark while the wind flipped through the pages. He seemed lost in thought or asleep. It was this lethargy she fought against. She thought of all the times she'd heard of men dying shortly after retirement—men lying around with nothing to do. It would be a sad ending.

Her father's trusted soldier, Gregory, lay on a lounge chair nearby, a ludicrous picture of a beached, hairy walrus wearing shades and a fedora. He was huge, and his only allegiance was to her father. She had no doubt the folded towel on the table next to him would hide his custom-suppressed Colt .45. Ever vigilant, few would be able to approach the pair unchallenged.

She took a moment to fill her lungs with the breeze, gazing out at the ocean. "Good morning, Father."

His voice was high-pitched and articulate, nothing like the soft, lazy drawl of the islands. She'd often wondered when the switch happened, men to high voices, women to low. Old movies had it the other way around. Of all the men hitting on her at the resort and adjacent nightclubs, she doubted if there were an ounce of testosterone among them. But to yearn for better days would not be realistic. She had to make them.

"You're late."

Alina shrugged, unconcerned. "I'm not running a schedule. It's the tropics. Everything is late. What are you reading?"

Glancing at the book in his hand, he shrugged. "Some apocalyptic novel uses Springfield, Missouri, as a center point. Guy's an idiot—thinks just because the big rigs stop doing deliveries, people will starve. His premises would never happen. The government would step in."

"You'd rely on the government? Since when? By the time they passed a law to cover their collective asses, it'd be too late." She chuckled, trying to see the cover. "So why are you reading it?"

"I don't know...can't seem to put it down." He glanced around the beach a moment until his gaze landed on her. "You've decided then?"

She shouldn't have been surprised. Nothing of importance got by him. The subject was hard. She knew it would be. The luxury and splendor of the beachfront villa should be inviting. Their secluded home had all the accoutrement money could buy. All her father's money was available here, not back in the States. Still...she had resources to draw on. She wouldn't be an Ivanov if she didn't. That heritage left her with an uncanny aptitude for landing on her feet in uncertain circumstances.

She nodded, again gazing at the ocean. "I'm going back."

Gregory sat up and watched her with an unblinking stare before commenting. "Not a good decision. There are dangers. You'll have no support. No backup."

She nodded and shrugged. "I think those dangers will stay in St. Louis. I talked to Donatello. He gave me assurances as long as we stay out of his business."

Anton Ivanov raised his hand to stop the comments

from Gregory and directed his attention toward his daughter. "You trust these people? I sold my interests to the Italians. That doesn't mean I trust them. Those bastards will cut your throat if given a chance."

Her smile was cold. "Donatello and I have moved into an equal destruction agreement. It's in his best interest to leave me alone."

She shook her head. "As for Jim Lane? Crazy as it seems? I love him…always did. It's my eternal shame that I treated him with so much disrespect." Her shrug was expressive, her gaze holding on her father. "If there are dangers…so be it."

Concern shone in his eyes, more than she'd ever seen. "You know you can't have him. He's too straight arrow."

"Maybe. We're a lot more alike than he knows. I just need to convince him. But if that doesn't work? I can be close. If nothing else, that will have to do."

He settled in his chair with a sigh, and Gregory gazed out to sea, shaking his head. Anton continued. "I spent millions refurbishing that place through anonymous donations. I gave them a lot. We paid for their misfortune and I still feel guilty. Now I'm giving them my daughter? It's too much." He locked his gaze on hers. "You have money?"

"Enough." She inclined her head and was surprised to find her eyes welling with tears.

Anton stood with a sad expression. "A hug for your father?"

She watched him a moment, startled because he'd never been touchy-feely around her, before conceding with a smile. "Well, this is a first. Kinda scary."

He shrugged. "Goodbyes are hard when you feel they may be permanent. This could be the last time we see each other. I can't go back to the States and stay alive."

When they parted, Gregory stood, arms wide, fingers wiggling in a 'come here' gesture. "What about a hug for me?"

She laughed as she shook her head. "Me wearing a bikini and you with more hands than an octopus has tentacles? I don't think so."

He sat, grumbling. "Octopuses don't have hands. They got suckers."

Shaking her head, she laughed again. Theirs was never a close relationship, though they'd worked together often. "Even worse. Thanks for making my point. Nice try, though."

As one of her father's trusted soldiers, they'd known each other a long time, and she realized this was as close to affection as they'd ever get.

Anton tried again. "It's been over a year. Last I heard, Lane was still hung up on that lady sheriff. Anything changed?"

Her gaze was far away for a moment. "No. Not really. But..." Her smile turned predatory. "My informants tell me, for some reason, she hasn't nailed that down—they're not married or even engaged. I've heard she won't commit. If there's trouble in paradise, I need to find out why."

"Still...we've harmed that man enough."

"Don't worry, Papa. I won't break them up. But if I'm presented with an opportunity?" She smiled and shrugged. "Who knows. A little nudge, one way or another? Stranger things have happened."

Gregory gave her a serious look. "Don't kill that sheriff."

"I've given that life up. You should know that. I'll be an independent lady of means living on a lake. What can be more innocent than that? The feds have always wanted you guys, not me. I've been invisible."

He lay back on his beach recliner, settling the fedora over his eyes. "Given up that life? Sure you have. I'm thinking you're like a vampire. You need the blood and the adrenaline rush. One more thing." Gregory gave her a direct look. "When we left, the drug cartels were moving into the meth trade—they'll be out in hillbilly country trying to take that away from the home folks. Don't mess with them or get in the middle of that. But if you do? Take my advice and don't negotiate. Don't talk. If you run into them, either side, kill them. If you want to stay invisible, no witnesses. There's no other way to deal with those people."

She shook her head and rolled her eyes. "I don't do drugs, never have. You know that, but thanks for the advice. It won't be an issue."

"That's enough, you two." Anton sat up and faced her. "Remember, Alina. If you need to contact me, use the old email address for a drop box. You have my number for short conversations. We'll have to move our location again as a precaution. With you back in the States, Donatello may regard that as a breach of contract and reach out."

She sighed and finally met his gaze. "Understood, and I'm sorry to cause problems. I have to do this."

Her father chuckled. "Don't mention it. It'll give us something to do. I miss the old life. It's hard to step away. And if the Donatello family makes trouble? I may come out of retirement."

# FIVE

SMALL WAVES quietly tapped against the pontoons. Driven by a battery-powered trolling motor and heading into the wind, the boat barely moved. It was a quiet day for Stockton Lake, known to be perfect for sailboats but also for choppy water when the wind was up. Motoring close to shore was much easier than the open water.

Josh Barnes lounged on a deep-cushioned seat at the bow of the boat. Watching the shoreline under the shade of his John Deere gimme cap, he spoke over the small amount of wind they were generating.

"Jim, when are you going to name this aluminum tub? It's a ship on the water and gotta have a name. I could help you come up with something. Maybe paint a girl on the front with big jugs? And then you could call it a jug boat. You know, like for jug fishing?" Barnes grinned at him. "I have lots of ideas."

"Oh, you'd love that." Jim Lane shook his head. "I can just imagine you interviewing girls to use as models. Sounds like a recipe for disaster. Just how long has your wife been gone? You need some stress relief."

Wifey, as Barnes called her, was notorious for going to visit relatives when displeased with her husband. Jim watched the depth finder, looking for a shelf between warm water and cold—a place fish would feed. "Besides, I'm not going to name it."

"What?" Barnes turned to give him a disappointed look. "Why?"

"If someone wants to report my boat, they're going to have to read off the whole registration number. No short-cuts. By the time they get through it, I'll be gone. It's my rebellion against The Man."

"Yeah, I can see you in a high-speed chase over the water. The water patrol's scuba diver could catch us with one fin on his foot. We're doing what? Two knots? I can't tell if we're moving."

Jim's reply was interrupted by an excited yell from his fishing partner.

"Wow. Would you look at that? Topless cliff diver, port side, ten o'clock high. I think she's gonna do it!"

Jim rolled his eyes, shaking his head. "If your blood pressure spikes and you have a heart attack, what reason should I give your wife? Besides, we're not in the Navy, and we're sure as hell not flying."

"Could have fooled me. Damned boat is big enough, at least for the Missouri Navy." Josh Barnes started whistling the theme song from an old comedy, *Gilligan's Island*.

Jim Lane looked where his friend was pointing and then couldn't stop watching.

Considering the girl's launching platform was a lichen-covered limestone ledge hanging fifty feet above the water, it was a beautiful dive. That she was an athlete was evident. The strength of her legs giving her that half-second of hang time with arms spread wide, hands bent upward at the wrist, and fingers stretched to the heavens to clutch at one more millisecond of suspended flight, chest thrust out in a classic gravity-defying swan dive.

In that split second of weightlessness before she dropped toward the water, her sternum blew out in a silent mist of blood and bone. Long black hair streamed behind her as she plummeted toward the water. But her arms didn't come together. She didn't point her hands or make a fist to slice into the water. She would have won the belly flop championship at the local pool. It was an awkward ending to a beautiful start, and if there were a 10-score to be had, she didn't come up to claim it.

Her audience numbered everyone they could see—she was that beautiful. He'd bet every male and most females tracked her all the way down until she hit the water. But from their angle of sight, the onlookers wouldn't see what was observed from the boat.

Barnes stood a moment, mouth open, before he flinched, a movement that was way too late to do any good. A plume of water had erupted just beyond their bow from the round passing through the girl. Still looking at the point she hit the water, his face slack with shock, he whispered. "Well, shit. Now what?"

When she launched into her dive, Jim Lane thought she was Rita until he took a closer look. His intimate knowledge of that particular topography dispelled that notion. He knew better, but not so much that his heart didn't stop a moment.

His stomach roiled as he stood on the deck of his pontoon boat checking the shoreline, looking for smoke

—a doubtful occurrence considering the dense brush and trees that bordered the shore. No one was acting like they'd heard a shot.

While Barnes looked at where the girl went under, Jim's attention was on the water in front of them. He'd seen the splash the bullet made. If they hadn't slowed down to watch the girl?

Jim looked at his friend. "Did you hear anything?"

"Nothing but heavy metal boomboxes. There ought to be a law against those things, especially in nature."

When nothing else happened, and there were plenty of targets for a shooter if they wanted more, he relaxed a bit and responded with a tired sigh. "I guess we should go over there."

"Yeah, I suppose." Barnes, hand on hips, peered at the water around them. "Dammit. The crappie are going to start biting. I can feel it in my bones. This new Marabou Jig I got from Bass Pro was going to bring them in."

"They'll be there tomorrow."

"Maybe. But will we?"

A good question and one he didn't have an answer for. Jim's fishing buddy was Josh Barnes, a retired Missouri highway patrolman. Combined with Jim's history of military police and then working for the Shepherds, both had seen enough of this sort of thing to last several lifetimes and knew it was just another chapter in the dirty book called humanity. He felt a moment's regret that they were so jaded, a girl's murder didn't cause anything more than dull anger and feeling of inconvenience. And both knew there was no hurry—no rescue or saving a life. It was too late for that before she hit the water. All that was left was the cleanup.

A suppressed weapon must have killed the girl. But

suppressed weapons are not silent, especially rifles. Although there wouldn't be much sound around the shooter, the bullet was still supersonic—hence making a clap of sound when it broke the sound barrier. From their actions, it appeared most people didn't know anything had happened and wouldn't have seen anything from the victim's back anyway. The shouting and catcalling between drunk kids continued, music blared from heavy duty sound systems on the high-end pontoon boats. Party central. Dance 'til you die.

With a shrug at his raised eyebrows and 'really?' expression, Jim engaged the electric trolling motor and slipped up to the other pontoons and party boats attached side-by-side making a party pier attaching them to the shore. Getting close, he realized he'd already lost the 'my daddy's boat is bigger than yours' contest, enduring the sneers of a couple of drunk college-aged boys as his smaller boat drifted up. After a couple of minutes, the rubber side-bumpers nudged up against the outermost boat filled with silent kids looking at the water. Some were pointing, but not many. Apparently, all they knew was the diver made a poor entry and didn't come up.

He stepped from the front of his boat onto the water access of the nearest pontoon, one hand on the rail. The other held his cell. Rita's number was speed dial number one.

Not giving her a chance to say anything when she answered, he gave a quick report to get her on the move. "Rita. You've got a shooting and fatality out at Chicken Rock. One vic in the water. Hell, I don't know. It just happened a couple of minutes ago, and all your witnesses are gonna scatter like quail."

Her questions had come fast and furious over road

noise while she drove. Being a small county and short-handed, she was never in the office. Still, it would be a half hour before she'd arrive. A lifetime for an active crime scene.

Barnes was backing the boat as he spoke. "I'm going up the shoreline and put in. Maybe I can flush the shooter back this way."

He looked at his friend for a moment and then shook his head. "Not much point."

"Because?" Barnes was swiveling his head around, looking at different points of the landscape.

Jim sighed. "She was shot in the back." He paused, the visual burned into his brain. "And big bore. You saw the splash where the bullet hit the water. The shooter had to be perpendicular to the shoreline. Could be a thousand yards inland up that big-assed hill."

"Okay. You're right. Guess that's why you get the big bucks." His gaze scanned the bluff and shoreline. "Maybe I'll just sit here and enjoy the show."

"Funny." With Rita's mood lately, they'd both be lucky to not get thrown into jail, just for being here. "Why don't you get to the top of the rock and start talking to those kids before they decide to disappear. Rita's bunch is on the way, ETA thirty minutes. Maybe you could use your cell and take a bunch of pictures of kids and vehicles. Someone had to have seen something, but I'm betting they won't stick around to tell about it."

Barnes fished his phone from his waterproof pack. "Do you remember who you're talking to?"

"Yeah." Jim was flipping off his deck shoes and removing his shirt. "A washed-up, retired highway patrolman who's scared his wife will find out he's fishing with me instead of mowing the yard."

"Oh, shit. This will be on the news." Barnes shuddered and shook his head. "We have to leave before the cameras get here or I'm dead."

Oh, and this will be on the news," Jim Jackson
talked, and shook his head. "We have to leave before the
authorities get here." Jared

# SIX

THE PARTY ANIMALS finally realized something was wrong and were watching the spot where the girl went under. Jim was amazed at the cries for him to hurry. Yet, none of them dove into the water. Given the amount of alcohol consumption, that was probably a good thing. And hurry? They didn't see her chest blow out.

A standard nylon rope was connected to the side of Jim's pontoon boat. One end had a rescue float attached. Grabbing it, he tossed the ring into the water. Making a quick loop of the other end of the line, he threaded his wrist through it. The water was reasonably clear with the sun nearly straight above, so he felt there was a good chance for retrieval. There was a small reason to hurry, but not for saving her life. Since there wouldn't be any air in her lungs to help buoyancy, she'd sink. Every lake has a current down deep, moving cold water to warm water. If the body drifted into the rocks and caves under the shoreline, they might never find it. Some parts of the lake even had abandoned towns. He took a few deep breaths to hyperventilate and then dove into the water.

The shock of cold water and quick exertion made his brain try and convince him he was already starved for air. Wouldn't that make a great headline? Underwater for thirty seconds, an out-of-practice, out-of-shape middle-aged swimmer drowns in futile rescue attempt of a dead body. Film at eleven. Trying to calm his panicking lungs, he swam toward the girl's entry point and found her at once.

She was suspended about twenty feet away, feet down, arms akimbo, with half-lidded, vacant eyes. Her expression looked surprised, but he doubted she had time for any thoughts at all. Everything stopped when that large-caliber bullet blew through her.

If not for the wound in her chest, she might have been an underwater siren luring him deeper to his death with a wave and smile. Her hair fanned lazily above her while blood congregated close to her body. There wasn't much since her heart stopped in mid-flight. He grabbed a handful of hair to pull her toward him. Taking the rope off his arm, he attached it around one of her ankles and cinched it tight. Now she couldn't get away. One more look confirmed the entry and exit wounds. What a damned waste.

Glancing up, he was thankful for the sun to give him direction. Even trained divers can get disoriented in murky water and swim the wrong way. Releasing a little air to relieve pressure, he followed the air bubbles and rope tied to the float. He surfaced like a breaching whale and gasped for air. Treading water a moment to catch his breath, he yelled at a young man standing on the nearest pontoon boat.

"Throw me a rope."

The young man picked up a coil of white cotton rope that lay on the cabin roof of his boat and tossed it to him.

Disgusted, Jim glared at him. "You threw me both ends of the rope, shithead."

The man shrugged. "Not my job to help. I'm outta here—you can keep the line."

Jim tied one end around the rescue float. The dead girl would keep better in the cold water and he'd let Rita and the water patrol do the actual retrieval.

He swam to the pontoon boat anchored nearest the shore and climbed the access ladder to the deck. Tying the rope to one of the rails, he stalked up to the captain's chair and took the keys from the console. At least this boat wouldn't take off unless they wanted to hot-wire it.

Now, the girl's body was anchored to the float, and the float was tied to a boat for easy retrieval. Community service done for the day.

People clapping brought his attention to the shoreline and ledge above. Standing in his tighty-whities, he shivered as Rita strode out to the edge of Chicken Rock and yelled down at him.

"What the hell are you doing?"

He gestured out at the water. "Oh, a little fishing. I swim around looking for them, it's cheaper than sonar. Got a little retrieval operation going, that sort of thing. Kind of a sideline. I like keeping busy."

"Well, get up here. I need to talk with you."

Apparently, she didn't appreciate his humor. "Yes, ma'am."

"And put some pants on!"

———

TAKING HIS TIME, he swam back to his own boat, doing a slow, perfect crawl for the onlookers, drying off, and then motoring around the bluff to a more reasonable-looking shore. He'd be damned if he was going to climb that cliff with the rest of the kids. The macadam road followed around the bluff at this part of the lake, so he strolled along it through the deep-shaded canopy of oak and maple to the staging area built for the Chicken Rock scenic view and campsite. Cars still lined the road while Rita and her deputies had the local girls-gone-wild club herded together with their fans and enablers.

Stopping a moment to admire the scene, he sometimes wished he could be so clueless—not a care in the world but the latest party site and how many kegs they could empty. Nothing slowed them down, not even murder. He turned and looked toward the place he figured the shot must have come from. Well, maybe. The shooter had to be a certified tree climber—he'd call him squirrel man for now, at least until he had a name. At first glance, this should be an easy case for Rita. All she had to do was check the girl's list of admirers and see who was seriously mad, and a shooter.

He looked up the hill again. The slightest thing will ruin a long-range shot. Wind, leaves, twigs, errant birds and dragonflies. Even getting the yips like in golf by not using a smooth trigger pull. Anything. He couldn't see a clear lane for shooting.

So, not long-range? Maybe not in a tree? It didn't matter. The shooter made a damned good shot. Close to the road were several flat sections of limestone, made when the Corps of Engineers blasted out the road around the bluff. He strolled over that way, hands in pockets, looking for any movement. There was none, and he didn't expect any.

A prolific growth of poison ivy surrounded the rocky area. Water runoff carved a slight trail around the boulders. He thanked several deities when he heard Rita calling him, interrupting his thoughts of climbing and checking out the rocks. He'd got into some poison ivy last year and didn't want to try it again. Ever.

Walking back to Rita, he ran into the munchkin, Allison Crewes. If she listed herself at five feet tall, it would have to involve high-heeled boots.

She nodded. "Hey, killer."

So, not a fan today. "Hey, Munchkin."

She stopped. "Last time you called me Big Al. Are you getting 'old timer's' disease? Forgetting what you call me?"

He grinned at her and was glad to see one in return. "Nope. I've been rethinking your nickname. I might change it to Smurf. A blue uniform would suit you, maybe a little blue face paint and blue scarf."

Before the deputy could reply, Rita was in front of him. Rita was not happy. Rita was firing on all cylinders in sheriff mode. He'd always relied on humor to deflect her anger. This was not going to end well.

"Hey, Rita. I missed you last night. You never stopped by for that chat."

"I got busy. Unlike you, I have a job."

He pulled an imaginary arrow from his chest. "Ow. That hurt."

"Funny. What's your part in this, Jim? We talked about this before. Seems like every time there's a problem I look up and there you are. It's déjà vu, all over again."

Trying to keep his temper down, his answer was curt.

"Asked and answered, Sheriff. You know exactly what I'm doing here. Anything new to ask? Like, how ya doing? How ya feeling? Did you almost drown recovering the victim? Do you need counseling for seeing such a horrible and graphic killing that destroyed your snowflake status and left you depressed? Things like that?"

She stared at him and he could imagine several scenarios of his being drawn and quartered running through her mind by her expressions.

"No, I guess not." She sighed and ran her fingers through her hair. "Sorry, but you look okay to me. You always do. I doubt this has disturbed your inner self at all. Thanks for the call-in."

Not getting help with the rescue still rankled. All those kids just stared, like they didn't care at all. Who raises people like that? "Well, I have a question. It appears like there's about fifty people here. How many 9-1-1 calls did you get from the helpful masses?"

She glared at him a moment. "None that I know of."

"Then maybe you can dial back the attitude a bit. I'm just trying to help." He could hear the siren of the water patrol boat coming in. He could never figure out why the sound of the siren seemed to bounce along with the boat.

Shaking her head, she was turning to go when he stopped her. "Why water patrol?"

The Stockton Lake Water Patrol was manned by Missouri Highway Patrol and there was a lot of frequent head-butting between the patrol and the sheriff's department.

Rita glanced at him. "Why not? We need a dive team for a drowning, that's standard procedure. Do you have a clue where they should start?"

"You didn't hear a word I said, did you?" He shook his head, amazed she'd discounted his words about retrieval and hadn't seen the float. "So, yes. I do have a clue. My suggestion is to not dive at all. There's a rescue buoy floating around out there, painted red and white, so you can't miss it. The dead girl is tied to it."

Reaching into his pants pocket, he retrieved the keys to the party boat and pitched them to her. "The buoy is tied to the rail of this guy's boat, it's right by the shore. Just look for someone really pissed off because he can't leave. Easy peasy."

Barnes picked that moment to walk up to them. "Hey, Rita. I just sent you a movie file of all the cars and people here. It's a big-assed file."

Her gaze shuttled between us. "Oh god. You're involved in this, too?"

He took off his hat and scratched his thinning hair. "Involved? I'm damned sure we didn't shoot anyone. Hell, we were just fishing when this happened. Thought we'd lend a hand. Professional courtesy."

"This is not a John Wayne western. Even money says you were watching the girls." She snorted at his expression. "You were, weren't you? It figures. The last thing I need is Heckle and Jeckle looking over my shoulder during an investigation. Neither of you belong here. The sheriff's department will handle this."

"Hey, you know damned good and well those girls have to take off their tops, or they'll just lose them when they hit the water. It's physics." Barnes raised his hands in surrender. "I'm out of here. The crappie are biting. Or they were."

He turned to Jim. "You piss in her Cheerios this morning?"

"Nope. We haven't done mornings in a long time." He gave Rita a sad look. "Oh, by the way? Save your deputies some trouble and have them look at that ledge behind us or the next one farther up the hill." He pointed across the road. "It's about the only spot a shooter could use to get the angle."

Her gaze met his. "Well, finally something you're an expert on. I'll send you a consultant fee. Dollar about right?"

He looked at Barnes and shook his head. Cheerios indeed.

As they walked away, he stopped again—couldn't resist. "Send your steroid junkie PJ up there. He can stand and flex on the rock while he's looking around. The girls will love it."

She looked at the limestone outcropping. He knew she could see the poison ivy. Though she didn't reply, he saw a ghost of a smile turn her lips.

Barnes watched the byplay with a puzzled look. "What do you have against Officer Rails?"

"He stopped me twice in one week for speeding."

"Do the crime, do the time…or dime in your case." He glanced across the road. "He'll see the poison ivy."

"Nah. City boy."

———

LATER, they sat on the deep cushions of the pontoon boat, enjoying a beer and watching the deputies trying to manage the drunken party—herding cats into a plastic bag came to mind.

"Feels good, doesn't it?" Barnes sighed and stretched.

"We get to live out the old saying—not my circus, not my monkeys."

Jim nodded. He didn't envy them. Other than a dead body, he suspected there would be no sign of the shooter. That was just too good a shot. Whoever it was, they were good—and long gone. Maybe they were careless enough to leave something of themselves behind, like a shell casing, footprint, letter addressed to them, or DNA sample, but he doubted it. It was one of those seemingly random shootings that drove law enforcement crazy.

He was military police before working for other agencies, so he knew what Rita and her deputies were going through.

"I guess we could stay out until dusk and catch some crappie." There wasn't much enthusiasm in Barnes's voice. "We might get a few."

Although both men glossed over it, watching a girl get murdered in front of them didn't sit well. Even if they'd rushed to the shore to try and catch the shooter, they'd be long gone by the time the two men arrived. Both knew it, so didn't try. On the bright side, the aftermath of the shooting was being handled and wasn't their responsibility. Rita Morris was more than qualified to find the killer. If they took over the investigation, the water patrol had plenty of manpower to throw at the problem.

It had been over a year since the so-called Russian invasion of Limestone County by a segment of the Russian Mafia. It'd been a good year since, but the cracks in his relationship with Rita started when she was elected sheriff. She'd been appointed when her husband was killed on the job a couple of years before. Now, things were different.

Rita told him she didn't want the job, wouldn't do it if

asked. She was ready to retire and Jim was looking forward to it. And then, with no discussion with him, she ran in the election and won. Guess she wanted it. They could sit back and enjoy life and each other's company. Were there degrees of lies? Some worse than others? Politicians would say deception by omission was not lying, but only other politicians would believe that. The relationship between them hadn't been the same since.

"Nah." He finally answered the question, and his reply sounded depressed, which made him more depressed. "Let's just motor back and call it a day."

Moving to the steering post and preparing to start the twin Mercury outboards, Barnes glanced at him over his shoulder. "What was that Heckle and Jeckle comment from Rita? I remember that old cartoon. Hell, it's as old as the TV in your rec room—the one with the tubes in it. It was about a couple of wise-cracking crows that caused a lot of trouble. I think I've been insulted."

"You're just now figuring that out?"

"It just so happens that I'm slow. So, what do you think?"

"Depends."

Barnes threw his empty can toward the trash box. "On what?"

"Which one of us is Heckle."

# SEVEN

SHERIFF RITA MORRIS STOOD, hands on hips, listening to the rapid-fire speech of the twenty-something girl in front of her. Before her eyes glazed over from trying to understand the girl's speech, she held up her hand.

"Whoa, stop, back up a minute. There's not enough coffee in the world to help me keep up with what you're saying. Start over. Speak slowly. Think of English as your second language and concentrate on each word. Now, your name again?"

"Alisha?"

She couldn't stop watching this girl. If this was an example of what colleges were putting out, the country was in deep trouble. "You made that a question. Are you unsure of your name? Do you have identification you could look at, maybe a stencil on your shorts?"

The girl returned a puzzled stare, slowly shaking her head. Trying to avoid a palm slap to her own forehead, Rita asked. "Do you have a last name, Alisha?"

"Oh. Yeah, sorry? It's Jones?"

"Okay, Alisha Jones." She jotted that down. They were finally communicating. Yay. "How old are you?"

"What does that have to do with anything?" The girl's bored eyes were tracking a young man in a sagging swimsuit, who walked across the pavement. His flip-flops were beating cadence like a drummer on a watermelon.

Rita waved her clipboard at the girl to get her attention. "Well, we have these little blanks we need to fill in on our investigation sheets—the ones that came in the cereal boxes? So we could inconvenience people? You know, after someone has been murdered?" She stopped. Mimicking the people around her, she was starting to end every statement with a question. God.

"Oh, of course? I'm eighteen?"

"Alright, Miss Jones. See how easy that was? Now, what did you see?"

"About the accident? Nothing? I mean, I was standing over there with some people?" She pointed vaguely over her shoulder. "I wasn't paying any attention?"

Rita nodded, not doubting that for a minute. Everyone had the same answer, using the three-monkeys defense against evil. No one saw anything at all. No one heard anything. No one knew anything. All they knew is the girl dove off the ledge and didn't come up after she entered the water. That's all, which was no surprise, given how self-absorbed the witnesses were in cell phones and beer bottles.

She put her hand on the girl's arm to get her attention. "So, did you know her?"

"Who?" Her sand-blasted, red-veined eyes danced from one thing to another—never stopping, never seeing.

"Did you smoke weed by the pound today?" Rita

looked around and spotted her youngest deputy. "Crewes! Get over here."

When the deputy bounced up, Rita spoke quickly. "Look, this is Alisha Jones. If you can keep her awake, get her statement. Make damned sure she doesn't drive anywhere, maybe find her a box of Ding Dongs or something. The munchies are going to set in any minute, and she'll give up anything for a package of Twinkies. You might even get a confession. Once you're finished and everyone's ID is recorded, cut them all loose." She held up her hand. "But not before screening everyone to see if they can drive—pass that on to PJ and the water patrol."

Allison laughed, nodding in agreement. "Will do, Boss. I don't think we're getting much here anyway. What a mess."

Rita nodded. "Amazing, isn't it? A murder among at least fifty people and no one saw it? With all the boomboxes, grab-assing, screaming, and yelling, no one heard a shot. No witnesses. All we have is a dead body that fell out of the sky."

"Well." Crewes slid a glance her way. "You do have a couple of reliable witnesses."

She closed her eyes and shook her head. Josh Barnes and Jim Lane.

Barnes was retired Missouri Highway Patrol and Jim was...a problem. The two men had become friends a year ago during what they called the Russian invasion. She knew Barnes's inclination was toward law and order, and she shouldn't have snapped at him. He was a good guy.

Jim? His inclination was to blow things up, kill them all, and let God sort them out later. Once he got started, he made Rambo look like a Boy Scout. She had to keep him out of it.

The problem? She and Jim were lovers, although that had cooled—and it was her fault. She'd told him last year she was done with the sheriff's job. At that time, the county law enforcement was in shambles. Being the smallest county in the state, money was hard to come by. The Missouri Highway Patrol was going to have to step in to help, along with the surrounding counties. No one liked that scenario. She didn't want to leave the job in such a mess, so she ran for sheriff in the special election and was elected. It wasn't hard...no one ran against her.

Things changed. Anonymous donations started showing up, money given for the sheriff's department use only. New vehicles arrived from an unknown donor, along with money for a new building. She had her suspicions, but everything checked out as legitimate and she didn't look too hard.

Nodding, Rita finally answered her deputy. "We do, but they can only tell us what happened. Since we already know, it's up to us to find out why. Anything else those two contribute is speculation. There's no need to interview them."

"You sure? If you don't want to do it." Crewes grinned at her. "I'd like to do some speculating with your old squeeze. I'm betting he'd have some good ideas."

"Crewes?"

"Sorry."

Rita inclined her head toward the wannabe valley girl. "Your witness is drifting away."

With a sigh and dreaming of four little brown pills of I-Be-Loafen, what Jim called ibuprofen, to cure her headache, she walked out on the ledge of Chicken Rock. Water patrol had retrieved the body and was long gone. The party boats were gone, as were most of the non-witnesses and looky-loos behind her. In the distance, sailboats tacked with the wind while closer to her, a speedboat pulled kids on wakeboards and foam pads.

Arms folded across her chest as she watched, she envied their freedom. Even if they were oblivious to the things going on around them. Sometimes, she wished she were. Recapping her day so far, all she had was the placid waters of Lake Stockton and the body of a dead girl. She knew what would happen. State would take over the case, and guilty feeling or not, she wouldn't fight it. It was almost a relief. There were other fish to fry in Limestone County.

Her thoughts turned to Roman Fielding. She knew his game. That was easy. He was small-time, but there was a lot of money in that. He'd tell Dickie to deliver a message. Dickie would visit a friend. That friend would visit someone else. Somewhere down the line, product would be bought and sold. When they busted a meth lab, the people running it only knew some Good Old Boy that stopped by occasionally. A gift to some anonymous cause would be made and that money would travel up the chain. It was convoluted but highly effective. No direct involvement by the people at the top.

She sighed. Sooner or later, they'd make a mistake. They always do. The beating of Dan Hyatt might be the one thing to bring Fielding down. But that hope dwindled with every day Hyatt didn't wake up from his coma. It was a hot day, but she shivered. Everyone has a gut instinct warning them things were about to happen. The premonition of impending doom was beating on her like a drum.

# EIGHT

WHEN HIS RIGHT leg started throbbing and burning, Jim pulled up his pant leg to find a cut on the calf. The angry-looking scratch was about six inches long and had a puncture wound at one end. Cleaning it with hydrogen peroxide, he didn't remember hitting his leg on anything, but the proof was in front of him. Considering how dirty the rocks were in the lake, even though the water looked pristine, he decided to go to the clinic for at least a tetanus shot—maybe antibiotics.

Knowing it was the only medical facility in the area allowing walk-ins, he arrived at the Mercy Clinic in Lockwood, a small town west of White Rock. He checked in and waited among the mothers and children showing every symptom from the sniffles to the flu. Judging from the people around him, there was already a pandemic in progress and everyone was going to die puking their guts out. It was an odd occurrence for the middle of summer and gave him an uneasy feeling.

He didn't like crowds in general or waiting rooms of any kind. It would be better going to the local Farmer's

Exchange that had veterinarian supplies and buying some streptomycin. It was the same medicine used for humans, but with different dosages. Google would help with figuring that out. But that wouldn't get him a tetanus shot. While he watched, a small girl, maybe three years old, ejected snot all over her mother. How women did it, he'd never know. His heart hammered more than when he was underwater and panicked for air. Time to get out of Dodge.

As he stood to leave, a nurse opened a door and called his name—smiled as he practically ran to the door. Safely deposited inside the exam room, the nurse pulled up his records on the computer, then recorded his blood pressure. She'd already recorded his weight, temperature, and blood oxygen levels just inside the door. The nurse looked about twelve to him and yet did her job with quick efficiency.

"So, what are you needing to see the doctor about?" She waited with fingers poised over the keyboard, anxious to enter the information into his chart, tapping her foot.

Jim didn't say anything, just pulled up his pant leg and pointed.

"Nice." The keyboard rattled. "Okay. They'll be in shortly." With that proclamation, she grabbed a handful of hand sanitizer and bounced out the door. Thinking that was a good idea, he grabbed some for his own hands.

Taking out his iPhone, he started surfing the web. Catching all the headlines and bullet points on Drudge and Whatfinger News, it was confirmed. They were all going to die. If not by plague then by EMPs, poisoned water, global warming, global cooling, Yellowstone volcanic eruption, or simply because the world was tired of humans.

He was so wrapped up in the news, it startled him when the door opened abruptly and Dr. Bartelli swooped in, followed by a nurse. Without saying a word, both began disinfecting their hands.

"Uh, I'm just here for a tetanus shot guys." Neither of them stopped applying the foam from the dispenser. "Hey, we haven't been exposed to the Kung Flu, have we?"

Bartelli grinned over his shoulder at him. "No, but trust me. You don't want to be contaminated with what we're seeing today. That coronavirus is getting all the hype, but the type A and type B influenza are doing quite well. Even strep throat. The odd part is it's happening in the summer. We don't see that much. Let's hope the three viruses don't combine and turn us all into zombies."

Dr. Bartelli nodded toward the nurse. "This is Jacy Mane. She's in nurse practitioner training, so she's following me around learning bad habits. Is this the same leg we sewed up last year?"

Jim shook his head, marveling at how the doctor always seemed to be moving at high speed. "Nope. I'm starting a new leg. The other one is all used up."

The doctor turned to Jacy. "You remember the small war that never happened and never made the news over at White Rock last year, around the lake? This guy was the chief recipient. He's ex-military and ex-contractor." Bartelli glanced at him. "You don't have any more exes I've forgotten, do you?" He directed his attention back to Jacy. "Anyway, don't trust him."

Jim smirked. "Alright, Bartelli. Just because you're

still active National Guard and I'm an ex-whatever, no need to get chippy about it."

Jacy interjected with a small smile. "If you boys are through insulting each other, we have a lot of patients waiting."

He looked at her, big-eyed. "Is this an outbreak? I've seen the movie and your waiting room is packed."

"No outbreak, at least, not yet." She glanced at Bartelli. "He's not real comfortable around doctors, is he?"

Bartelli laughed. "No, he is not. And he should be, considering how often he needs one."

"Hey, this is a dangerous place. I read somewhere a sneeze leaves the body at over a hundred miles per hour. That's dangerous. There's a kid out there that could shoot right through the walls. We may not be safe in here."

By this time, Jim was on the exam table with his leg up, exposing the wound.

"How'd you get this?" The doctor watched closely as Jacy shaved his leg around the wound with what seemed like the dullest razor she could find and then pulled out a suture kit.

Jim flinched from the disinfectant as she irrigated the wound, deciding to fill them in. "There was a shooting at the lake today, over at Chicken Rock. I went into the water to retrieve the body and must've hit my leg on a rock getting out."

"A shooting?" The medics glanced at each other. "We hadn't heard. Anyone we might know? Jacy is from over there."

"I don't think so. It was a young girl from the girls gone wild party animal set." He thought a moment, but didn't see any reason not to tell them. "She was shot midair as she dove off the rock. Hell of a thing. And a damned good shot from someone. The sheriff was there with the whole crew when I left."

"You and Rita still a thing?" Bartelli was looking at something on his phone as he talked.

"Who knows? It's hit and miss lately—mostly miss. She told me that we need to talk, so I figure I'm about to get my walking papers. Thanks for asking."

Jacy looked up at him. "You said midair? Like a snapshot?"

He nodded, gaze suddenly sharp. That was not a term most would use. "Yeah. High caliber, like a .308 or maybe even a .50 cal. Hit her in the back close to a horizontal line and blew her chest out. Huge exit point, but that may have been from the angle. You might keep that under your hat a day or so, at least until official notice. Rita is looking for any excuse to arrest me."

"She likes you in cuffs?" Jacy tried to hide her grin.

He snorted. "Lately, she doesn't like me at all."

A quick knock on the door announced a nurse poking her head into the room. "Dr. Bartelli, we need you in exam one right away."

Bartelli shook Jim's hand. "I'll leave you with Jacy to get patched up. She's more than capable. We'll get you a script for an antibiotic plus your tetanus booster. That should fix you up. Nice to see you again."

Jim shook his head after Bartelli closed the door. "That man goes at top speed all the time."

Jacy was bent over his leg, blotting some blood from the two stitches she'd sewn in. "He's a fast mover, all right."

He started putting it together. Snapshot. Fast mover. Both military terms. She was not a young nurse, maybe in her thirties. She wore a short-sleeved smock, and he glimpsed the bottom of a tattoo on her left arm. What he saw was the bottom of a knife blade with snake tails entwined around it, on top of a red cross. He'd bet most anything that the knife was a K-Bar.

"So." He spoke softly as he watched her work. "I'm going to go out on a limb and guess you're 86 Whiskey."

She stood abruptly and looked at him with gray, expressionless eyes—not startled, just an assessment like he'd been scanned, cataloged, and filed away for future reference. "I don't spread that around. Most people around here wouldn't know what you're talking about." She chuckled and shook her head. "I just tell the other nurses that see the ink not to get drunk and wake up in a tattoo parlor. If they do, pray they took a liking to Daffy Duck."

He nodded, remembering a few of those days. "Good advice. Seems we're all exes here. Army?"

In the few seconds he'd matched her level gaze, he knew all he'd ever need to know about Jacy Mane. She'd been there. Not only was she a nurse and in training for a practitioner, she'd been a combat medic. Designated 86 Whiskey, combat medics didn't stay in the rear with the gear. She fought alongside her soldiers, protecting them, patching them up, eating the same dirt they did. No job in any of the services deserved more respect than a combat medic.

"All I can be." She nodded and checked her sutures again.

He held out his hand. "Thanks for your service."

"I never get used to that." She shook, holding his hand a moment. "I know who you are. Most people do. You're kind of famous in a 'what in the hell did that idiot do' kind of way. And we're neighbors. My husband and I have a small ranch down the hill from you, past the grove of trees. We're raising horses and kids."

"Well, hey neighbor. That sounds nice and normal. I'm envious. How many?"

Her laugh was soft. "One husband, about twenty horses and colts we train for barrel racing and three boys. I'll give you odds on which are the most difficult to deal with."

"Huh. Not taking that bet. We'll have to talk sometime. I'd like to have a horse or three. Maybe you or your husband could come over and tell me how many heads of horses my little valley could support. I don't want to overgraze."

She gave him an appraising look. "You'll have to feed them in the winter regardless. You want to raise them to sell, or just have them to watch?"

"Dunno. Don't think I need it for a business. I just hate to see all my grass going to waste."

"Okay. We'll talk about it later. I might have a mutually beneficial idea." She snapped off her gloves and tossed them in the trash. "I think you're good to go. Keep some topical antibiotic on that. Silvadene, if you have it. As active as you are, I couldn't put in sutures that absorb and go away. I'll need to take those out in a week or so. If you want, I could drop by...since we're neighbors. Hand me your phone and I'll put my number in."

Using his phone, she called hers. "Now we'll be in both our contacts. You can call me when you have time." She glanced at the door. "I doubt if Bartelli would care, but just so you know? I'm trying to raise money for school. If you know anyone who needs a house call, off the books, let me know. I can handle most things."

He nodded. "I'm sure you can. I'll keep it in mind."

About that time, another girl brought in a tray. Jacy thanked her and turned around. "Now for the good stuff. I'd recommend taking the tetanus shot in the hip."

He stood and slid his pants down enough for the injection. As she pulled the needle out, she raised his shirt, did a double take, and then raised it to his shoulders.

"Jesus, Lane." Her fingers traced some of the scars on his back. "How are you still alive?"

"Eh. That's what they all say." He shrugged his shirt down. "I've used up all my cat lives."

"And then some. You're working on your second cat." Jacy handed him a yellow sheet. "Hand this to the receptionist on the way out. She'll get you squared away. And don't forget to pick up that script at the pharmacy."

"Thanks, Doc."

She stopped, shaking her head. "I'm not a doctor."

He put his hand on her shoulder as he went out the door. No military veteran, active or retired, would ever call her anything different. Especially after seeing she was an 86 Whiskey. "You've earned that title. Wear it with pride."

Pausing at the door, he snagged another palm full of disinfectant from the dispenser. He gave her a sheepish look. "One more thing."

A raised eyebrow was the only reply he received.

Vigorously scrubbing his hands with the foam, he craned his neck to see down the hall. He handed her a five-dollar bill, which would cover his copay. "Can I bypass that waiting room? I don't have a hazmat suit."

"Coward." Jacy pointed toward the back door and laughed as he made his escape.

# NINE

JIM LANE CARRIED his laptop computer out to the front porch, settling into a cane-backed chair in front of a sturdy plank table. He took a deep breath of air, holding the freshness in his lungs as long as possible before expelling a deep sigh. Mornings were the best time of the day, with sleepy birds calling on soft winds, the cool breeze before the sun started boiling the world. For most people, it was an uncomplicated time before the day's spring started winding them up like an old clock.

There were trails left behind on the dew-covered grass. The clearing he'd built his house on was a popular place at night. He imagined that every animal in the forest was curious enough to check on him after dark and scavenge for food.

Movement in the valley drew his attention as a white-tail buck raised his magnificent rack and stared up the hill at him. Jim felt a moment of sadness. The meat would be tough to eat, but that rack might grace some-one's mantle after deer season. But then, the old boy was smart enough to grow old. So, who knows? Dodging fate can be an art form.

Things had changed after the debacle of the last year. Maybe he'd finally come face to face with his mortality. The last ten years with the Shepherds ended with one incident that gutted him. One little blip in life that ended with a rescue gone bad, resulting in his killing a woman so used up by torture and grief that she begged for release. She was holding her dead child, and he'd never seen such supplication in the eyes of a human. He gave her what she wanted and often wondered if she knew the price exacted upon his soul for that favor? It left him hollow and empty for a long time. Her face hadn't lost any detail in his memory over the years.

Retired and living the dream, with a house on the lake and nothing but free time, he thought he'd found a lady to share his time with—until he didn't. The Russian Mafia came knocking on his door. The body count was horrendous as folks discovered the one thing he was good at and it wasn't fishing. He'd made a few friends along the way and fate offered him another lady, though his hold on her was tenuous at best.

Thinking of his life, it was time for a reset, a new beginning. And he was ready.

One failing he seemed to have was reading and being a news junkie with satellite TV and internet. It was easy to become isolated from most of the outside world in their little corner of paradise called Stockton Lake. But every year, the Doomsday Clock took another click toward ringing the bell.

The regime in North Korea wanted the United States dead. Hell, they wanted everyone dead. The only way to keep control of their people was to promote fear of attack and siphoning every resource from the starving country into the military so they could strike first. Recently they'd demonstrated they had the means for delivery. Not good.

The culture in the Mideast was a complete shambles that was spreading across the world. Europe had fallen. Migration was assailing other countries and regions. Once enough numbers populated a region, the Trojan Horse of Hijrah turned into Jihad.

In Jim's humble opinion, the US should pull out of Europe and the Mideast completely. We didn't need their oil or gas, natural or refined. Of course, the rest of the regions would fall into war. Hell, they'd been fighting since the twelfth century anyway. The US could deal with the victor after the dust settled.

And then along comes COVID-19, the novel coronavirus out of China, or Europe, or the USA, depending on who you listened to. The blame game pointed in all directions. A high mortality rate if you happened to be over sixty years old. Was it coincidence that the outbreak happened close to a Level-4 Biocontainment lab? One newsie extrapolated, tongue in cheek, that a cockroach crawled out of the lab and was eaten by a bat. Then the bat soup delicacy transmitted the virus to humans, but who knew? There were different strains on the left and right coasts. China claimed the virus came from the USA. Politics made sure no one would ever know and inhibited any progress for curtailing it.

The book he was writing wasn't about a global outbreak, but if he wanted it, the outline would be in the headlines. All he'd have to do is re-order them and fill in the blanks. As usual, some news sources gave it full coverage while others ignored it. Maybe he should start his book like Snoopy from the Peanuts cartoon. *It was a dark and stormy night.*

He shrugged his shoulders, his rotating neck sounding like popcorn, wondering if he should just disconnect altogether. Websites that carried good news were few and far between. It didn't bode well for the country or the world when everyone was mad about something. And they were. What had the alien said in the movie *Independence Day*? Peace? No peace. What can we do? Die.

His new house was unique, with the ills of the world kept in mind. An apocalyptic novel he'd read recently was written by a former high-ranking government official. In the preface and three-book series, it was obvious that the author and the government he used to work for considered anyone who was prepared for disaster, and were armed well enough to protect themselves, domestic terrorists. Back to peace, no peace. He feared there was a New World Order coming to the USA, and no one would like it except for those in power.

Before building the house, they'd drilled a well and then poured the basement floor and walls. The well house, or pump, was in the basement and protected. He had a windmill, but it didn't pump water. It was a backup power system. The main power to the house came from solar panels concealed on the bluff behind trees, not visible unless you flew over. Sewer was a common septic system. Water from the well went to the tank behind the house and then into the house. Instant water pressure plus an emergency supply if the well pump went belly up. If the tank were compromised, it was switched out of the system and water came directly from the well.

The house was tight with extra insulation and double

gas-filled windows. A small HVAC unit supplied air conditioning and heat when needed, although the fireplace could heat the house in the winter. His house was so tight, his kitchen stove, burning propane, could heat it. Domestic terrorist? No. Prepper? Yes. Last year he'd been ill-prepared for anything, caught flat-footed and not able to defend his home. He'd vowed to change that.

Last year, he'd have been watching the lake come to life through a cool mist over the water. Today, that mist was curling around the trees in the valley below, only disturbed by a few passing deer heading for their bedding ground. A silhouette passed high in the sky. Eagle or turkey buzzard? It was large enough to be either.

He took another deep breath. It was a good day to be alive. Barring any distractions, he'd get some major work done.

# TEN

THE SUV POLICE Interceptor slowed enough to make the turn into his drive on two wheels and then started raising dust in his direction. Okay. Getting work done on his WIP—work in progress—was out the window. He glanced at his watch. Seven a.m. Early for Rita to be out and about. She didn't usually start her day until after eight. She would win the prize for the first distraction of the day.

He said the first thing that came to mind when she walked to the porch. "You look tired, Rita."

"Try a few twenty-hour days and see how you look."

She was in jeans and untucked shirt, the tail hiding her pistol and badge clipped to her belt. With a big sigh, she settled on the porch steps and leaned against the post, closing her eyes. The morning sun painted lines and shadows on her face as she relaxed a moment. Her department had taken to wearing small, business Stetsons, but she must have left it in the car. She was a beautiful woman. Sometimes he ached just from wanting her.

She smiled. "You have any coffee in there?" A second look made her frown. "You look down, Jim. Feel okay?"

"We make a great pair. You're tired, and I look depressed." He stood to go to the kitchen. "I'm fine. Just doing too much reflection on life and not seeing many ways to change it. And I doubt you're here to lift my spirits this morning."

Returning with two cups, he gave her one and set his on the table. "So, what brings you out here so early? Are you starting or ending your day?"

Holding the cup with both hands, she smelled the coffee before taking a sip. "Oh, that hits the spot. I'm just starting after a late night. Tying up some loose ends on the shooting yesterday. The girl was Monica Lewis from Springfield, so State is taking the case. We finally found someone willing to admit knowing her. I'm trying to clean up leads on this end. Getting a lot of nothing."

"How'd State get it? It's your county. The crime scene is here." He wasn't surprised. Barnes warned him this might happen. In fact, he guaranteed it.

Rita nodded, conceding his point. "The girl was in the water, so I got trumped by water patrol. Hence, the State boys. I was told their workload was light and they have a lot of officers with nothing to do and looking for any excuse to visit the lake."

He folded his hands and leaned back in his chair. You'd think there were enough killings to go around and different departments wouldn't have to fight to take the case. "She was shot in the air. Why don't they bring in the Air Force?"

Rita snorted into her coffee cup. "That's good. I'll bring that up at the next meeting. Knowing them, they might follow that advice. It would let them add another layer of bureaucracy to the circus."

He had visions of that advice going up the chain of command in a completely serious manner, like someone calling a military headquarters and asking if they'd page Captain Tiberius Kirk to the phone.

Shaking his head, he said. "Since they have the case, I'd also tell them to do their own grunt work. You're shorthanded as it is."

"Tell me about it." She gave him a long gaze before speaking again. "Look, Jim. I'm pressed for time. How about a new subject?"

"Figured you weren't here for polite conversation." He shrugged, giving her a wary look. "Fire away. It's your visit."

"Okay." She glanced away, seemed to realize the body language mistake and caught his gaze again. "I know things haven't been easy between us for a few months."

"Easy?" Guess that was the first shot across his bow. He couldn't wait for the torpedo. "Try non-existent."

Holding up a placating hand, she replied. "I know. With the election and all—"

He couldn't stop himself. "Which you weren't supposed to do. How was that again? 'Even if chosen by write-in, I will not serve?' You became a politician with your first lie."

She inclined her head with a sigh. "—and getting the department back on an even keel, it's been tough and time consuming. It's not going to get better in the short term. The way things are going...maybe never."

When he didn't answer, she continued. "I'm trying to say I'm sorry and not doing it very well."

He took a sip of his cooling coffee. "It's a piss poor

apology, as a matter of fact. You could have said something to me, talked it out. Instead of running in for a one-night stand occasionally and then leaving before daylight so you don't get caught. If you want out of whatever we have, then get out. I'm a big boy. I can take it."

She wouldn't meet his gaze. "I thought that was every single guy's dream relationship?"

"A hit and run in the middle of the night? Not mine. We had an agreement. Look, we're too old to play these games. I have enough money from retirement and investment funds to keep us in good shape. You promised to give up the sheriff's job. If you'd done that, we'd be sailing happily into the sunset, hand in hand."

She gave him a guilty look. "There's an old saying. Agreements made during pillow talk are not binding. The light of day shreds their logic. You should know that."

"Been reading Shakespeare again?" He rolled his eyes. "So, what's the bottom line? You're wanting plausible deniability in case someone asks? An association with me not good for your image? What?"

"Dammit, Jim. It's nothing like that. But admit it. Your reputation puts some people off. All they remember are dead bodies. The bottom line, as you put it, is that I'm officially not living with you."

"You haven't been, so officially, that's not a problem. What are you doing? This is the damnedest breakup I've ever heard. Is there someone else? Keeping Mr. Right chained to your bed in town?"

He watched her complexion pale.

"You're an idiot."

"Ah. Deflection. That's not good for the home team." He sighed and gazed at the valley. "Alright. You win. I've tried and been rejected. The new situation is noted. I'll live with it. Any other business this morning? Otherwise, get the hell out of here. I need to get my thousand words a day done. That's a promise I made to my pillow."

Her stare could have boiled water. As he watched her hand creep toward her pistol, he folded his own hands and leaned on the table. If she came unhinged, he couldn't shoot her—well, maybe wound her? They both had tempers that got in the way of reason. They were their own worst enemies—temperamental people carrying guns.

With an effort, she finally relaxed. "Fine. Have it your way."

"My way? My way would have you padding around inside making breakfast, barefoot and pregnant. My way would have us working together to build something here —build a life for the next thirty or forty years. You pull away from me, for reasons I'm still not sure of, and then infer it's my fault?"

"Well, that's not how I see it." After several deep breaths, her gaze faltered as she looked away again. "Let's have another change of subject. Everyone knows, or at least suspects, you have an arsenal of weapons here. I'd like to see them. For the record."

Now, the real reason for the visit popped up. "Rita, that change of subject was damned near psychotic." He watched her close for a moment. "Well, let the interrogation begin. Do you just want the weapons here, or in all the hidden locations around the property? You know, buried supplies like preppers do?" He knew taunting was bad, but couldn't help himself.

Anger rekindled in her eyes. "Here will suffice. You're too OCD to leave weapons buried somewhere. You can't clean them."

"Got a warrant?" He held up his hand to stop her reply. "It's a fair question. It begs another question. Why are you doing this? I'm not a suspect and you know where I was when the girl was killed. I'm not your shooter."

"The coroner's preliminary report couldn't nail the wound down to anything other than large bore, given the amount of damage to the body. That girl looked as if someone used a can opener on her. I think we both know what does that kind of damage. I know you have a .308, probably several. Hell, every deer hunter in the county does. But what about something larger, say a .50 caliber? Maybe a Bushmaster or Barrett? After being shot at last year, I can imagine you wanting to bring in a big boy."

"My Henry .44 caliber is big enough to cause that damage, but you already know that." His gaze was level as he conceded. "I also have an M-2 Browning on order. Belt fed ammo for the MA Deuce is hard to find, but I have a few leads. But again. Why are you looking at me for this?"

"That's not funny, Jim. I hope to hell you're joking. Look. I'd just like to check your gun locker to verify a few things. If you have one, it could have been stolen."

"If something is not there, how do you know if I had it? Or, if it was stolen? You're not making sense."

Receiving nothing but a hot stare, he reached into his pocket and tossed her a key ring. "You know where it is, right by the bed you used to like bouncing around on."

She flinched away and turned sharply toward the door. It was a half hour before she came out of the house, her eyes red-rimmed and puffy. She tossed the keys to him. "Jesus, Jim. Are you figuring on starting a war?"

"Nope." He grinned at her. "But, fondly remembering

last year, I want to be better prepared if one starts. I like to do my part."

"Why the Barrett? That's only good for one thing."

He took her by the shoulders, ignoring her flinch—what was going on with that? The fragrance of her hair made him ache for what he was losing. Turning her toward the valley, he pointed toward the tree line. "I have the room to raise a few cattle, more likely a few horses, been talking to Jacy Mane about that. See the wooded area about a mile away? When the coyotes come for the foals, I'd like to be able to deal with it."

She shrugged his hands from her shoulders. "But a fifty caliber?"

"It makes sense. No wounded animals running around, suffering. Don't have to allow so much for wind and it gives me a pretty flat trajectory to the target."

Her eyes were big as her gaze bore into him. "That's a damned expensive coyote gun."

"Let's call it a varmint gun." He shrugged dismissively, couldn't keep the sarcasm at bay. "You never know when varmints will crop up, or how many at a time. Some travel in herds."

"You're a strange man, Jim Lane." Turning, she gave him a sad look.

"Circumstances breed character. You should know that. I guess my secret's out. I'll be forever dubbed the strange man. The recluse that lives on a hill."

"Well, smartass. There's one other thing that brilliant mind of yours may not have thought about. That murdered girl was running before she dove. That makes for an extremely hard to hit target with a scoped rifle. Damned near impossible. So, let's forget her a moment. If you draw a line from the top of the ridge behind Chicken

Rock, through the point where the girl was hit, what was at the end of that extended line?"

He stalled a moment, not liking where this was going, and finally nodded. "A couple of fishermen minding their own business?"

"Bingo." Rita nodded, watching realization dawn on his face. "You think about that. Let me know when you come up with a name—let me handle it."

She looked around the front of the house. "You know, there's something new every time I come out here. You've got raised beds with veggies?"

It took him a minute to catch up with the segue. He'd have to take notes to remember everything they'd covered. "I need to grow something so the deer don't starve. I can fatten them up, and it's fresh meat on the hoof if I need it."

"Why here?" She made a half-circle wave toward the valley. "I always thought you'd rebuild on the lake, or fix up your old house. It was a good spot. I loved the back deck. Why'd you turn into a hermit out here in the boonies?" She checked her watch, edging toward the steps to make her getaway. "And what's with the laptop?"

"You're asking questions that would take hours to answer." He shrugged and shook his head, trying to keep up with all the twists and turns of the conversation. If she really wanted answers, she wouldn't be leaving. "I thought you'd know the answer to that. To make it simple, last year took a lot out of me. I'm tired of fighting. Getting old, I guess."

"Tired of fighting? Right. Tell that to Dickie."

"That's different. I call it exercise, but I'm done with that and shouldn't have been doing it. Dickie isn't the problem, his boss is. I think we both know that."

He continued, knowing if he paused, she'd jump in and defend Roman Fielding. "As far as the lake property, I still own it. Maybe I'll fix it up and rent it out. The lake is busy and noisy most times and I like the solitude here. Never was much of a people person anyway. Plus, keeping distractions down helps me write."

Her head whipped around so she could stare at him with a smile. "Write? What, a book? What's it about? Can I see it?"

"Secrets and lies—and no."

She glanced back toward her vehicle, trying to hide the tears. And the anger. Maybe she needed medication to keep up with the bouncing balls of her mood swings?

"Well, let me know when it's out. I do read on occasion, especially fantasy and fiction."

He chose to ignore her comeback. Arguing nuances and shades of conversation was never his strength. "Don't get your hopes up. Unless I self-publish, I'm sure it'll be years. Once the manuscript is done and if I'm lucky enough to find a traditional publisher who wants the story, it will still be a year or more. The only stories that hit the fast-track are romance and even those are hit and miss."

"Wow. I didn't realize it took so long to get something out." She gave him a skeptical look. "Of course, you have to finish it first. I'll believe that when I see it. Well, gotta go. Take care, Jim."

"What's the hurry? It's early. We're still friends and you can relax a little. Have another cup of coffee."

"No can do. I've heard of an amateur meth operation in a trailer house out by Twin Bridges. They're close enough to the road to blow up some tourists, along with themselves. Bad for the economy. The tourism committee of the Chamber of Commerce is already on my back, with the shooting at the lake. I need to check out the lab before the tweakers wake up. Meth heads are not early risers, so I need to get out there."

"Need help?" He couldn't keep the concern from his voice. The only thing more unpredictable than a tweaker, was a tweaker woken from a drug-induced coma. "I can give you backup."

She gave him a long look and finally shook her head. "I got this, Jim. Really. And I do have deputies."

Deputies? With her twenty years of military police, she was more than qualified. Her deputies? Not so much. "Are you taking them with you?"

"Nope. They're busy." Hands on hips, she gave him a stern look. "Let it go."

Though he wouldn't tell her, his opinion of her deputies was a good example of what you get when you always go with the lowest bidder. You get what you pay for.

"Okay. Sure. Been nice talking to you. Stop in anytime and all that."

Her eyebrow raised at his sarcasm, but she didn't comment. She left in a rattle of dust and exhaust fumes, leaving him sitting at the table staring at a laptop screen...wondering how to feel. She hadn't really told him anything. Like a good interrogator, she'd drawn him out and turned all his questions back into themselves. What did she want from him?

And a law enforcement officer doing drug busts alone with no backup? That was a recipe for disaster. He knew she had a lot on her plate—that was also a bad recipe. Distractions could be the third strike at the plate.

# ELEVEN

HE'D STOWED his laptop in the house and was climbing into his GMC Sierra when Josh Barnes pulled into his drive. Jim's new truck was bought after he saw a commercial highlighting the new tailgate. It had a man-gate with steps and everything—opened sideways or up and down. Make fun all you want about a man's truck—those were damned convenient. The end gate on his old Dodge weighed a ton, or seemed to. Plus, the Dodge V-8 turbo was noisy. He'd sound like a small-engine airplane coming in for a landing. On this day, the silence of new vehicles might be the best choice.

Barnes stepped up to the passenger side of the truck with a smile. "Where are we going?"

"We?"

The man shrugged, losing the smile for the moment. "Wifey somehow got bent out of shape when the news report came out yesterday. I didn't see anyone taking pictures, besides me anyway, so I thought it was safe. We're sitting comfy on the couch watching the news on our giant wide screen TV, when there I was at a crime

scene in all my glory, notebook out and looking official."
He shook his head with a rueful expression. "That did
not go over well. She used some brand-new words I
wasn't aware she knew, and gotta wonder who taught
them to her. Anyway, she's visiting relatives in KC for a
couple of weeks, even after I begged her not to leave me
alone and promised that I'd use you for a boat anchor. I
can't figure out why she left. She knows I get bored at
home by myself, and I always get into trouble."

Of all his attributes, making him laugh was the best
one. "You're bored already? It's been less than a day since
the shooting. Read a book. Go fishing. Knit some socks."

"Hey, I'm high maintenance, and fishing wasn't all
that restful yesterday. After what the water patrol pulled
out of the water, if I catch a catfish, I gotta wonder what
it's been eating. I may be scarred for life."

"You know catfish are the garbage fish of the lake,
don't you? They're bottom feeders. That's all they eat."
Jim grinned at him. "Okay. Hop in. I can always use your
sage advice. We're going to do overwatch on a drug bust.
Maybe."

"Whoa." Barnes hesitated, gaze sharpening. "All
things considered, I'd rather not."

After he explained what Rita told him about the bust
and no backup, Barnes shook his head. "So, we're just
going to innocently cruise by and see if she needs
help?"

"Pretty good plan, right? Just drive by and happen to
notice her car. We can always stop to report a litterbug or
something. Trash along the highway is bad around
there."

"Swell. We sound like a couple of teenagers who just
happen to drive by some girl's house, maybe fifty times."

Barnes scrambled into the truck. "You know where we're going?"

"I have an idea." Jim recalled seeing a single-wide mobile home near the road and west of Twin Bridges. If he remembered right, the front yard looked as if a junk-yard exploded. "We should be there in about twenty minutes."

"You ever notice how you always have to try all the bad ideas first before you ever come up with a good one? So, why are we doing this again?" Barnes pulled a pistol from under his shirt and checked the magazine. "Not that I care...asking for a friend."

He snorted and shook his head. "Yeah, right. A friend. Look, I worry. It's that simple."

"About Rita?" Barnes kept his gaze on the bridge coming up. "Well, bud, pardon my saying so, but that doesn't seem like a two-way street to me."

"Yeah, she kinda gave me my walking papers this morning. I think. It's like she wants to tell me to get lost...but doesn't really want to tell me. I guess she hopes I'll take the hint."

"With your hard head, that can't be going well."

A few minutes later, he glanced over at Barnes. "I've been doing a lot of thinking lately. Do you have a position or philosophy of life?"

Barnes jerked his head around. "Oh, no you don't. I'm supposed to come back and ask if you're drunk, like in *Chuka*, that western by Richard Jessup? I re-read that the other night after I stole it off your kitchen table. I ain't falling for that unless you just want to play trivia to pass the time. Boring as hell, but go ahead."

He glanced at his friend. "So, no?"

"No. Well, there is one thing. Stay out of other

people's business and don't play Looky Lou at a drug bust."

"That's two, so we'll throw out the last one."

It was a bright and shiny day and the road noise changed to a high whine as they crossed the rough-textured east bridge over Stockton Lake on Missouri 215. The sun winked off the choppy waves below and the morning sailboaters were taking full advantage of the wind. Fishermen would be anchored in protected coves. Lake Stockton was famous for wide open water and windy days.

Rita's new, shiny SUV Interceptor was nestled among four rust-bucket cars parked in haphazard fashion, fronting a dilapidated trailer. He steered the pickup into the short drive, finding an open space to park between two dented and bullet-punctured washing machines, being careful not to block the drive. Allowing for one person per car, Rita could be seriously outnumbered.

The old single-wide trailer perched on cracked and broken cement blocks with part of the roof rotted and caved in. All the windows they could see were covered with aluminum foil. The residents may as well have posted a sign "doing drugs here." The home was surrounded with debris that ranged from overstuffed chairs and couches, old hot water heater tanks and abandoned propane cylinders. The highlight of the yard was bird-spotted clothes flapping on a clothesline.

"This must be one of the new tourist lodges on the lake shore. I've been thinking of investing in that market," Barnes commented, shaking his head. "We must be in the high-rent district."

As they got out of the truck, the door of the trailer slammed open, smacking against the side of the building.

A barefoot, emaciated man dressed in jogging shorts leaped through the opening, tripped on the porch rail, and landed face down in front of them, squirming like he was trying to swim. When he started to rise, Barnes casually put a foot on his back to hold him in place.

"Stay put, pard." Barnes held his nose against the man's stink. "You know you can't fly. Why'd you try that?"

The man twisted his mouth out of the dirt, panting like he'd run a mile. "Lemme go. Lemme go."

"Well, at least we don't have to search for weapons." Jim looked at his friend. "You know you're going to have to throw that shoe away, don't you?"

Two women walked out of the trailer, hands zip-tied behind their backs, stumbling down the rotting steps of the leaning deck. Both had stringy hair and were partially dressed—the lack of clothes showing off the untreated sores dotting their bodies and protruding ribs for anyone interested enough to count. Like moles forced into the light, they squint their eyes against the sun.

Rita gave the two men an irritated glance as she shepherded her charges toward the SUV. Both women had red welt marks on their foreheads that may, or may not, have matched the tip of Rita's Talon baton.

Looking at the two women, Barnes shook his head. "How do we unsee that? This is going to be burned on my eyeballs forever."

The woman leading the small parade was using a man's jockey shorts for a halter top, donned upside down with her arms through the leg holes and her head stuck through the pee-hole.

"You wanted to tag along." Jim suppressed a grin, shaking his head. "You have to applaud the ingenuity. I wouldn't have thought of that in a million years, still can't figure out the mechanics."

After depositing her charges in the back of her SUV, Rita walked over. "What are you two doing here?"

Jim raised his eyebrows. "Just passing by and saw your vehicle. When we saw all the cars, we thought we'd lend a hand. Is the trailer cleared? Lotta cars here."

"It's clear. I wouldn't be out here waltzing around if it weren't. You don't think I can handle this?" She knelt and zip-tied the man Barnes held captive. "You shouldn't have stopped. Your lack of trust is not endearing."

Barnes snorted. "What about this one? He was leaving at a high rate of speed. Were you going to let him get away?"

She shrugged. "Get away? I was hoping he'd run all the way to White Rock so I wouldn't have to put him in my vehicle. Thanks for messing that up, by the way."

"Anytime." Barnes took his foot off the man, put a hand on Jim's shoulder for support and examined his shoe. "Your department owes me a new shoe."

Rita laughed. "Fine. Submit the proper paperwork, and I'll fast-track it. I don't think I have enough in petty cash for your brand of boots."

"Where do I get that paperwork?"

She grunted, helping the man to his feet. "Dunno. Never seen it."

They were interrupted by a low, dull whump from inside the trailer, and flames melted through the foil-covered windows. A small spiral of smoke rose from the collapsed part of the roof.

"Should we call rural fire?" Jim was edging away. "No telling how many propane tanks are in there."

Shaking her head, Rita pushed the tied man toward

her SUV. "I'd wait a bit. Make sure the damned place burns good. No point in endangering any firefighters."

"Brushfire?"

"Not likely. We're surrounded by green foliage and live trees. Not much brush to burn. It'll take EMS a half hour to get here anyway."

Barnes flinched as another muffled explosion rocked the trailer. "Well. Alrighty then. You're the boss."

"Jim?" He was getting that look from Rita again. "I know you're concerned. I get that. I know we have history. I get that, too. One last time. Stay the hell out of my business. I won't warn you again."

One of the women in the back seat of her vehicle vomited into the floor well, immediately followed by the other. Their man was cursing and screaming at them while butting his head against a window, leaving a bloody smear. Rita sighed, shaking her head. "That'll never clean up. Looks like PJ gets a new vehicle. I'd better call EMS for these idiots before they drown themselves. If it makes you happy, I'll even call rural fire. How about you boys take off before the circus arrives."

When they didn't move, she tried again. "If I arrest you for interfering with a crime scene, I'll have to put you in the back with them. It's gonna be crowded."

She stood wide-legged with hands on her duty belt, beautiful as ever. He locked his gaze on her cobalt-blue eyes for a moment. He wondered if a blood test would show she'd taken some kind of mind-altering drug.

"You'd actually try that? What's happened, Rita? What's going on with you?"

When she didn't reply, he sighed and turned to Barnes. "Let's go, Heckle."

# TWELVE

THEY RETURNED to the homestead to find Jacy and a Pancho Villa lookalike sitting on the porch. A couple of dusty four-wheelers were parked in the shade of the house.

"Hey, Jacy." He pointed his thumb at Barnes. "This is Josh Barnes. He's confused about his role as my sidekick, but generally a good man."

She gave him a quick, cataloging gaze and then laughed. "Hi Barnes. Nice to meet you. Jim, I remembered you talking about horses. I have a proposition for you. This is Pablo Estevez."

They shook hands all around before Jim spoke. "So, what's the deal?"

"Pablo works for us sometimes, but I'm going to have to let him go. His work at Roberts Farm is slowing down, and he needs a job. For me, sales are down on quarter horses, and feed prices are up. I have to admit, we're in a bad place." She looked around. "You have a nice place here, and I wondered if you could use a good man to get it into shape. There's a lot you need before you run a few head of horses or anything else out here."

Jim looked him over. The man was as stereotypical Mexican cowboy as he could get. He was short, brown, and had a huge mustache. The Stetson he wore was wide-brimmed and dirty brown, with a sweat line around the band. His sleeveless shirt allowed a Marine Corps tattoo to show on his arm. Quizzical brown eyes watched the proceeding closely, with no hint of being uncomfortable with the scrutiny.

Several dormant ideas popped into his mind. If he wanted to turn over a new leaf and change the direction of his life, there was no time like the present. Up to this point, he'd just been treading water, waiting for life to happen. It was time to turn the whole basket of leaves upside down and shake it. Hell, why not? He almost smiled. If there were a flag denoting a plot twist, he'd hoist it on his flagpole.

They were waiting patiently. "You vouch for him, Jacy?"

She watched him closely, a curious look on her face, and nodded assent. "One hundred percent."

"No reservation? No quibbles?"

"Quibbles?"

"He can't help it," Barnes interrupted, and he, too, was all attention seeing a change in his friend. "He's being an idiot."

"Alright." Jacy nodded and smiled at them. She gave Jim a serious look. "No reservations. He's a good man. I'll leave the quibbling to you."

"That's high marks." He grinned and cut a sly glance at Pablo. "Can I call him Pancho?"

Jacy and Pablo answered in unison. "No."

"Dammit."

Barnes interjected. "You know, I don't know what's going on here, but this is a good idea. If anyone needs a caretaker, it's Jim. I'm a busy man and can't watch him every minute. It's like a full-time job."

Jim stuck his hand out again. "Mr. Estevez, you're hired. Providing you can put up with me. Anytime you feel the job is too much, you can walk away. We'll have to talk about how much I can pay you and what your duties may be. Do you have a family?"

"I do. My wife Juanita and two little girls. We have a shack in town until I can find something better." He took a deep breath, giving an expressive shrug. "Money is tight for everyone, and I don't blame Jacy for letting me go. I appreciate you giving me a chance."

"I'm sure you'll be worth every penny. Jacy, if you have time, why don't we kick back with a tall glass of Red Arrow tea and discuss some ideas that have been bouncing around my brain pan."

Barnes slapped Jim on the shoulder. "Okay. I'm out of here. Can I use the pontoon? I might do some night fishing."

"You know where the keys are. And find someone to go with you. No night boating alone. The way you navigate, you could be motoring in circles all night. Them's the rules."

"Yes, mother."

Jim filled large glasses with ice and grabbed a jug of tea from the refrigerator. Once the glasses were full, he raised his toward them. "Success."

"Success," they replied in unison, more than a little confused and trying not to be conspicuous with curious glances at each other.

It took a moment to get his thoughts together while they watched him over the tops of their tea glasses. "I have come into some money...not gazillions, but enough. To make things clear, I'm looking for good friends and partners as well as hired help. You may think it strange, but after last year's fiasco, I'm well on my way to becoming a hermit of sorts. Crowds of people don't interest me anymore. Listening to the news every day, I'm also becoming interested in being prepared...long term. We need a buffer zone in case the world goes...um...bad."

"That sounds sensible." Jacy shrugged and smiled at his red face, refilling her glass. "In the Army, we called it 'tits up.' How about you, Pablo?"

"The same." Pablo nodded. "Jim, I agree with your thoughts, but like Jacy and her family, we haven't had much chance to act on it. Without money, it's hard to prepare for anything. It's easy to store good intentions, but we have no place to put anything else."

"Well, now you do." He smiled at them. "Pablo, you're going to be a busy man. Like I mentioned, I've recently come into a good bit of money. In my opinion, money in the bank is stored in the same vault as your good intentions. Since I'd rather have things that are worth something, instead of money in the bank, I'd like you to help me spend it."

"Well, since I've lost my helper, I have work to do." Jacy stood, finishing off the glass of tea. "I'll leave you men to it."

He quickly put his hand on her arm. "Please stay if you have the time. I can use your advice."

After she sat back down with a curious look, he continued. "I don't necessarily need to own horses, but I'd like to see some roaming around. If you guys need more pasture, I have plenty available. Since I don't know much about this, I need advice from both of you. I assume I'll need a fence down by the road. Gate or cattle guard?"

Jacy glanced at Pablo before answering. "Gate. An electric motor with a solar charger to open it works pretty good."

"Okay. So, Pablo, it looks to me like we'd better get your new home in here before the fencing goes up. Agreed?"

He gave Jacy a quick look, who just shrugged back at him. "My what...?"

"What did you think? I'd make you live in a tent? Now, I'm notorious for knowing nothing about women. You'd be surprised how many people tell me that. But you'd better take Juanita along. I think the manufactured double wides would be quickest. I've looked at some, and they're nice. The only requirement I have is if you can find one with a fake log exterior to blend in with the landscape, that would be good. If not." He shrugged. "It's not a deal breaker."

He rummaged around in his wallet and pulled out a debit card. "Use this. If there are any problems, have them call me, which I'm sure they will. Today would be a good time to start."

Pablo was stunned, and Jacy had tears in her eyes. Pablo finally spoke. "And where shall I put this new home?"

He waved his hand at the valley. "There's a limestone outcropping down by the tree line. It's a good, cool spot with a natural spring. Anyone coming in the drive wouldn't even see your house or know it's there."

Pablo still looked stunned. "And this is important...why?"

Jim grinned. "Look down the valley toward the highway. See those pretty, white rocks along the side?"

Shaking her head with a small smile, Jacy whispered. "Well, I'll be damned."

"I see them." Pablo nodded, looking at her a moment.

"Well, using your experience as a door-kicker and someone who likes to blow shit up, about how far apart do you think those rocks are?"

He didn't turn to look. "One hundred yards. I noticed them coming in."

"So, a ranging tool...just in case?" Jacy still gazed out the window, slowly shaking her head.

Pablo turned quizzical eyes on him. "And my home situated where you want...?"

He shrugged. "Crossfire, just in case. If things ever deteriorate to that level, I want nothing left to chance."

Jacy laughed, shaking her head at him. "And you seemed to be such a nice man."

"Oh, I am."

Pablo shrugged and continued, seeming to be taking everything in stride. "Water and sewer? Power?"

"I have a plan." He grinned at them.

Jacy interrupted. "How long have you had this plan?"

He glanced at her. This girl was sharp. "Fair question. I just made it up, so we'll need to flesh it out as we go. Any input is greatly appreciated."

"We'll need a barn, maybe some outbuildings." Pablo glanced from his old boss to new.

"Luckily, that's not my deal. You're in charge of that." He paused. "Just one thing. Try and situate any other buildings with their backs butted up against the bluff. We wouldn't want anyone hiding behind them with a good field of fire, and the bluff is good protection in the winter from the north wind."

Pablo's steady gaze locked on Jim's. "This is a godsend for my family. Not knowing me, how can you trust me that much?"

"I know Jacy—"

She interjected sarcastically. "We just met."

"—and I'm a pretty good judge of character." He gave the man a direct look. "You gonna steal from me?"

Pablo set up straight. "Of course not."

"Then it's settled. Start today, make it happen. Sooner is better than later. If you run into problems, solve them or call me."

Pablo palmed his hat and rubbed his head. "I have no phone."

"You're still not getting it." Jim sighed and then patted his shoulder. "Pablo, that debit card is to a special farm account. Even I can't believe how deep it is. Use it for what you need and what you think we may need. Itemize your bills and give them to me once a month. For now, instead of a salary, use the card. If you or your family need something, buy it. Food, clothes, phones...I don't care. I'd appreciate it if you could take care of all this. I have other things to do."

They watched as Pablo jumped on his four-wheeler and tore off toward the bottom of the valley.

Jacy stood and shook his hand again, a not-quite smile painting her face while she searched his eyes. "You're a little crazy. Sure you know what you're doing?"

He'd hoped it would be Rita helping with the planning, but that wasn't to be. "You're not breaking new ground with that opinion. Everyone tells me that. Some in not-so-kind ways."

"But all that money?" She had a look of wonder as he watched her think about it.

"Look. There are things I've been wanting to do but didn't know where to start or have the motivation to do it—just kept it all on a back burner. Sometimes things fall in your lap. After last year, a certain player in not-so-legal circles caused me some life-threatening problems, and I think because of his daughter, grew a guilty conscience. To make himself feel better, he gave me a lot of money. It's not hurting him. If he runs out of money, I suspect he tells someone to go get some more and they do it. Maybe it's dirty money, but who cares. I've decided to get off my butt and do some good with it."

He paused. "Next question. I count you as a friend, and I'm wanting to build something here. Do you or your family need help?"

She stood, staring at him with a flat expression until it turned soft. "Like I said, it's been rough. The economy is in the crapper. We're struggling, but so is everyone else. It's hard to find a rodeo that gives out actual prize money anymore. You can't eat buckles, so our customers aren't investing in good horses. The days of barrel racing or goat roping may be gone. The kicker is that the markets may force us to switch to beef cattle, but we don't really have the acreage for it. That's why I'm trying to build on my nursing degree. But no, we don't need help. At least, not now. Thank you for offering, but hubby would never go for that."

"He sounds like a proud man. With you beside him, it's easy to know why. He should be popping his buttons.

I'd like to meet him sometime. Look, I can put you on the payroll as an adviser if that helps. Or my ranch nurse."

She shook her head, laughing. "We'll see." Taking a moment, her gaze took in the valley with a slow, meticulous look ending with him. "So, what are you trying to do here? I mean, really."

"The short answer is, I'm trying to build something worthwhile. I had kind of an epiphany a while back. I've been close to death a lot. Mostly, I've looked around and seen that when I'm gone, I'll leave nothing behind. I thought there was a woman who'd share all this with me, but now that's gone away. Be glad you have a good husband and your children. That's a legacy. You'll be remembered. Me? Not so much. I can't keep women interested over five minutes before they put me at arm's length and just want to be friends."

She shrugged. "Some people aren't meant for a double harness. It doesn't mean they're bad people. Do I need to put you on suicide watch?"

"Not yet." He grinned at her. "But thanks for the thought. And like you said, the economy is in the crapper, the world is on the brink, and I'm tired of getting run over by things I can't control. Simple as that. I'm taking control, at least of what I can."

"What about your lady friend, the sheriff? Is she the one you thought would share this?"

Jim shrugged, gazing at a circle of buzzards wheeling in the distance. The correlation between them and his love life wasn't lost on him. "For some reason, Rita wouldn't piss in my mouth if my tongue was on fire."

She grinned as she looked away a moment before giving him a sad look. "Is there another man involved? There usually is. If a woman has something she wants, if she's satisfied, she won't usually drift away unless there's something pulling her—or pushing her. Are you pushing?"

"I think she views my pulling as pushing. And someone else? I don't know. I haven't noticed because I haven't been looking. Hell, I hardly see her anymore. When you trust someone, you don't look. But it doesn't really matter. That's a decision she must make on her own. I won't muddy the waters."

"Oh, it matters. More than you know." She looked at her watch. "Well, in true southern fashion, I've said I'm leaving about four times. Maybe I'd better do it."

He stared across the meadow at a deer bounding away from the trees. Dogs or coyotes must have spooked it out of its bedding area—or a cougar. He'd heard one the other night. There were a lot of things in the dense forest surrounding the lake that most people wouldn't normally associate with it—black bear and panthers, to name a few. Maybe Sasquatch.

He shrugged and smiled. "I heard a song last night and can't get it out of my head. It was my epiphany, and I woke in a bad mood. I'm sorry if I've pushed that on you."

She gave him the hand-palm, shaking her head. "Please don't put a song in my head. I have enough banging around in there. When I get home, it'll be nothing but SpongeBob SquarePants."

"It was Sean Rowe singing, 'To Leave Something Behind.' It's like Johnny Cash singing 'Hurt.' Sticks with you. I call it tortured voices."

Staring at him a moment, she finally shook her head. "Well, shit. I've heard that song. No wonder you're depressed. And now I'm depressed. Thank you for that."

She gave a finger wave as she left. "I'm outta here. Don't forget the suicide hotline. Maybe they can help."

"Will they fix my love life?"

She stopped and studied him. "Given that I don't know you all that well, this may be out of line. But I'm thinking nothing is going to fix your love life." She grinned before turning away. "Sorry."

Once again, he sat in front of his laptop, but words didn't come. Watching the sun warm up the world around him, he slammed the lid down.

"Another day in paradise."

# THIRTEEN

IT WAS STILL early in the day when Jim thought of Dan Hyatt and his family. On impulse, he fired up Google and got an address for their farm. Google Maps routed him south of White Rock, west through Lockwood, north a few miles, and turn right on State Road BB.

He jumped in his truck and took the closer route by returning to White Rock, turning west on county road BB and stopping at the last place on the right. Take that, Google.

A long, narrow lane nestled between waist-high corn and no-till beans peeking through wheat stubble led him to a white farmhouse with a green metal roof and playground equipment in the front yard. The lane, two bare tracks with grass growing in the middle, was narrow and gave him no opportunity to turn around when he saw the number of cars in front of the house. A cold knot gripped his stomach, thinking of all the reasons for the gathering.

Pulling into the barn lot, Jim stopped and was looking for a place to turn around when a man tapped on his window.

"Help you, mister?"

Lowering the window, he looked the man over. He appeared friendly enough, standing with a curious smile waiting for an answer. "I'm Jim Lane. I thought I'd check on the Hyatts' welfare, but it looks like a bad time. That's what I get for doing things at the spur of the moment."

"Yeah, should'a called." His feet shuffled in the grass as he stared at Jim. "You from the welfare people? It's a sad thing when you have to accept that."

"No, I'm not from the county." When the man didn't elaborate, Jim prodded. "Anything serious? I know Mr. Hyatt is in the hospital."

"Not anymore." The wind ruffled the man's hair, what was left of it, above the tan line from the cap he probably wore every day.

No secret is ever safe. The revealing of it just depends on the force applied to retrieve it. That was a hard and fast rule, yet there are exceptions. If Jim ever wanted a secret kept, he'd give it to this man who would drive an interrogator crazy.

"Did Mr. Hyatt come home recovered?"

The man stood a moment, concentrating on an answer while looking over his shoulder toward the house. It was agonizing to watch.

"Okay." Giving up, Jim sighed. "Look, this is obviously a bad time. I'll turn this rig around and head on out. Sorry for the intrusion."

"Mister!" A voice caught his attention, and he recognized the little girl he'd met at the Hot Spot running toward him, bolting from a group of people congregated by the front porch. "Mister? Please wait."

He put the truck in park, shut off the engine, and stepped out. "Janie, isn't it? How are you doing?" He made a small leap of intuition. His glance at the people congregated around the porch didn't reveal any happy faces. "I'm sure sorry about your troubles."

She ignored his hand and hugged his waist hard, face turned and buried against his stomach. Stepping back and kicking at a rock with her patent leather shoes, she wouldn't look at him. The silence stretched a moment, neither of them knowing how to fill it. Finally, she spoke and it nearly broke his heart. It was also something he thought about as he grew older. In the heat of battle, you take a life. How many leave someone missing their daddy? What would it be like to have someone to miss you? Would that responsibility be incapacitating?

"My daddy went to heaven." Her voice was soft, barely audible. "He couldn't hang on any longer. Momma said he tried really hard, but just couldn't stay with us. I know he wouldn't have left without trying the best he could. He was just hurt too bad and couldn't even say goodbye." She looked back toward the house, so he barely heard her. "Momma is really sad. She's trying to hide it, but I know. I loved him, too."

Glancing up at the secret keeper before kneeling in front of the girl, anger flashed through him, followed by sorrow and then the unavoidable conclusion that the man responsible for this girl's grief was going to pay. He'd made that promise in hot anger, but it was a cold promise he would keep.

He reached out and touched her shoulder, wondering how he could be this involved with someone he didn't know. "I'm sorry. You know he loved you, too, and didn't want to leave. Remember the good times, and the bad will go away. I know these things are hard to understand, but you'll come through it. Just give it a little time."

She gave him a tearful nod. Before she could say anymore, footsteps brushed through the grass and then crunched on gravel as a man and woman stopped beside him. The woman pulled Janie against her as she spoke in a tight voice, rough from crying. "I'm sorry, but I don't know your name."

He pulled his hat off, bunching the brim in his fingers. "Jim Lane, ma'am. I'm sorry for your loss."

She nodded once, cleared her throat, and continued in a soft voice. "I'm Jana Hyatt, and this is my daughter Janie—seems you two have already met." She gestured at the man by her side. "This is Pastor Tanner."

After handshaking all around, she spoke to the pastor. "This is the man who gave us a rather large donation." She met Jim's gaze. She'd been crying, but he'd have to adjust his estimate of ten miles of bad road by a good margin. Somewhere between plain and beautiful, her sturdy appearance and manner projected a calm strength. What surprised him was the icy-blue eyes— eyes he'd never want to look at him across a gunsight. He'd seen eyes like that before, and it startled him to think of Alina.

She continued. "I want to thank you for that. It helped a lot and came at just the right time. We were really down in the dumps, and it was much appreciated."

"You're welcome." He reached into his pocket and produced a card. He'd had them made on a whim, showing the Lazy J Ranch with his name and cell number. "If you or Janie need something, I'll be upset if you don't call. Anytime."

Maybe she wanted to say more. He felt she did, but her shoulders shook and after a grateful look, she guided Janie back toward the house. The woman looked back at him once more, over her shoulder, and gave him a half-smile.

Starting to leave, he hesitated and spoke to the pastor. "Will they be taken care of?"

Pastor Tanner nodded. "I believe so. The neighbors are finally stepping up to help. Funny, it took a death to bring that about. Before, all people knew was that Dan got beat up in a bar fight and didn't want to get involved. Probably looked down their noses a little. Now they are helping."

"As for Jana?" He shrugged. "I believe she has a sister in Kansas City that they'll stay with. Maybe. It's hard to tell with her. She's a tough nut, doesn't have many friends and is kinda standoffish. Probably why people didn't step up quickly. No telling what she might do. As far as money? Insurance will kick in, and I'd be surprised if she doesn't have a few offers for the farmland after the funeral. If they don't owe too much, she might break even. So, yeah. It's a tough time, but she'll get through it."

Watching the mother and daughter blend back into the crowd of well-wishers, he didn't envy them. To him, grief and mourning were private things and the last thing he'd ever want was a crowd. But people are voyeurs, even if they don't mean to be. They can't help it. Especially at funerals, they watch to see how you're taking your grief, if you're crying, if you're holding up. Few of them are actually concerned. His attention came back to the pastor.

"Well, I'm glad of that. It was a terrible thing that happened. Senseless."

"That's true." The pastor sighed, shaking his head. "It's too bad they didn't catch the people responsible. Poor Dan never regained consciousness to name his assailants. I'm not sure law enforcement is getting the job done on this one. But those responsible will pay for their sins. It may take a while, but it will happen. We have to believe that."

"Yes, sir." Jim's gaze took in the farmhouse and peaceful surroundings—the mowed lawn, the purple martin house taken over by sparrows, pin oak and maples bending before the wind, the young groundhog sitting by the corn, unperturbed by the crowd.

He finally returned his attention to the pastor. "As a matter of fact, they will pay. And sooner rather than later. We can't blame the sheriff. I know a little about this case, at least her end of it. Legally, there's no evidence she can act on and she won't do it any other way. No one is talking, no one saw anything. I suspect those responsible for Dan's beating have a pretty good grip on the underbelly of Limestone County."

His comment drew a sharp look from the pastor. "I hope no one takes revenge for this. I've told his friends and family the same thing. Let the law do their job and the Lord will take care of the rest. Those that take revenge leave their own souls in peril. I hope you know that. There's always the chance of punishing the wrong people."

Jim shook the pastor's hand in parting. "I'm certain the Lord will pass judgment on them. Maybe that process should be sped up. It's my thought a more corporal judgment will come. Justice isn't always found in a court of law, Pastor. The souls of the damned are already forfeit, so there's nothing to lose. Revenge isn't always a bad thing. Good day, Pastor."

He reached out and rested his hand on Jim's arm. "So, this person who believes his soul is lost, thinks he can take another soul since there's no downside? Their souls are lost anyway. Interesting concept."

The pastor gave him a quizzical look. "I'm not sure I understand what you said, even though I paraphrased it, but I'll figure it out. Before you go, I'd like to invite you to Sunday services." The man handed him a business card for Immanuel Lutheran Church in Lockwood. "I think you'd enjoy the fellowship. We're a friendly bunch." He paused. "And I'm always up for a good riddle."

Jim paused with one foot in the cab, arm hanging out the lowered window in the door. "Sorry, Pastor. I don't think so. I'm not much of a people person. Besides, I've been to his house...the Father wasn't home. At least, not for me."

"Well, okay then." The pastor smiled and nodded. "That sounds like a catchy line from a country song. Being somewhat an expert on the subject, I can assure you of one thing. He holds your soul in his hands, Mr. Lane. What you do with it is up to you. But know this. No matter what you think, the Father was with you when you came into his house and with you when you left. You think about that. Oh, and don't hesitate to call me if you have any more one-liners. I can always use them in one of my sermons. It keeps the congregation from going to sleep." He paused before continuing with a smile. "Well, most of them."

Jim backed his truck around to leave and glanced toward the people on the porch. Little Janie waved to him, and he responded with a quick double-tap on his horn. Driving the lane toward the highway, he had a nagging feeling he'd just been spanked and wasn't quite smart enough to know it.

# FOURTEEN

IGNORING Roman's warning to not come back, Jim parked across the street from The Gallows Bar and Grill, crossed the highway and threaded his way through the cars in the jammed parking lot. He gave a half-wave to Deputy Rails. The man stood by his cruiser, gazing at all the vehicles and looking confused. If his job were traffic control, he may have just realized it would be like herding chickens chasing grasshoppers on a windy day.

Pushing through the door, blasted by heat and a heady aroma of beer, sweat, and some cowboy's liberal application of aftershave that smelled like bug spray, he stopped in his tracks. On the raised dais set aside for the night's entertainment was a Sean Rowe lookalike, right down to the tortured voice and beat-up guitar, doing covers. Dammit! Just what he needed. Haunting, gut-busting songs and alcohol.

He found a place at the long western replica bar, complete with brass foot rails, and got Ruby's attention. When she approached with a wary eye, he smiled. "Looking for Roman. Seen him?"

She shook her head, giving him a JB on the rocks, without asking. "Ain't seen him since we heard that farmer died. That kind of news travels fast. I did see Dickie cruise through a while ago." Putting her hand on his arm, she squeezed hard. "Don't start anything tonight. It's too crowded. Some innocent bystander might get hurt."

He studied the amber liquid through the clouded glass before knocking it back in one swallow. The burn only lasted a moment. "C'mon, Ruby. Point out one person in here that's innocent. Excluding you and me, of course. Your innocence is legendary."

Shrugging, she shook her head as she gazed around the bar. It took a moment before she finally spoke. "Well, you won't find the cast from *Happy Days* in here, but it ain't Sodom and Gomorrah either."

He set the glass down and held his hand up in surrender. "I'll try and be on my best behavior."

She snorted. "Yeah, but you're best at breaking things."

After stopping at the Hyatt farm, conflicting thoughts were rampant. The little girl had pulled his heartstrings and woke yearnings in him that he thought were buried deep. Hearth and home. Children. Then there was the pastor who wouldn't take his crap—in a nice way, of course. Jim's world of black and white, no middle-ground, take no prisoners, was starting to show some gray around the edges. There were cracks in the foundation. Thinking back, he realized things were a lot simpler when he had no friends.

The music ended and the floor cleared as people sought refreshments. Waitresses scurried between tables and the bar. The girls might not be college grads or economic geniuses, but they knew the correlation between high alcohol content and increased tips. Add cleavage, tight jeans, and a big smile? A week's wages could be made in one night. For some, he was sure a quickie trip to the parking lot wasn't off the table.

The big question was, why did he stop at the bar in the first place? It was like watching the half-time show at the Super Bowl. A lot of purists hated it. If you don't like that sort of thing, don't watch it. Coming to that conclusion and exercising his freedom to not like crowds, he was about to leave when he noticed Jacy Mane being led off the floor by a thin, wiry cowboy about her height. Both were in country dress-up—jeans, boots, pearl snap-button shirts and short-barreled hats. Short-barreled meaning the brim was narrower than a regular hat worn while working and wider than the little black hats the Mennonites wore.

The man's hand was around her waist, and she was smiling over her shoulder at him. Jim felt a moment's envy. That's the way life should be. Two people anchored together. Laughing at small talk, they sat at a table and kicked back longnecks while the band tuned up for another song.

Trouble played the next tune and Dickie was singing the song as he strolled up to the Mane's table, holding his hand out in invitation for Jacy to dance. Standing in front of them, his size blotted out everything but their faces— Jacy firmly shaking her head and her husband's expression going from neutral to full outrage.

Never having seen a bouncer in The Gallows, Jim came off the stool and grabbed Dickie by the collar before things got out of hand. Every man and most of the women in the bar were armed in some fashion. For Jacy's husband, it was a belly knife. Anyone who rode horses in rodeo or worked cattle stood the chance of getting tangled in rope, or baling twine or netting, that was attached to some two-thousand-pound animal. Most carried a short, heavy-bladed knife right next to their belt buckle to cut themselves loose, usually with a fat, bone handle that was easy to grab. Hidden from Dickie's view under the table, Jim caught the shine of a blade coming loose from its scabbard.

He pulled Dickie backward and off balance. "Little Dickie? What a surprise. I didn't know you could dance. Hell, you couldn't walk the last time I saw you. We need to talk about a few things, so how about I buy you a drink over at the bar? I think Ruby can still make a Shirley Temple. Would you like pink or lime green?"

It didn't help that someone guffawed in the background. His confused face turned a mottled red, but before Dickie could answer, Jacy's man was on his feet. "Back away, Mr. Lane. I believe I have a prior claim, and I stomp my own snakes."

Jacy stood next to them, ignoring Dickie. "Jim, this is my husband, Donny Ray."

Jim held out his hand in front of a bewildered Dickie to shake hands. "Pleased to meet you, Don." When his hand was ignored, Jim slowly drew it back, eyes narrowed, glancing between the couple. From the White House to the outhouse, even your enemy will shake your hand in public. Especially if you're country folk. What the hell was this about?

"It's Donny Ray, not Don. Why don't you go back to the bar, Mr. Lane?" Donny Ray's voice was sharp. "I may not be a professional killer like you, but I can handle this tub of lard."

"As you wish." Jim stared at the man a moment, nodded once, raised his hands in an "I'm clear" motion, and retreated to his barstool. Professional killer? He didn't remember turning pro—didn't know there was a league for it.

Jacy didn't admonish her husband to apologize, didn't speak to him at all. She turned to the table, sat, and drained her bottle. Slamming the bottle down on the table, her gaze met Jim's, and she mouthed, "sorry."

Finally finding his senses and not to be ignored, the tub of lard picked up Donny Ray, not Don, by his neck and crotch, tossed him into the band, and ruined a good set of drums, turning a microphone stand into a question mark. The squeal of the unseated microphone blasted everyone into silence until someone yanked the power cord of the amplifier out of the wall socket.

When Donny Ray came staggering off the bandstand, his next feat was to find himself lying unconscious by Jacy's feet. Dickie shook his hand from the pain of laying a straight punch to Donny Ray's forehead, took one look around, and stomped out the front door.

Jim stood to help, and Jacy looked over at him and shook her head, her disgusted gaze settling on her husband.

"Ruby, fix me another JB and a long neck for Jacy." He glanced back at her table and noticed a woman joining Jacy. What the...? A cold knot formed in his stomach. "Add a water glass filled to the top with vodka—your cheapest brand."

Moving over to their table, he side-stepped Donny Ray, who lay blinking at the ceiling with a blank stare, and set the drinks down.

Jacy laid a napkin over Donnie Ray's eyes, so they

wouldn't get dirt in them and then gave him a smile. "Thank you. Jim, this is Alina. She's a new friend of mine that's new to town."

A new friend? He forced his attention back to Jacy. "Do you need to check on Donny Ray?"

"You mean Mr. Glass Jaw, or forehead, as the case may be?" She snorted, glancing at her husband. "He's been bucked off too many times, so he's concussion prone. He always seems to lead with his head. But the idiot has a pulse. That's all I care about right now. I'll take him home later and stick his head in an ice bucket. Sorry about what he called you."

He forced himself to shake the other woman's hand, staring into ocean-blue eyes. "Alina? I used to know a woman with that name—kind of a bag full of monsters, but nice enough in her own way. You remind me of her. Been in town long?"

"Not long." She squeezed his hand, lingering with the touch, before taking the glass. "It's not surprising that you haven't seen me. I'm kind of an invisible girl. One of my strong points, I guess." Alina, gaze holding on his, put the glass full of vodka to her lips and drained it without expression before setting it on the table.

Jim shuddered as he watched. Was the trick not to breathe after chugging vodka? How could any human do that?

"That wasn't water, was it?" Jacy watched her new friend a moment. "Do you two know each other?"

"I don't know. Maybe our paths crossed at some time or another." Jim threw back his JB, toasting one of the strangest nights in memory. "I used to know someone like her, but I'm not sure who this is. Do you believe in the legends about shape-shifters?"

Donny Ray stirred, trying to hack up a lung, so they helped Jacy pick him up and plant him in a chair. The band had regrouped, sans drums and a pissed-off drummer, and were cranking out a slow song. Jacy held out her hands. "Please?"

They drifted out on the dance floor, moving smoothly on the polished hardwood. Her scent was mostly overpowered by smoke and beer, but enough was there to tease him into impure thoughts. Jacy did not dance with the customary polite inch or two of separation. A quick glance revealed Alina trying to engage Donny Ray in conversation, handing him another napkin as the man sat drooling. Seeing no danger from that quarter, he settled into the saddle and lost himself for a few moments.

Her voice startled him. "I'm sorry about the ruckus and what he called you. I've been talking too much."

"No harm done, at least not to me." He nodded toward the table. "Dickie's not too bright, but he packs a punch. He's not your normal barroom brawler. You might want to get Donny Ray's head checked."

She moved against him, and he felt it from his thighs to his chest. "I shouldn't be doing this, but maybe it's just payback. Hubby lets his mouth get way ahead of his brain. Comes with the cowboy hat, I guess. It's been worse since money got tight. He's prideful. We'll pull through this, but he doesn't see it that way."

"Easy, now. I'm wearing a hat."

"Yeah, you're country all right. But you're no cowboy." She snickered, glancing up at him. Her expression sobered. "At least, not that kind."

Sometimes his own mouth got him in trouble, but

he'd been agonizing in self-reflection lately. "What kind am I?"

"Sure you want to know?" She gave him an appraising look, stepping away while holding his hand before settling back into him. "We saw a few like you in the sandbox. There was one in particular. Our squad was taking a break inside a gutted building. You know the type, most of the buildings looked the same. All mud and rock walls, blown-out windows, and no roof. The ones that make our slums look like mansions.

"Our Overlook, what we called our sniper, radioed that a friendly was coming in. A man walked through a doorway, looked us over, nodded once and settled into a corner, asleep in seconds. He was a walking arsenal covered in dust and dried blood, with a couple extra AKs slung over his shoulder. His plate carrier was torn and punched with holes. A flap of Kevlar was hanging from his helmet. Most of his clothes looked as if they'd been through a blender. I started to get up to see if he needed medical and our Top stopped me. Sarge said the man was a cowboy who'd been out killing, reducing the enemy, I think he called it. That was the man's only job. Move behind the lines and reduce the enemy. When the man woke, he'd be gone to kill again. He said it was best not to wake him because he was too dangerous to approach while asleep. A few minutes later, I looked around, and he was gone. He'd left us the captured rifles.

"We all had our jobs. We were door-kickers, clearing out the neighborhood. My job was watching their backs and patching them up. Our Overlook was a sniper who never missed, or if she ever did, we didn't know it. She loved to catch sappers setting IEDs so she could give them a premature detonation. The cowboy? We saw him from time to time—called him Pale Rider. We never knew him, never saw his face when it wasn't covered with goggles. He must have liked us because he always dropped off captured weapons. The AKs packed a lot more punch than our M4s, and we used them on occasion."

His thought was the cowboy might have stayed around them because that's where all the action was. Whether they knew it or not, he was the point of their spear.

"Nice story." He gave her an uneasy look. "That ain't me. You must know that."

"Um hmm." She nuzzled his shoulder. "Long as the monster stays asleep, it isn't. It's buried deep inside, but I can see it, feel it." She raised her head to look at him, nostrils distended, still with the quirky smile. "Smell it."

"Like PTSD? I'd admit to that, on occasion."

"No. I sense something deeper. Like something you keep in a room with the door nailed shut. You only let it out when you want a lot of something dead. An instructor I had called it the Hulk Syndrome, after the Incredible Hulk."

He pulled her closer than he should, given she was someone else's wife. Maybe the worms in his belly would go away with distraction. His hand drifted lower down her back before sanity prevailed, and he pulled it back into safe territory. "What kind of doctor did you say you wanted to be?"

Laughing, she shook her head. "Not that kind. I won't pop your lid to look inside. I have enough monsters of my own to manage."

"I'm surprised you didn't shoot Dickie." He'd felt the

bulge of a pistol in a paddle holster under her shirttail and hoped to God she hadn't felt him.

"It was close, but I thought hubby would last longer. He's tough. Then it was too late. Besides, he'd never forgive me if I stepped in. Like I said. Prideful."

"How much do you know about Alina?" If there were a joker in the deck of cards called his life, she was one. The only reason he could think of that would bring her here, he didn't want to think about.

"Not a lot. She doesn't talk that much about herself. She came out to the place asking about riding lessons. We kind of hit it off. Now that I think on it, I don't even know where she lives."

His glance at their table found Jacy's new friend staring at him. He nodded to her while whispering to Jacy. "I'm not sure she'll make a good friend. She has a hard look to her and may not be someone to get crossed up with."

"I knew it. You know her." Jacy laughed and shook her curls. "I'll stay on her good side. My radar still works pretty well. I'm thinking you're two of a kind. She might have the same monsters you have—just hides it better."

"Well, that makes three of us with monsters. Maybe we should form a club."

The guitarist was getting bored with the same three chords, and the singer was repeating the refrain, so the song was winding down. The air conditioner wasn't keeping up with body heat being generated, and a trickle of sweat coursed its way down his spine. Or maybe it was fear. Nothing is scarier than a female dissecting your mind.

With a serious tone, she spoke again. "Maybe I'm speaking out when I shouldn't. I do that a lot. But Jim,

you're a lost soul and a good man going to waste. You
need to find an anchor."

Her hip accidentally, sort of, nudged him in the
crotch. "And just so there's no misunderstandings? I'll
take this as a compliment. I want us to be friends. But
just that. This dance is a one-off and a bit of fun. I'm
married with children and have a short-tempered partner. I'm settled. Understand?"

"Yes, ma'am. If that's your story, I hope you can stick
with it." He shook his head. "All the women I know have
somewhere else to be, something else to do. Story of my
life." He'd just been flayed open, inspected, and put back
together by an expert.

She laughed again, giving him another appraising
look. "Hey, that's a better tagline than we're getting from
the podium—a country song in the making. You'll make
millions of pennies."

They got a staggering Donny Ray into the passenger
side of their dented F-150 pickup. Jacy drove off with a
wave as Jim whirled on Alina.

"What in the hell do you think you're doing? Why are
you here?"

She was still sweating from the humid interior of the
bar, and one step brought her heat against him. "You're
not looking into breaking up that girl's marriage, are
you?"

That was a worry for her? "Never entered my mind.
She's a good woman. What's your interest? Whatever
you're planning, you need to disengage."

"Nope." She laughed. "How do you like that? This
country stuff is getting to me. Nope. I can't find any kind
of contraction or euphemism that justifies that word.
Anyway. I'm not working any angles, and I have a right to

a life, too. There is only one interest for me around here and you should know what it is. I like this area and Jacy is becoming a good friend. Both of us need lady friends. A couple more blows to the head like her husband got tonight, and she may be a widow soon. See you around, boy." She finger-waved as she drifted off into the darkness of the back parking lot. He heard a horn chirp when she hit her key fob.

"Dammit." He exploded a ridge of gravel with his boot. "Dammit to hell." When that didn't feel right, he kicked a tire, setting off the car alarm.

Finally, he looked at the sky and screamed. "Shit!"

A heavy hand on his shoulder stopped his tantrum, and he turned to find the steroid junkie, Deputy PJ Rails, looking concerned. "Is there a problem here?"

"Shut the hell up."

# FIFTEEN

TRADER JACK'S was about as far into the boonies as you could get, yet hiding in plain sight. All you could see from the road was a welded pipe swing-gate and dirt road that disappeared immediately over a hill. When Jim pulled off the road and up to the gate, he noticed a call box on an extended metal arm. He backed his pickup and maneuvered over to the box. Pushing the silver button, he waited for a reply. And waited. After a minute or so, he took out some aggression and pushed the button several times. Still no answer. But he did get a response.

A man appeared on the opposite side of the barbed wire fence from the call box. Dressed in Cabela's finest computer-generated forest camouflage, he wore the latest tactical orange sunglasses from the '*but wait*' commercials and a plate carrier vest, minus the ceramic plates. The butt of a pistol was showing in its MOLLE carrier, and his suppressed M4 was held in a ready-down position. What the hell? The guard looked as intimidating as a cartoon character.

"State your business." The man spoke in a menacing drawl.

Jim watched the man closely. In this situation, the more amateur a man was—the more dangerous he was, prone to doing stupid things. "I'm here to get supplies from Jack Snow. Maybe. I may just leave. This ain't much of a welcome."

The guard pulled out a small radio. "You got a name?"

If the radio signal made it over the steep hill behind him, he'd be surprised, but why not? "Jim Lane."

He rolled his eyes as the guard turned his back to have a private conversation on the radio. Once that was over, the man unlatched the gate and waved him through.

"Have a good day. When you come back, give me a honk. I'll let you out."

"What happened to the call box setup?"

The guard pointed to a solar panel with several holes in it. "A visitor didn't like to wait. We ain't got it repaired yet. There's just no patience left in the world."

The trading post was about a mile from the gate, circumventing two hills and a twisting drive along a dry creek bed, finally crossing a low water bridge. When he stopped in front of the post, he realized he'd styled his own home after this place. The store was built on the front of a cave, with most of the store inside. It made sense. Heating and cooling done by Mother Nature. A natural spring was in front, complete with koi and lily pads in the still water away from the spring. A wooden bridge was built across it, leading to the front door.

Taking his time getting out of the pickup, Jim noticed two more armed men loitering in the trees. He'd stepped into an armed camp. Curiosity might get him killed, but he had to wonder why. It wasn't this way the last time he'd visited.

Stepping through the front door, the smell of old leather and gun oil hit him, along with a heavy dose of cooking smells. The walls were lined with hats, boots, and camo for different seasons. The long guns graced the wall behind a long glass counter showing pistols inside. Ammunition was stacked in crates and boxes on tables. A pallet of MREs sat in one corner. He'd bet money that would be the last item to leave the place.

Even more interesting was a pallet of N-95 face masks and another of hand sanitizer.

Jim extended his hand across the counter. "Morning, Jack."

The big man grinned, shaking his hand. "What brings you out here? Surely you don't need more guns?"

"Do you ever have enough?" He shrugged. "Thought I'd pick up some ammo. And if I buy enough, maybe some information to go with it. Did you sell out of those new AR-15s?"

"Yeah. First day. But I do have something you might like. Got some Ruger Mini-14s. Sweet little ranch rifle."

"I'll pass, but thanks. I have a new foreman who's an ex-marine. I haven't asked what he'd like to shoot, so I'll hold off on that."

The man shoved up the sleeve of his shirt to show a tattoo. "No such thing as an ex-marine."

"Yeah, yeah. I won't get into that argument." Jim looked out the window as a man patrolled by. "What's with all the guards and firepower? Are you expecting an invasion soon?"

"Guess you don't listen to the news. I ain't sure if

North Korea is gonna EMP us, or if that Kung Flu Chinese virus is going to break out, but something's coming. I feel it in my bones. I'm just protecting my assets." He leaned hard on the ass.

Jim looked around, curious to see what Jack was stocking for his assets. "I don't think that virus is anything to worry about, do you? You can't shoot it anyway."

"Really? Nothing to worry about?" He stepped in front of a laptop sitting on the counter, pulled up a website, and turned the screen so Jim could see. "Then why did they just designate another twenty military bases as quarantine sites? And I'd like to point out that the article says ANOTHER twenty bases. If there's nothing to it, why are so many agencies running scared?"

"I don't know. Nothing better to do?" Jim watched the guard stroll by again. "Oh, I forgot to mention it. Your guard at the gate? Turned his back on me to radio in. Since he was on the other side of the fence and couldn't check me for weapons, I could have stitched him up and waltzed in here unannounced."

"Really?" He shook his head. "I'll have to talk to him about that. He's new and young." His grin widened. "Of course, you'd have had to get by the drone that was hovering around, and then there's my QRF, quick reaction force, you'd have had to deal with. I won't even mention the claymores and other surprises we have."

"You just did. Jesus, Jack. What are you dealing here? Meth? Heroin?"

"Nothing that will harm my fellow man...unless they come calling with ill intent." Jack sat on a stool with his arms on the counter. He motioned toward the door and another armed guard in the room walked out. He laughed at Jim's surprised look. "Got a false corner over there. Kind of my ace in the hole. So, what kind of info are you looking for? I assume this is a private conversation."

Jim shook his head. It would take air support to take this place out. "Roman Fielding. I need to know where he's hiding."

"Yeah, I heard about that farmer dying. That was a bad deal and for nothing. That Dickie gets wild in the head sometimes, and there's no stopping him. I hear you've been shaping him up a little. I'd have paid good money to see that. But you watch out. He ain't above a back shooting. Anyway, Roman and Dickie shack up with some Mexican woman named Bella, or something like that, out on H highway. It's about three miles north of White Rock. Got a mailbox looks like a largemouth bass, and the house is way up in the trees. You can't see it from the road. No telling how many men he has at a time around the place. They sell a lot of stuff, but don't make the mistake they're users. A man needs to scout that out real careful before he goes busting in there. That's all I can help you with on that matter and you didn't hear any of this from me. Ain't nobody going to miss that sumbitch if he disappears. He's elbow-deep in any kind of perversion you want."

He sat up straight. "Say, did they ever find out who shot that girl over on Chicken Rock? Heard she was a real looker. What a waste. And a strange deal."

"No, not that I know of. That's the kind of thing that never gets solved unless somebody talks. So far, nobody's talking. Rita says the state boys took that over and they're chasin' their tails. It was a long-range shot, and there's not much to go on."

"Well, I wouldn't discount the drug angle. Those kids got no sense." He shot Jim a side glance. "Speaking of Rita...probably a good thing you aren't still chasing that."

Jim's heart trip-hammered, but knowing Jack, he waited him out.

"Oh, shit. From the look on your face, that's bad information. The word's out that she's taking on more than she can handle, snooping into things that don't concern her. She's knocking off Roman's meth labs pretty regular. The Good Old Boys let it be known that if she dies, there's a lot of money and favors to be paid. Something could happen on her next raid, and I've heard that's today."

Jim felt lightheaded, trying to control his breathing. "Somebody from her office must be talking out of school if you know where she's going. I need you to find out who. I'd appreciate some help with that. The last thing this county needs is a deputy with a loose mouth, or a snitch. Any idea where that next bust is going to be?"

"Yeah, I heard it's a place just west of Bona, right past those two hills that drunks try to jump with their cars once in a while. Ain't one of them made it yet. There's an old, white two-story clapboard right on the highway."

He was speed-dialing Rita as he went out the door, praying she would answer.

"Hey. What about that ammo?"

# SIXTEEN

RITA MORRIS WAS CRUISING SOUTH of
White Rock following a canary yellow pickup that slowed
down to a crawl when she came up behind it. They might
be guilty of something, or just nervous. Folks did weird
stuff when being followed by a patrol car. She thought it
funny that the best way to slow down traffic was to park a
sheriff's vehicle beside the road and leave it. Some of the
more inventive departments put a blowup doll behind
the wheel. You could see the brake lights for miles.

The dispatcher at White Rock PD lit up her cell
phone. "Hey, Donna," she responded. "What's up?"

"Mrs. Chandler called and said you need to come out
there and maybe bring an ambulance—said PJ hurt
himself."

Deputy Rails had the K-9 unit for the day and had
been dispatched to the Chandlers to serve a warrant for
failure to appear. Since Mrs. Chandler was more likely to
cook PJ biscuits and gravy than do any kind of harm, she
figured something was wrong. "Okay. Show me
responding at ten twenty-one." She hit her strobes,

dodged the giant canary when the brakes were slammed and pulled into the front lane of the Chandlers within ten minutes.

"White Rock show me on scene at ten thirty-one."

The dispatcher responded. "Ten thirty-one."

Mrs. Chandler was trying to herd a cow through a gate that led to a pasture. Since the pasture was cropped down to the roots and the grass in the yard was a foot high, the bovine was resisting. It looked to be a Jersey and Rita remembered hearing they were unstable and downright cranky. It would have been fun to watch if it weren't for her deputy.

Deputy Rails was leaning on a fence post holding his head while the German Shepherd lay quivering next to him. She pulled his hand away from his head, looking for a wound.

"PJ, what happened?"

The man watched her with a blank look on his face. A red lump was already showing on his forehead. He tried to say something, waved uncertainly at the dog and then stared at her. He shook his head like he was trying to clear his thoughts and grimaced in pain.

Pulling her mini Maglite from her duty belt, she checked his eyes. Both pupils were equal and reactive, although he seemed to have trouble focusing.

Popping her back hatch, she grabbed a cold pack from the med kit, squeezed it to mix the chemicals, and placed it on his forehead. Four wraps around his head with a self-adherent wrap to hold the pack in place and that was all she could do for him in the short term.

After calling 911 to dispatch an ambulance for PJ, she turned and yelled at the woman. "What the hell happened out here?"

The woman gave up trying to herd the cow and finally came over. "Sorry about all this, Sheriff Rita. It ain't been a real good morning around here."

"I can see that. So, you want to tell me about it?"

The woman shrugged. "Well, your deputy was giving me those papers you sent, when his dog got out of the car and started barking. That old brindle cow doesn't like dogs at all. The wild dogs do that to them, chase them all the time out in the pasture, and it makes them skittish. Anyway, she came after the dog, busting through the fence. That dog commenced chasing after her. The cow was kicking up a storm and bawling to beat the band."

Rita was developing a tic in her eye. "So, how'd the deputy get hurt?"

"I'm getting to that." She glared at the deputy, hands on hips. "He was trying to get the dog to leave my cow alone. I'll give him that. At least he tried. When he couldn't, he pulled out that contraption with the wires on it and shot the dog."

"No." The corner of Rita's mouth twitched. A scenario full of cartoon characters was playing out in her mind. The deputy had stun-gunned the dog. Rita stood rubbing her face, wondering what a stroke felt like. Good Lord.

Finally finding her voice, she continued. "I think I understand. That takes care of the dog. What happened to PJ?"

"That's the weird part." She poked at the dog with her cane. "He bent over to take care of the dog—that dog ain't looking so good, by the way—and the cow kicked him in the head. I know how much that hurts, been there my own self, so I called for help."

Wondering why Mrs. Chandler didn't think tazing the dog was weird, she speed-dialed Deputy Crewes. The department's Energizer Bunny answered on the second ring.

"Hey, Rita. Wassup?"

"Allison, drop whatever you're doing. I need you at the Chandler place ASAP. PJ was serving papers and got hurt."

"Hurt?" Allison laughed. "What happened? Did she feed him too much, and now he can't get up?"

Through the cell phone's speaker, Rita could hear the motor of Allison's Dodge Charger Interceptor winding up. "No, nothing like that."

Rita stopped a moment, trying to get her giggle reflex under control. "Don't drive off the road when you hear this. He tazed the K9, which in most departments is like shooting a fellow officer and then somehow, a cow kicked him in the head. Anyway, the ambulance is on the way to take him to Mercy for a possible"—she looked at the deputy—"make that probable concussion. He's going to jump up and start claiming he's Batman in a minute. I need you to pick up Tucker at the office and bring him to drive PJ's car back to the station."

She looked at the dog. "And one of you needs to take the dog to the vet. He ain't looking so good. He's got a bad case of the quivers."

"The dog, too? Is that what we tell the vet? He's got the quivers? I can't wait to hear this story. It'll be a bit before I can get there. I'm over on the northwest side, south of Jericho Springs."

"We'll be here, unless some circus animals get loose somewhere and I'm called away."

RITA SAT IN HER SUV, waiting for Deputy Crewes. The ambulance crew had loaded a stupefied Deputy Rails up and carted him off to the hospital. She didn't know what this would do to him. He wasn't all that bright in the first place. Probably nothing. He had a hard head.

She'd tried to pet and reassure the dog, but he growled and snapped at her. Not that she blamed him. She'd be pissed, too. If the dog ever stopped shaking and wanted to be petted, she was sitting close by with her door open. That was about the closest she would get to a mad German Shepherd.

Earlier, Mrs. Chandler had listened patiently as Rita explained that, when a law enforcement officer gave her a speeding ticket, it wasn't an award for going fast. If she didn't show up and either pay the fine or talk to the judge, then she could be arrested—given they had time, on any given day, to do something like that.

Mrs. Chandler gave her homemade cinnamon rolls and a glass of fresh, cold milk, probably from that bubble-headed Jersey cow. Rita sighed. Why couldn't life be so simple every day? What was the saying? The only easy day was yesterday?

She had a murder in her county, but was only too happy to give that over to State. It was going nowhere. No shooter, no weapon, no brass, and no witnesses—at least to the shooting. There were plenty of witnesses to the result.

Dan Hyatt had died without waking up. That left them with no suspects to his beating. Most knew what had happened, but in the eyes of the law, her hands were tied. Again, no witnesses.

Now, she'd been notified a detective from Springfield would be visiting, checking on the murder of the girl at

Chicken Rock and possibly interviewing people about the shootings the year before. That could be a problem, depending who the detective talked to.

She could hear a car approaching in the distance and knew it was Deputy Crewes. No strobes or siren, just a souped-up Charger and Allison's need for speed. Leaving her cell phone on the holder in her vehicle, Rita got out to brief her deputy and help get the dog loaded up.

Once the dog was loaded, Deputy Crewes stood by Rita. "I smell cinnamon rolls."

Rita moved to block the door. "Yeah, I had some. You need to get going, Deputy. I'll be along once I take the plate back inside to Mrs. Chandler."

"Are there extras...to share?" The deputy was trying to see around her boss. "She wins first prize at the county fair with those rolls."

"Well..."

She forgot how fast her deputy was. Allison faked left and then pivoted around Rita, slid into the vehicle, and came back with a sweet roll the size of a volleyball. She was already chewing, guarding the roll from her boss as she moved to her own car.

"Gawd, this is good."

Rita was hoping to save that one. "Don't get your steering wheel all sticky and have a wreck. I may have to write you up for this."

"Really?" Allison gave the sheriff a concerned look. "Don't you feel even the least bit guilty about holding out on us?" The dog, suddenly feeling better, was already licking her fingers.

"Get out of here, Deputy."

# SEVENTEEN

JIM'S CALL to Rita went to voice mail. "Rita, don't go on that drug bust today. It's a setup. Call me."

Jack must have called his gate guard because the gate was open when he got there. Barreling north toward Bona, he kept to the speed limit. Between the hills and curves, too much speed meant you wouldn't get where you were going. Ever. The trip was about forty-five minutes of gut-wrenching worry, because she didn't answer his call. He passed the twin humps in the road going too fast, not liking the weightlessness or the workout his shocks got when he hit the second hill. The bottom of his grill chipped a piece from the asphalt.

The house sat next to the road and looked normal enough. A couple of trucks with flatbed, round hay bale loaders were parked in front. The pole barn in the back was half full of hay. There was no sign of activity when he eased into the lot. Maybe this was the wrong house? It looked like a working farm with nobody around.

Easing the safety strap from his holster, he moved toward the house. The upside was that Rita wasn't here, at least her vehicle wasn't, but he still needed to check. He was too exposed out in the open, so he hurried to the house, watching the windows for movement.

Pulling his Glock 22, Jim stepped onto the porch of the old run-down farmhouse and immediately saw exit holes punched through the wooden siding next to the door. A quick peek in a window showed four men down in the living room. Easing in the door and ignoring the obviously dead bodies, it took him a few minutes to clear the house. There was a back door in the kitchen, so he took a napkin and twisted the dead bolt closed. Anyone coming at him from that direction would at least make a little noise.

Where was the shooter? Glancing out the windows, all he saw was a tawny, yellow cat with one ear chewed off strolling toward the hay barn. A cardinal was piping in the trees, while a Carolina Wren, easily one of the noisiest birds on the planet, fussed in the bushes. As he watched, a blackbird swooped on the cat causing it to jump. Normal, everyday stuff. Except for the smell of death.

He stood for a moment in the doorway between the kitchen and the living room. There was no one in the house and he didn't hear anyone leave in a vehicle. Too many questions and no answers. Finally, he moved inside the room, keeping out of blood splatter. There wasn't much, all four had head wounds, but he didn't want to leave anything pointing to him that would confuse the investigation. This would probably go down as a multiple murder, drug or gang related. He didn't see any brass left from the shooter.

Looking at the men, he didn't recognize anyone. They were dressed in jeans and faded shirts, work boots and gimme caps. Just four country boys hanging out in a drug house. A couple of AR-15s sat on the coffee table and he was tempted to borrow those for his own collection—bad idea. Each had handguns stuck in their belts, except one. It was still gripped in his hand and it looked as if he'd got off a shot, which earned him an extra hole in his forehead. He didn't see any extra ammo laying around, or drugs for that matter. They were just sitting around waiting for something. Or someone. Rita.

His best guess was that someone came in the back way and popped them. Looking at them, it was a clinical hit. The two men sitting on the couch had wounds in the back of their heads. If you didn't see the hole in their cap, you'd never know it. He figured the shooter was moving left to right down the length of the couch. The third man caught it in the temple as he turned. The last man was hit just above the eye. Close range, but still uncanny marksmanship.

But then, the unexpected must have happened. An ambush inside an ambush. Possibly as the shooter left, someone came in from outside, behind them. It's always the unknown factors that get people killed. The exiting bullet holes must have come from this man's gun. Seeing it from the inside, he could tell the rounds weren't fired from the four victims. They hadn't moved.

A mystery. Who was the shooter? Did they bust up the ambush, or was this something else entirely? Opening the front door, he stood just inside the threshold...listening...watching. Nothing seemed out of the ordinary.

The feral cat crouched, a study of patience, watching the offending blackbird. If it got close enough? Lunch.

**ROLLING UP TO HIS CABIN,** the late model Toyota Prius was the most out-of-place thing he'd seen in a long time. He couldn't stop himself and did a quick, guilty look around. If anyone saw a Prius in front of his house, he'd never live it down.

Maintaining his country-boy status was the least of his problems. Glancing inside the car, Alina sat leaning forward against the chest strap of her seat belt, her bloody hands resting on her lap. Pushing down an unaccustomed moment of fear, he reached in and checked her pulse. It was strong and steady. She had a shoulder wound with a slow trickle of blood, meaning no artery was hit. Given that her complexion was ghost-white, he couldn't tell if she was pale. He speed-dialed Jacy on the chance she could help and had to leave a message. Zero for two on speed dials today. Not a good record.

He found a blue plastic tarp and put it on his dining table before he brought her in. She was still passed out when he laid her on it.

"Where's my pistol?"

Her voice was like a raspy, unused hinge, and he flinched at the sound. Well. Guess she was awake.

"I need it, Jim. Please."

With a sigh, he took it from his back pocket, cleared the chamber and set the safety. Already suspecting the answer, he didn't check the magazine for missing rounds. He'd bet anything there were five spent brass casings in her pocket. The Ruger Tactical SR22 was a nice weapon and appropriate for this woman—suppressed and lethal at close range. Anyone thinking a .22LR caliber pistol wasn't deadly hadn't met a good shooter, or the Israeli

Mossad. It had as good a one-shot stopping power as much larger calibers. A little something called ballistic shock. "Alright, here's your teddy bear. Against my better judgment."

Taking the pistol and laying it down beside her, she looked at him with a wry smile. "You don't have good judgment, or I wouldn't be here."

"What happened? Who did this?" The circumstances finally clicked in his mind. "Wait a minute. Were you at a certain farmhouse this morning?"

She grimaced as she shifted her weight. "It was a setup. I was trying to help."

He shook his head. "I can't imagine you trying to save Rita. That doesn't make sense."

"You idiot. She wasn't the target." She flinched again as she tried to shift position on the hard table. "You've lost your edge, Jim. Get your brain to working."

Mind whirling with the implications, he was staring at her when he heard the pickup arrive, recognizing the squeaking suspension of the old F-150. When the door opened, he didn't look around. "Hey, Jacy."

She walked to the table, wearing scuffed jeans and desert-tan combat boots. A stained smock was under an unzipped fisherman's vest with all the pockets stuffed full. The heavy army-issue canvas medical kit slung over her shoulder would drop most women to their knees.

She lowered the bag by the table, gaze scanning Alina's form. "Hi, Jim. What in the hell did you do?"

"Wasn't me, although I've been tempted from time to time. I'm sorry for pulling you away from work, but this can't be reported. All she did was get crosswise with some meth heads on my behalf. I owe her."

"I wasn't at work." She nodded. "I'll see what I can do. No promises."

Alina put her hand on her pistol, her weak voice strained. "I'm not sure about this."

Jacy's left eyebrow rose, along with the tail of her shirt. Her hand was on the checkered grip of her Beretta MX4. "I know we just met not too long ago, and I kinda thought we were friends. So let's get something straight. Regardless of that friendship, if you lay your hand on that suppressed assassin's wet dream you call a pistol again, we'll have a comparison test between my .40 cal and your .22. You won't like the results. Sweet gun, though."

Alina's gaze locked on Jim. "I like her."

He put his hand on Alina's good shoulder. "Listen to me. You probably know that Jacy is a nurse. Aside from that, you might say she has some tactical experience in your situation. Trust her. She also has three little boys and a husband that works his ass off trying to make ends meet. She's studying to be a physician's assistant, and she'll be a good one—and a doctor if she had the money and time. She'll take care of you, but you need to reciprocate."

He squeezed her good shoulder. "She's taking a big chance for you, so her money problems are over. Do you understand? She's good people."

Alina's gaze traveled between them and then settled on Jim. "She's too sweet looking to be a nurse...or a medic. Besides," she sighed, cutting a glance at Jacy. "I thought she just raised horses."

She tried to move and winced. "Somehow I doubt she'd do this for me. But yeah, I got it. I'll be good." She held out her hand. "Shake on it."

They did and then Nurse Jacy was all business. "Jim, help me get her blouse off, and then you can step outside while I take her bra off."

"She doesn't wear one."

Alina's voice was sharp. "He stays. It's not like he hasn't seen me before."

He laughed. "She also has control issues."

"Well this just keeps getting better and better." Jacy pulled out a syringe and drew liquid from a bottle. "Okay. You need to go to sleep."

Alina tried to squirm away, stopped with a gasp. "No way. Not happening. Don't put me out."

Jacy sighed and shook her head. "You need to trust me. I have to probe around in there, check for frags, pieces of cloth, bone chips—anything. And then irrigate the wound. If it looks too bad, I'll use a chemical cauterization, guaranteed to make you shit your pants if you're awake. Then I need to leave a drain in there, so you'll heal from the inside out. If that wound closes on the outside first, it'll trap all the pus and corruption inside and we'll lose you. This whole thing is going to hurt like a bitch and you'll be flailing around, firing your weapon and screaming bloody murder. That's more than we can handle. Once that happens, you'll pass out anyway because I'll knock your ass out. Might as well do it the easy way and save the concussion."

Alina looked at Jim. "Well...you'll be here. Right?"

He nodded to her as Jacy interrupted. "You allergic to any drugs?"

"Not that I know of," Alina replied.

"Good. I need to fill you with enough antibiotics that you'll grow mold in wet, dark places." Jacy grinned at her, patting her on the hip. "One good thing, though."

Alina rolled her eyes. "Don't keep me in suspense."

"If you die, this is off the books. I was never here. It never happened."

"Sweet Jesus."

———

AN HOUR LATER, Jacy came out and joined Jim on the porch. "Hubby's going to be pissed. This took longer than I expected. I'm supposed to be working cattle today."

"I appreciate it. Didn't know where else to turn. Have him call me if it helps. He can yell at me. And you're right. This is off the books."

She glanced back into the house. "What did I step into here?"

He brought her up to speed on Alina, including the Russian invasion from last year.

"So, she's a mafia hitman? Or person? Or what the hell ever? I told you at the dance I was getting a vibe from her. I must be losing my touch because that wasn't it."

"She's a good actress—comes with the job, I guess. And she is a used-to-be, kind of like us. I'm not sure what she is now. Or, what she's doing."

"She's dangerous?"

He knew she was thinking of her family. "She's not psychotic, but she's definitely dangerous if she has cause. I'd guess she's more like me than I care to think about. But she's not a problem to you or yours. How come you're not at the clinic?"

"I'm doing online classes and work at the clinic only a couple of days a week." Pausing a moment, she took a deep breath as she looked back toward the front door. "She's like our pet bull, then. But you be careful. Even a pet can turn on you. Seen it happen. I better get going. She'll run a slight fever. If she spikes, call me. I'd leave some pain pills, but I'm betting she won't take them. I hung a bag of Ringers on her. You know how to pull the pin when it's empty?"

"I can handle it."

"Good. You know, if it were me, I'd put a plastic sheet on your bed before you put her in it. No stains, you can always throw that away later—just in case."

"Plastic sheet?"

"Evidence. DNA. I read mysteries. She didn't get that wound cleaning her weapon. And throw away that plastic we used on the table."

"Thanks. And you're right. Someone will investigate this."

She smiled at him. "I'm not worried. I was never here."

He rubbed his eyes. "How long will she be out?"

"Another hour or so. We're lucky that nine mil didn't frag out. It's a good thing those gang bangers, and I'm making a big assumption here about gangs, can't shoot for shit. Anyway, I gave her a large dose of Ketamine." She giggled. "It'll be the worst hangover she's ever had. If I were you, I'd take her gun away. She is not going to be happy."

He gazed back inside the door trying to envision an unhappy and hungover Alina with a gun. "Point taken."

The door on her F-150 complained as she opened it.

"Army strong, Sarge."

"All I can be..."

Jim turned and walked inside, gazing at the mess, and a snoring and bloodstained Alina sprawled on the wide table. It was cleanup time.

"Well, hell."

———

HOURS LATER, staring at his outdoor grill, he waited for the other shoe to drop. He hadn't built his cabin for guests staying overnight.

After the Ringers solution bag was empty, he'd pulled the needle out and applied pressure. The puncture hardly rated a Band-Aid. Stripping Alina the rest of the way, he'd bathed her with warm, soapy water. Wrestling a long T-shirt on her, he deposited her in his bed. Her clothes went into the washing machine, blood spots and all. There were no clothes on hand that would fit her smaller frame. Rita was a six-footer, and he was taller.

He'd cleaned her Prius as well as he could and parked it behind the cabin. It would have been better to take it to the power washer in town, but that would mean someone would see him driving the Prius—he'd never live that one down. Her clothes were washed and dried and folded on the foot of the bed. The only thing left to do was wait for Murphy's Law and all the corollaries to descend.

The message he'd left for Rita was unanswered, so he figured she'd stop by. If she went to the crime scene, he was sure she'd stop—wondering what he knew and how he knew it. She equated him with every bad thing that happened in the county—and was right in this case. One thing was sure. Things were about to get interesting.

Flipping over the pork steaks and slathering them with barbecue sauce, he stuck a fork in the foil-wrapped potatoes—smooth entry, they were done. The first shoe drop came with the sound of borrowed flip-flops from within the house. The sun was setting, highlighting the valley below, leaving him cool in the shadows.

"What in the hell did that woman give me? I almost drowned in my own drool, thank you very much for checking on me."

He glanced at her. The tee had a couple of blood spots. He didn't remember having flip-flops in the place and hoped she'd at least put her panties on. Watching her sit gingerly on one of his ladder-backs, he got his answer.

"Feel like eating?"

"God, no."

Remembering days like this from better times, he went inside and fetched her a mug of coffee. "Feel like talking? And don't ask what about. I need answers, hopefully before the chief county gendarme shows up with fire in her eyes and weapon in hand. That will not end well."

She struggled to find a comfortable position. "It wasn't supposed to go down that way."

"That's the first lie of the day. Don't play me, Alina. Those boys never knew what hit them. I figure you got three of them before the fourth lit you up. Then you dropped him. There were bullet holes in the siding coming from inside, so I figure someone shot at you after you left. That means one got away. Getting close?"

"You should be a detective. Look, you know I have... connections. A little birdy told me you have a bullseye on your back. Somebody wants you gone. The contact told me where it would take place, but not when. Or how they'd get you there. Anyway, I decided to go have a word with them. I parked down the road and snuck up to the house. When I saw all the firepower they had, I couldn't wait...couldn't take a chance you'd show up. I was just lucky they were all together."

"What about the fifth? Man or woman?"

"Hell if I know. I was out in the front yard when someone started blasting away, so I beat-feet out of there. They must have been drunk or high because nothing came near me. They were firing wild."

"How'd you miss the extra person?"

"No clue. I didn't have much time to clear the house. Maybe they were hiding or outside and saw me go in. I just don't know."

"Cost you."

She nodded. "Thank you, Captain Obvious."

"And then you drove here?"

"Sorry. I didn't know where else to go. I've been living out of a motel in Springfield, so I couldn't go there. The hospital was out of the question, for obvious reasons. Please don't kick me out. I don't want to be far from my doctor." She gave him a serious look. "Or you. They'll try again, you know."

He pulled the pork steaks and potatoes off the grill. "You can stay for now. I'll try to keep Rita off your tail, but no promises. Once she sees those headshots, comes up with .22 caliber and then sees you here? She's not stupid."

Alina held her hand out so he could help her stand. "Actually, she is. She's damned stupid."

He stared at her for a long moment, trying to figure out where she was going with that comment. "How do you figure?"

"I'm here and damned near naked, drinking coffee on a beautiful evening. She's not."

"Not happening, Alina."

She smiled and it was one he hadn't seen before—maybe reserved for a favorite pet? "One other thing we need to think about. How'd you wind up at the ambush site? Who told you?" She moved gingerly back into the cabin. In a few moments, the bedroom door closed with a soft thud.

Sitting back in his chair, he watched two deer bolt from the tree line. A group of feral dogs gave chase, but in the open field, the deer quickly outdistanced them. That was another problem in the area. Along with feral pigs, there were wild dogs that ran in packs like their ancestors. They were all large animals. The smaller ones became food.

He knew who sent him to the farmhouse for the ambush. That was easy. He had one bit of information to add to his list. Jack Snow was dirty and had knowingly sent him to be killed.

# EIGHTEEN

**MORNING BROUGHT MORE DISTRACTIONS.** The first was trying to get the kinks out of his back from sleeping on the couch. It was not built for overnighters. The second was Barnes pulling up with a big grin on his face. The third was activity down at the tree line, in front of the limestone bluff. Jim sighed and gently closed the lid of his laptop. The gods of chance did not want him to write a novel.

"Morning, Barnes. You're looking bushy-tailed this morning. Did you take Ex-Lax last night?"

Barnes settled himself into a chair, giving the laptop a curious glance. "Very funny. Nope, just feeling good. What's going on down in the valley?"

"Looks like they're digging holes for a footing. My guess is that's where Pablo's house is going to be." Two four-wheelers were zipping around, a couple of men were measuring and marking spots with a paint can, and a tractor with an auger attachment was drilling holes.

As one of the ATVs started toward them, Alina walked out on the porch. She yawned and did a one-arm stretch, making her tee rise with her shoulder. "You didn't wake me, Jim. I don't like to sleep late."

"Holy Mother of God." Barnes breathed as he leaped to his feet, hand sweeping for a holster that he must have left in his truck.

She gave him an unperturbed glance. "Good morning Officer Barnes. Nice to see you."

Jacy climbed off the ATV, grabbing a med pack off the rack. "Alina, you should be in bed." She gave the men a jaundiced eye. "And dressed."

Jim suppressed a grin as he watched Barnes's head swiveling between the two women, finally finding his voice. "I leave you alone for a couple of days..."

Alina gave Jacy a wave. "I heal quick. Can we jerk that drain out of me today?"

He watched the women walking into the house discussing the wound, waiting until they were out of hearing range before turning back to his friend.

Distant thrumming of the tractor's auger drilling through rock and soil drifted to them on a light breeze. Taking a deep breath, he turned to Barnes. "Things have happened."

Barnes was still looking at the door the women had disappeared through. "No shit. Things? Really?"

It didn't take him long to bring his friend up to speed about his trip to Trader Jack's and the thwarted ambush at the farmhouse.

"That's a lot of bodies in one pile. The good thing is no one will miss them, but the one that got away worries me. This isn't over." Barnes shook his head. "You know, a year or so ago, the killing of four people would have put me in high gear to bring someone to justice. Then I met you."

Barnes dug a cell phone out of his pocket. "Wifey is coming home, and I was all in a good mood about that. Gonna be fun times around the old homestead." He gave Jim a pointed look. "Now, I'm telling her to stay put for a while."

He watched the man stroll out to his car in animated conversation with his wife. He came back, put his hands in his back pockets, and stretched. "She asked me a question I had trouble answering, wondering why I stay around you—maybe at the cost of my marriage."

"Then you should go. There's nothing going on here worth that. You need to keep her happy. Remember? Happy wife, happy life?"

"You're one to talk about keeping your significant other happy." Barnes shook his head. "Is that what you would do? Just leave a friend when he's in trouble? Refresh my memory. We are friends, aren't we?"

"I hope so. You're probably the only friend I have. What did you tell her about staying?"

"I told her you were the only one I knew with a pontoon boat and the fish are biting. Speaking of which...?"

"No time for that. Not yet." Jim sighed. "There's another wrinkle."

Barnes stood with his mouth open a moment before settling into a chair with a deep sigh. "Of course there is."

"Rita pointed out to me that a line drawn from the hill behind Chicken Rock, through the murdered girl, would end up in our boat, if not deflected by the girl's body."

Tipping the chair back on two feet, Barnes seemed to be running it through his mind. Finally, he looked at Jim. "That's a sad little factoid. I don't like it. Given your circumstances from yesterday, she could be right. Which means the girl just got in the way? What a damned waste."

He paused. "You know? Maybe I should go visit my wife—surprise the hell out of her. She'd love that."

Jim shrugged. "I told you."

"No...I just mean for right now. Or maybe take my ass fishing."

"Why now?" His curious gaze watched his friend's nervous behavior.

"A black sheriff's interceptor just two-wheeled into your drive, did a doughnut on the gravel, and about ran over your foreman. I'm thinking it's Rita bringing some chaos. I'm gonna need some popcorn for this." He glanced at Jim. "Are you the spider or the fly?"

"You ever see a bumble bee caught in a web?"

Barnes laughed. "Oh, you ain't no bumble bee. The bumble bee is coming up the drive, and I'm betting her stinger is bigger than yours."

They watched Rita get out of her cruiser and walk toward them. She stopped at the bottom step. "Hi, guys. Jim, what the hell's with all that loose gravel down there. 'Bout killed myself."

Barnes stood. "Hi, Rita. I'm going in for some tea. Can I get you something?"

She gave him a puzzled look. "Anything cold, thanks."

"Just visiting, or is this official?" Jim leaned his elbows on the table, squaring around to face her.

She made the peace sign with two fingers. "I took the rest of the day off. I thought maybe we could just hang out, mend some fences."

She gave him a quick peck on the lips, gaze searching his eyes. "Are you interested?"

Ignoring all the warning bells, thinking she must have more personalities than he could count, he pulled her close and nuzzled her hair. Always a hard body, she was strung tight as wire. Not a conjugal visit, then. He held her at arm's length a moment, staring at her. "Interested? Maybe. Curious? A lot. Give it up. What's going on, Rita?"

"Don't make this difficult. Please." When he didn't answer, she squirmed out of his grasp. "Okay. I thought we could have some alone time and we could talk. But it's your choice. Besides, Barnes being here puts the damper on that. I was hoping for more privacy. There are some bad things going on. What's with that crazy message you left me yesterday?"

Her gaze bored into him, and he almost smiled—except for his churning stomach. This was the Rita he knew. Deflect and fake him out with concern, keeping him off balance. Let the games begin. His eyebrows rose at the way she slipped the question into the conversation.

"Great segue. But to answer your question, I think it was somebody's bad idea of a joke."

Her voice seemed artificially upbeat. "So you went rushing someplace to try and protect me? I guess you really do have feelings for me. Where did this fake ambush you called about take place?"

Now he had the answer to Barnes's question. He was the fly. All he had to do was avoid a very sticky web. "A place west of Bona, just past the double-dip on the north side of the road."

She stiffened, her voice soft, words spoken distinctly. "And what did you find?"

Her deep-blue eyes gazed at him, intent on his reply. The description of an icy stare wouldn't do it justice. If he wanted compassion, it wasn't there. The subterfuge was ended. "Some Good Old Boy gang bangers and meth heads, all tatted up with no place to go. Enough guns to start a small war."

He held her gaze. "They were already dead when I got there, Rita. Who reported it?"

"That would be filed under none of your business. Why didn't you report it? You should have done that at once. Do you mind telling me what's going on?"

Voices drifted from the window—a laugh stifled before it became full blown. "I don't know what's going on, at least concerning that farmhouse. Wish I did."

Arms folded across her chest, she gave him a sharp stare. "Try again."

He tried to deflect with humor. "I really, really don't know?"

She wasn't buying it and he had the fleeting thought she hadn't bought anything of his in a long time. He held his hands up in surrender. "I was told you were going to do a drug bust at that house and would be ambushed because you've been busting up too many of Roman's meth labs. Since it's obvious you didn't know anything about it and didn't answer my call, I can only assume it was a setup to take me out. The reasoning behind that can only be guessed at. As far as I know, I haven't made any new enemies."

Wind ruffled her hair and she shook it out of her eyes. "Really? No enemies? Do I need to remind you about threatening Roman? He's not a man that will ignore that."

"Roman? Are you and that airbag Fielding on a first-name basis now?" He stared at her a moment. "Besides, I said new enemies. Is he the one that reported the bodies?"

He thought he knew Rita better than anyone alive. She was always direct and held eye contact while talking. Those eyes slid away a moment before coming back in white-hot anger.

"How dare you insinuate...who I talk to as sheriff of this county is none of your damned business." She stood rigid before him, her jaw clenched tight enough to make white spots on her cheeks.

"Why are you so angry, Rita? It seems you protest too much. You've kept away from me for months. Maybe it's time you told me why? Our communication skills are nonexistent and we're too old for this soap opera."

"Fine, Jim. I'm afraid. Okay? This whole thing is starting out like last year. Dead bodies show up, and suddenly, there you are. I will not let this happen in my county again."

She was searching his eyes, and he couldn't explain her expression. What she was looking for. Whatever it was, she wasn't finding it. Their verbal duel was interrupted.

Barnes used his butt to open the screen door holding two glasses of iced tea, and came out sporting a tight grin. "Here's your drink, Rita. Nice and cold. Sounds like you need it."

She turned to speak but froze with her mouth open and looking over his shoulder. Her hand swept to the pistol in the paddle holster hidden under her shirt, hung up on her shirt tail a moment.

"Son of a *bitch*."

Being the closest, Jim reached out and stopped her

from pulling her gun. He knew Alina would respond, and the situation would go downhill from there.

Jacy and Alina had come out behind Barnes. Jacy held a puzzled expression, while Alina had an easy smile planted on her face.

Alina was the first to speak, putting her hand on Jacy's shoulder. The other was behind her back. "Don't worry, Jacy. I don't think you're the bitch she's referring to." She squared around to face Rita. "Hello, Sheriff. Long time no see."

"What cavern of hell did you fly out of? My understanding was that you'd never come back to the States and sure as hell not back to my county. We had an agreement."

"No. That's not true. I told you I'd be watching and why." She shrugged. "Well, I have, and here I am. There's nothing complicated about this, at all."

"Jacy, you need to step away." Rita looked relaxed, but her hand hadn't left her pistol as she addressed Alina again. "Alina, you've no business here. I should arrest you, right now." Her head cocked to the side. "By the way, what kind of pistol are you carrying?"

Alina turned sideways, presenting a smaller target while gently pushing Jacy away. "Oh, I've upgraded. You'd get a bang out of it."

Jim stood, stepping between them. "Stop this. Both of you. For the moment, Alina is my guest. No arrests are going to be made here, Rita."

She whirled on him. "Are you crazy? This woman is an assassin, a damned killer, and I have a job to do. If her pistol matches up with ballistics—"

"We owe her, Rita," he interrupted, hands on her shoulders, trying to make her see reason. "You, me,

Barnes—none of us would be alive if she hadn't intervened. You know that. Maybe you don't believe in blood debt, but I do. She is not your enemy."

Alina snorted. "Well…"

Jim pointed at her. "Shut up."

"Jim, I'm betting she murdered those men. The scene has her signature all over it." Rita's voice was hard. "Right down to the .22 cal casings we found. You're getting sloppy, Alina."

"Things change. So do barrels and pins."

Jim sighed and shook his head. "Rita, I doubt you could prove she was there. It would just mean her gun was there, not her. What did you tell me the other day to get a look at my gun safe? Someone could have stolen it. But if, hypothetically, she did this…it was to protect me. They were waiting to kill me. And that's the bottom line."

Rita relaxed, shrugging away from his grasp. "You don't know that. Starting a war is the only thing that can come of this."

"I'm starting a war?" He shook his head. "Arrest Dickie and Roman Fielding for the murder of Dan Hyatt."

"There's no proof." Rita looked at him for a moment. "That's the problem, isn't it? Between you and me? We're on different planets."

"You know," Barnes interjected, surprising everyone. "You could look at it this way. The only people that died were drug pushers. People selling shit to kids, Rita. I know it's a hard pill to swallow, but no one will mourn their passing. It's hardly a blip on your radar."

"That's your solution?" She stood gazing over the field with her back to them for a few moments before she turned to stare at them. The silence stretched out long enough to be uncomfortable before Rita spoke again. She was the authority, and they were skating on thin ice.

"This ends here. No more killings or unexplained bodies. The line gets drawn right here. Got that? We've got investigators crawling all over the county dealing with that murdered girl at Chicken Rock. One sniff of this and the bloodhounds will be loose."

She pointed a finger at Barnes. "And you. You were law enforcement. How can you stand by for this? You should be on my side."

"I wasn't aware we were picking sides." Barnes shrugged. "But in this case, it's because he's right and I stand by my friends. It's a bitter pill, I know, but you need to swallow it. We're both old enough to know there's a whole lot of gray in law enforcement. Nothing is simple anymore."

She stared at him a moment and then her shoulders slumped. "I give up. Y'all are nuts." She directed her pleading gaze to Jim. "Do not force my hand. Please."

"I'm sorry, Rita. I think that hand has already been played. Where can I find Fielding?"

Her expression was hard, eyes narrowed. "No way. Stay away from him. He is not your problem."

How could she miss the connection? Why would she miss it? "He and Dickie killed an innocent man for no reason. Left a widow and child."

"You don't know that for sure." She was shaking her head, staring at him.

"Roman ordered it, playing his games. Dickie was just the instrument. Same thing." He shrugged and tried to smile—and failed. "You're right about us being on different planets. We have different levels of proof required."

"So, once again, you're going to be judge and jury? Gonna cowboy up and bring justice? You'll end up in jail...or dead."

He nodded, slump-shouldered, knowing what he was losing. "Some stories have no good ending. This may be one of them. But I looked a little girl in the eyes. You should have seen her. She was trying so hard not to cry, hands gripped into little fists, fingernails cutting her skin. Missing her daddy. How do you let that go, Rita? How?"

Watching her leave in a flurry of gravel, Barnes shook his head. "That girl must go through a set of tires every month."

Jim looked around at his circle of friends. "Well, that was fun. Jacy, can I ask you to forget you heard all this? It's probably more information than you need to know."

She shouldered her med kit. "Forget it? This is more fun than a box of monkeys. If you don't call me for the next meeting, I'm going to be pissed. Besides, from the sound of it, you might need my services."

As Jacy mounted her ATV and motored off down the valley, Alina yawned. "She's good people. Well, that little dust-up wore me out, so I'm going to lie down." She smiled at Jim. "Join me? Just for a cuddle?"

After the confrontation with Rita, the sight of Alina striking a pose and batting her eyelids was surreal. He shook his head. "I can't decide if that would be like cuddling a porcupine or climbing a Hawthorn tree. I can't imagine doing either. Bottom line? No cuddles. No bed. Nothing."

"So you say." She shrugged. "Porcupines must do it some way, or there wouldn't be any little porcu-puppies running around. There's always a way."

Barnes sipped his tea as he watched her leave. "For a

minute, I thought we were going to have a replay of Doc Holliday and Ringo. I could hear the theme music in the background. Damn, that was close. If someone had said '*say when*,' I'd have shit my pants." He shook himself, or maybe shivered. "So, what now?"

His gaze was still on the dust trail Rita had left. "Like to take a little trip?"

"You thinking of Fielding? You got a line on this man?"

"Yep. Maybe. I know where he's supposed to be staying. It's a big maybe."

Barnes gave him a guarded look. "What's your confidence level on the information?"

Jim grinned at him. "Well, the same man who set me up for the ambush is the one who told me."

His friend looked like a bug-eyed cartoon character, his cheeks round before he expelled his breath. "Okay. Swell. You ever feel like a puppet?"

"Most days I do, and it seems everyone I know has a set of strings. Right now, I'm more into cutting those loose."

# NINETEEN

MOVING NORTH ON H HIGHWAY, they pulled into the first drive with the largemouth bass for a mailbox.

"So, who is supposed to be here?" Barnes watched the narrow, brush-choked lane they traveled. "Two ribbons of dirt with a strip of grass in the center does not constitute a road. Looks like we're getting into *Deliverance* country. The first twang of a banjo, and I'm outta here."

"I don't think your ass is what they're looking for." He laughed at the sharp look his friend sent his way. "But I could be wrong."

Jim continued. "The word is that Fielding and Dickie shack up with a woman named Bella. I don't know her last name and don't care to. To keep house with those two, she might be a little rough around the edges."

They stopped in the bare dirt and gravel parking space in front of the house. No other vehicles were in sight, and they sat for a moment, letting the dust settle.

A huge dog watched them from the porch. Barnes spoke softly. "You a dog lover? That brindle pit bull could be a problem. I'm betting he tops ninety pounds, and most of it is teeth."

Jim watched the dog for a moment. He'd heard a discussion once on talk radio. Veterinarians said pit bulls were an unstable breed. People that raised them disagreed. Of course, most folks can't agree on their favorite color of gummy bears.

"Looks like a pussy cat to me. See how he's smiling at us? He's showing us all his teeth."

"Sorry, if that were a big tomcat, I still wouldn't go near that porch. One of those is more dangerous than a dog. Got the scratches to prove it."

When they approached the porch, Jim held his hand out—palm down. The dog sniffed and then gave a lazy-dog tail thump of approval. "Well, who's a good dog?" Scratching the indolent sentinel behind the ears, he glanced around the porch, noticing tufts of rabbit fur anchored to the floor by blood. "And well fed, too."

Barnes returned from looking through an open window, holding up one finger. They went through the front door quietly, guns drawn. A woman lay sleeping on a black, fake-leather couch. Despite the heat, she was covered with a light KC Chiefs fuzzy blanket. Jim kept his gun trained on her while Barnes cleared the rest of the rooms. It wasn't a big house, no upstairs or basement, so it didn't take long. He returned within minutes carrying a .308 complete with suppressor.

Leaning the rifle against the wall, Barnes commented. "I always wanted one of these."

Jim grasped the blanket and pulled it from the woman. Startled, she came awake. When she sat up, a snub-nosed revolver slipped off the couch and onto the floor. He kicked it under the couch when she reached for it.

Gazing open-mouthed between the two men, her voice slurred. "Wha-what do you want?"

What he really wanted was for her to take a bath. Trying not to take a deep breath, he asked. "Are you Bella?"

Nodding, she tried to stand, but he pushed her back to the couch. Bella was dark. Olive-skinned, black eyes, black hair, black painted fingernails, and according to the gaps in her torn tee shirt, dark everywhere.

"We're looking for Roman and Dickie."

"Ain't here." She leaned back and crossed her legs slowly, every move lazy and calculated. Needle marks on her arms were barely visible except for the fresh one showing red.

"We can see that. Know where they went?" He motioned Barnes toward the windows to keep a lookout. This place was giving him the willies.

"All I know is we were getting ready for a good time when Dickie got a call. They both left like their tails were on fire."

He tried to not look when she uncrossed her legs—failed miserably.

"You boys want to take up where they left off? All the same to me."

Bella wasn't that good looking and what beauty she did have would only last until her fix ran out. Then she would become feral until her next one and do anything for it. It was a cycle old as time.

He shook his head, trying to not show his disgust. "No, I think I'm good here. You good, Barnes?"

"It's a struggle, but I think I'll pass." Barnes rolled his

eyes and headed toward the door. He paused to make sure the .308 was unloaded. "I think we're done here."

"You pigs got names? You know, so I can tell them who came calling?" Somewhere she'd found a cigarette and was searching the cushions for a lighter.

Jim smiled. "Did you think we were law enforcement? Maybe the DEA or some other alphabet agency? Sorry. We're just a couple of citizens."

She nodded, finally lighting up, gazing at them through a smoky haze. "Then get your citizen-asses out of here. You fool with Roman or Dickie and you're going to be dead."

---

JUST ON THE chance Roman might be at his business, they stopped at The Gallows. It was mostly deserted as they nursed a couple of Bud Lights. Jim didn't know the girl behind the bar or the two sweeping and mopping the floor behind them, banging chairs around in time with whatever music was filling their earbuds. If they were eighteen, they hid their age well. It looked as if there had been a turnover in personnel. Roman must be looking for the teen market—legal or not.

He looked at the bartender's name tag again before speaking. "Marsha, have you seen the owner today?"

"You mean Mr. Fielding? He cruised through a while ago. Said he had business to take care of and left." She shrugged. "We're all new here and don't see him much. Can I take a message?"

He wondered about the changeover and made a mental note to put a bug in Rita's ear, assuming she would speak to him. The job here was more exciting than a job at the seed company running forklifts or bagging birdseed, but the dangers were real. He knew Fielding would have these kids turning tricks to keep their jobs. Either Roman or Dickie would get them in money trouble, or drug trouble, and offer them a way out.

"Nah. We'll catch up with him later." He placed one of his cards on the bar. "If you would, please call me when you see him next. I'd appreciate it."

She shrugged and popped her gum. "Okay. Holler if you need something."

"How old are you?"

"Why? You got an itch for little girls?" Her flat stare told him all he needed to know before she moved away.

After Jim recapped the last few days, Barnes glanced at his friend. "Jim, you're not stupid, and this has to stop. Now. You realize how this looks? You're not an investigator. You have no standing here. The sheriff's department is undermanned, outgunned, and too prideful to ask for help. The fact that you think the sheriff is your woman tells me you're no investigator, because you have no clue. It complicates things, and she'll arrest your ass if you try to help her in any way. I think she has a perverted desire to put you in cuffs. She hasn't already, has she? You know, the ones with the pink fuzzy manacles?"

He stopped a moment to take a breath. "There's also the not-so-small matter of a love-stricken Russian assassin, possibly reformed, sneaking around and trying to protect your back. It's starting to look like the Three Stooges being chased by the Keystone Cops and I don't want to get hit in the crossfire. If it weren't so serious, it'd be funny. You've got a bunch of redneck meth heads shooting speedballs and trying to rewrite the TV series *Justified* so they can win for once."

Barnes paused, staring intently at Jim. "Is there any scenario rattling around in that head of yours where this will end well?"

When Jim didn't reply, he continued. "My wife will kill me if I try to help. I'd like to think that's a joke, but it's not. She's got the whole year planned out. Wants to buy an RV and hit the road. I'm medically retired from the Highway Patrol from that last dust-up and you're the reason."

Jim rolled his shoulders, looking around the room before he glanced at his friend, giving him a slow smile. "You seem depressed."

"Depressed?" Barnes's slow drawl turned sharp. "I'm thinking that starting a drug habit isn't a bad idea, but I can't afford it. Dammit, Jim. What are we doing here?"

The big question—what was he doing? It didn't make sense, even to him. "Of course, you're right. I've made a few changes, but have been just reacting to things as they come. That's not much of a plan. I'll let Rita know I'm out, for real this time. Although, the killing of that farmer got under my skin. I don't think she realizes what Fielding is, but I guess that isn't my problem. Looking at it from the outside, I have enough to do with the building projects at home to keep me busy without getting involved in her problems."

"Well, thank God for small favors." Barnes seemed to relax. "I agree Roman and Dickie are probably responsible for the death of that farmer. But I don't think it was intentional, and so far can't be proved. If they're in charge of this Good Old Boy gang selling drugs..." He looked around the room at the young girls. "...and prostitution, they'll get wrapped up sooner or later."

"Look," he continued. "I need to be gone a couple of

days. Checking into RVs and some personal business. You going to be okay on your own? Stay out of trouble?"

Jim shrugged, thinking of Alina. "Sure. Remember, I got protection at home."

"What about that? She's dug in like a tick on a coon hound."

"She's going to get her walking papers."

"Really?" He snickered, rolling his eyes. "Yeah, well. Good luck with that. Careful that your protection"— Barnes did air quotes at the last word—"doesn't turn against you."

"I'm going to tell her to leave. Honest."

"Uh, huh. I heard you. I just don't believe you."

# TWENTY

JIM HEARD Rita make her usual entrance into the drive leading up the hill to the cabin, throwing creek gravel and dust as her four-wheel drive kicked in. It might be a good idea to put bumper guards just inside the gate—just for her. Wondering why his mornings were always so busy, he was chasing the last Cheerio around the bowl of sugared milk when she walked in the door. She wasn't much for small talk.

"Look, Jim. I know who's behind that bedroom door." She gave him a long look. "I do not approve. But I can't do anything about it...or understand it. Well, maybe I could if I suspend belief like for a science fiction movie or congressional hearing. If we ever had a chance for a relationship, you're killing it. Killing it dead."

"Rita, what are you doing? Following your line of thought is like catching balloons in a windstorm. Remember? You shot that in the foot the other day. Besides, do you honestly think I'm tapping what's behind that door?" He shook his head as he poured the excess milk down the drain, running water to clear it from the trap beneath. The last thing he needed was the smell of sour milk.

She stared at him a moment, breathing heavily before she finally calmed down, turned her head, and shouted, "Alina, get out here. You need to hear this, too."

Jim almost laughed as Alina moved through a creaky-hinged door with raised eyebrows and less clothes on than she'd worn the entire time she was there. Somehow, she'd smeared her makeup and tousled her hair into that bedroom look that screamed they were tearing up the sheets.

Rita busied herself inserting a memory stick into his laptop and pretending not to notice. Discerning eyes could see the red flush climbing up her neck and shoulders. Her jaw was clenched so tight, white spots appeared under her ears.

He chuckled, wondering at his choices. Should he make popcorn, or run like he stole something? How could Alina make herself up like that in such a short amount of time? Given that everyone in the house was armed, running seemed like a good choice. Maybe dive behind the counter.

"Oh, for Christ's sake!" Rita turned to face Alina. "Really?"

Rita took a big breath. Didn't work, so she took another. "Listen up. We need to forget all this and get serious. Jacy Mane came to my home early today. Real early. Before daylight early. This is a recording from our interview."

She took another deep breath, wiping tears from her eyes. Clearly, she was upset and needed blood pressure meds. And anger management. "I don't know what else to do. This is not legal. I am not here doing this. If any of this gets out, I'll be in deep shit and that rolls downhill. Do both of you understand?"

He'd heard about the feeling of someone throwing cold water on you—never felt it before now. He rubbed a suddenly nauseous stomach full of curdled milk. When he glanced at Alina, her face had gone blank, her sharp eyes tracking Rita's every move.

"I won't play this for you now," Rita continued; sadness replaced the anger in her voice. "Wait until I leave. I don't want to see this file again. Ever."

She took another deep breath and continued. "Jacy's been making extra money patching people up who can't afford the clinic or hospital. I'm sure you both know that. There are no prescriptions involved, just cuts, scrapes, and stitches. It's not strictly legal, but she needs the money. Hell, you know all this."

She paused to take another calming breath. "Dammit, I'm babbling. Anyway, last night, she went to see a couple of low-life meth heads who called her about an injury. She got raped for her trouble."

The only sound was Alina's sharp, indrawn breath. When Jim glanced at her, she returned his gaze with a flat stare while slowly shaking her head. Barnes and Rita would not get their wish. The body count was going to go up.

Rita leveled a brittle stare at them. "She identified them. We talked about it. At first, I wanted to arrest them and prosecute. Jacy was willing, but the more we talked, I tossed that idea. Our judicial system is not kind to victims of this kind of assault."

Pausing, she gave Jim an anguished look. "I can't believe I'm doing this. Jim, she has three little stair-step boys and a husband that worships the ground she walks on. She's in school to better herself and her family. Even if she wins the case, she could lose a lot here. You know how people are. They'll never look at her the same. She needs justice and closure. The low-life element in this county needs to know this won't be tolerated. Retribution will follow. I know she's a friend to both of you. That's all I have to say about it. I don't want to see any of this cross my desk. My copy of her report has disappeared. End of story."

"Is she hurt?" Alina's voice sounded like a handful of gravel in a grinder. "Physically?"

Rita gave her a long look. "Not too bad. Hurts like hell and bruising. She has a goose egg on the back of her head where she got popped. So, physically she's okay. She's tough in ways I'm sure most people wouldn't understand—except us. But where her mind is? I have no idea. I'm surprised she got into a situation like that, given her training and background."

"It can happen." Jim was already punching a speed dial labeled 86W. "We got this, Rita."

"Sorry to lay this on you." Her voice turned bitter. "Although it seems to be right up your alley."

She got up to leave and glanced at Alina. Her voice would have made a drill sergeant proud. "Put some damned clothes on!"

———

THE CALL to Jacy was picked up on the second ringtone. "Hello?"

"I..." For the life of him, he didn't know where to start. "Jacy, Alina and I just talked to Rita. Are you okay? Where are you?"

Her sigh over the airwaves didn't have much expression. It could have been wind passing over her speaker, a lifeless passage with no direction. "I'm home. Feeling stupid. Glad to be alive. Pissed. Psychotic. All that."

"I'm sorry this happened—can't imagine. You call the shots, Jacy. Whatever you want, just tell us. Nobody will know, if that's the way you want it."

When she didn't answer, he continued.

"Can you give me directions to the house? I'm going to visit those boys."

Jacy's voice hardened. "No, you will not. This is my problem, not yours. I'll take care of it."

He was shaking his head, glad she couldn't see it or see his expression. "It doesn't have to be that way. You have friends, Jacy. Friends with a particular skill set. Let us help you."

"I know, and I appreciate that." She paused. "Look, Jim. I'm not suicidal. I have way too much to live for. Last night, I was afraid I'd lost it all, that they would kill me. I was so damned scared. But they didn't kill me. It's not often we get second chances. I promise to rest today. I'll tell hubby I've caught a bug and we'll farm out the kids to his parents. I'm on my way to see Dr. Bartelli. He'll check me over and do an STD test, at least for the short-term stuff. He'll give me a morning-after dose, just in case. That will take care of today. I'll come over tomorrow and we can talk. I may need to borrow something."

"Anything you need. Say hello to the doc for me and I'll see you tomorrow." Disconnecting the call, he turned to Alina. "She's being very clinical and withdrawn about the whole thing. I don't know what's normal. She won't tell me who or where. The info I need is on the memory stick, but I'm not going to listen to it. We'll do it her way. She's supposed to come by tomorrow to talk. That's it."

"If you think that's it, you don't know women very well." She raised an eyebrow at him. "Which defines you pretty well, come to think of it."

He looked her over and knew she enjoyed the scrutiny. She was beautiful and knew it.

"How's the shoulder?"

"Functional." She rolled it around, moving her arm up and down. "The bullet didn't hit any bones, so...not bad. Hurts some."

"Good. I'm glad you're healing so fast. Since you can function on your own and don't need help, get on your phone and find a place to live. We're not a thing, Alina. And we're not going to be."

Leaning against the doorjamb, her voice turned soft. "Sure you mean that?"

He could feel his resolve breaking down and didn't like it. A picture of a fish caught on a hook came to mind. "Yes, I do. I'm trying to make things work with Rita. You're not helping."

"Not my job to help with that. Besides, you're not winning her over. Everyone but the two of you can see that." Her laugh was low and throaty. "Maybe she's mad because she knows that possession is nine-tenths of the law."

"You don't have possession. Look. I know you can turn on that sex appeal like flipping a switch. Turn it off. You need to vacate in the next few days. I'm serious. When Jacy comes over tomorrow, have her check you out if she feels up to it. Then you're gone."

It would have made a good cover for a romance novel. Beautiful, scantily clad woman leaning against the door

—a *come and get me* look on her face. A hard-eyed, shirtless hero staring at her. But this was not a book cover. Even though he'd told her to leave, it was a mere formality before capitulation. She was already through his defenses and well into sacking the castle. And she knew it.

He turned away and walked outside. Please God, make her go away. But the devil on his shoulder whispered that he wasn't pushing very hard to make that happen.

———

IT WAS ALMOST noon when Jacy stood just inside his screen door. Outwardly, he could see no sign of the trauma she'd faced and was surprised. She wouldn't look at him directly, maybe she was looking for Alina? He had no idea what to do, how to act.

"Would you submit to a hug?"

"No." Her expressionless gaze was steady, and she got right to the point. "Do you have an M4 I could borrow? Hubby and I are wanting to do some target practice. I'd just need it for this afternoon."

That was unexpected. "Target practice, huh? Why am I skeptical of that?"

"Can't help how you feel." She seemed withdrawn, her gaze drifting everywhere while she talked. He'd seen it before. In combat. She was a claymore waiting for someone to trip the wire. Hopefully, he'd be behind her when she faced the enemy.

"Jacy—?"

She gave a violent head shake, not meeting his gaze.

He tried again. "I'd be glad to take care of that

problem for you. Even Alina volunteered. We're particularly good at shooting targets."

Alina walked into the room in time to hear the comments. "Jacy." She went forward and hugged a very stiff and unresponsive recipient. "I'll be glad to set up targets for you. Let me help."

Jacy's gaze finally met his as she shook her head. "I can shoot my own targets. I can set up my own targets, or anything else. I do not need help."

She followed as they moved across the room to a closet in the bedroom that held his gun safe. He saw her glance at the rumpled bed that hadn't been made, but didn't comment.

"I actually have three M4s. They're each configured a little different. You're welcome to borrow any of them."

She stood looking at the array of weapons in the safe and shrugged. "Any will do."

"Why an M4?" Alina's voice was soft, like she was afraid to startle her.

Jacy's tone was even and listless. Her gaze was cataloging the firearms with practiced ease. She shrugged. "I'm comfortable with that shooting platform. Which one doesn't matter."

"Well, if you're going to practice shooting targets, how about this?" He took out his AA12 shotgun, which looked like a firearm in a science fiction movie. Fastening the drum magazine on the bottom. Giving Jacy a careful look, he held it out to her. "This is for targets inside buildings and tears them up with extreme prejudice. It's semi-automatic and loaded with slugs surrounded by 00 buckshot. They're called zombie loads, in a twenty-five-round mag. I've never had it jam. It will ride up a bit, so be ready for it. This has the same platform as the M4, so it should be comfortable. I'm thinking it may be more appropriate for the job. Sometimes targets come in unexpected bunches."

"It's light." She grasped the gun. "Zombie loads?"

His smile was more of a grimace as he glanced at Alina. He knew she'd remember his use of the weapon the year before.

"They do live among us."

Jacy didn't respond to the joke. Maybe because it was just a matter of definition. Zombies or aliens. A new normal was defined every day. He watched her carefully. Her expression was peaceful, almost serene. They may as well have been discussing tomatoes at the local market. It was obvious to him—she'd made her peace with what she was going to do. He couldn't blame her. His concern was her safety and coming out of it without repercussions.

"Jacy?"

She turned her attention away from the shotgun to look at him.

"We're not against what I think you're going to do. Give me a time and place. You need someone to watch your back. Nonnegotiable."

Her gaze was level as she nodded acceptance. "I guess that makes sense. How about two o'clock?"

After she gave him directions, she slowly drove away.

"Well, that was awkward." Alina stood watching after Jacy left. "You ever wonder why all your friends seem to have a screw loose? Jim, watch yourself around her. She's wound way too tight. Once she starts shooting, her targets may become anyone of the male gender. I'm not sure I'd want to back her up."

He didn't have a good response, wondering how his world had degenerated to the point that murder was okay. The justification came quickly. In this case, not murder. More like cleaning out feral hogs and other detritus to the human condition. If people insist on acting like animals, then treat them as such.

"I'm not wild about it either, but I doubt we could stop her."

She laid her hand on his arm, squeezing to get his attention. "I should go with you."

He shook his head. Seeing she wouldn't accept that, he said. "It would be too hard for her to keep track of both of us. Like you said, she may come unglued and not be able to stop shooting."

Alina moved around in front of him. Her serious question rattled him. "If that happens, if she goes crazy, can you kill her...to protect yourself?"

He held her gaze a moment before breaking it and looking down. "I don't know."

"Make up your mind to it, or don't go. Let me go instead."

Her hand on his chest didn't stop him from pushing past. "No. She'll expect me. That's who she'll get."

# TWENTY-ONE

AT STRAIGHT UP TWO O'CLOCK, Jim stood amid carnage, trying not to lose his lunch and wondering about going back to his truck to get his rubber boots. He was surprised any of the inside walls of the cabin were still standing.

The run-down shack had been easy to find. It had a largemouth bass for a mailbox, and he and Barnes had been there yesterday. The only things missing were Bella and the dog—and Jacy.

The Darth Vader theme music woke up his cell. He seriously thought about not answering, probably shouldn't have. He slid his thumb over the screen of his smartphone.

"Hey Rita. How's it going?"

Stepping over an out-flung bloody arm, he did a double take when the fingers twitched, but one look at the body told him it was reflex. Like a frog leg still twitching in the skillet. That thought about sent him out the door.

"What's going on, Jim? I'd like to talk to you, but you sound a little distracted."

He was distracted by the stuffing from the couch sticking to blood spots...everywhere. The place looked like someone tossed a fragmentation grenade inside a room full of live chickens and then closed the door. Or placed a tomato in a blender and pressed chop. Or...he closed his eyes a moment and willed himself to stop making comparisons.

He was just a few minutes late to the party, and that pissed him off. His mind finally caught up with her question. "Oh. Same old, same old. Doing some research for the book."

Rita snorted. "Yeah, like that'll ever get off the ground."

He feigned being hurt, wasn't sure if it was fake. "Thanks for the support."

She laughed, and he wasn't sure how to take Rita in a good mood. He hadn't seen much of that lately. "How about supper at my place tonight?" she asked. "We need to catch up. Don't make me beg."

"Sounds like a good idea. Maybe you can lose the attitude for a while? I miss the old Rita. We need to remain friends, and I may need a hug."

She groaned a little. "I'll see what I can do. I know I've been bitchy, and I'm sorry. I don't want us to be this way. We need to be friends. Oh, not to change the subject, but can you pick up some ketchup on your way? I'm home today and don't want to get out. Every time I leave the house, I get caught up in something. Air fries and shrimp sound okay to you? Maybe a nice salad?"

Gourmet cook, she was not, but he liked a simple fare.

His attention couldn't leave the room. Blood streaked the walls amid pellet holes from the shotgun blasts—big bore like double-ought buckshot and larger slugs. Zombie loads. As he watched, a piece of...something... succumbed to gravity and slid down the wall. Five people posed in death, limbs outstretched in panic and supplication. Violent death had its own signature. Mix the olfactory cocktail of rotten eggs, gunpowder, and voided bowels in an unventilated room—shaken, not stirred. You can't blow your nose or blink your eyes enough to make it go away. Some investigators use a dab of Vicks up their nose, but that just adds insult to injury.

His mind caught up with her again. His voice sounded feeble in his own ears. "Ketchup? How about I bring Chinese? Ketchup is not really good for me right now."

He didn't disconnect, and neither did she. Breath sounds filled their ears as they hung on like preteens doing their first boy-girl call until she finally broke the silence in a tremulous voice.

"Jim? My Spidey-sense just twanged into the hot zone. What's going on?"

This was going to be hard, but there wasn't any way to sugarcoat it...and she needed to know. "Remember that little item you wanted handled? Nothing crosses your desk? Well, that may not be possible."

Her response was almost too soft to hear. "Dammit, Jim. What did you do?"

So much for a friendly supper. He was beginning to think his real name was "*dammit Jim*."

Her voice turned hard and clipped. "Where?"

"You know where. It's your buddy Roman Fielding's place, but he's not here...at least, I don't think so."

"What in the hell is that supposed to mean?" The calming breath she took sounded like a hurricane over his phone. "Alright. You were never there. But, Jim, if there's evidence pointing to...someone, I can't ignore it. I hope you understand that."

Before he walked out the door, he noticed a pistol still encased in a paddle holster partly under the shot-to-rag-dolls couch. Without hesitation, he bent and picked it up. It was a customized Beretta PX4 Storm. Placing it in his back pocket, he drifted outside to await his own personal version of hell-on-wheels.

Once outside, he realized he'd made a mistake by not clearing all the rooms in the house. It would be impossible to do from the inside without leaving tracks, so he walked around the house peeking in the windows. There wasn't much to see until he came to a bedroom window on the opposite side of the house from the bodies. It was busted out from the inside, glass and part of the frame lying on the ground. Someone dove through the window. There was blood on some of the glass, especially on shards that hadn't broken loose.

There was a sixth person, and they'd escaped. He didn't know if that was good or bad. Given the company they kept, whoever it was, wouldn't be likely to talk.

———

RITA ROLLED up before the mosquitoes made a complete feast of him. No strobes or sirens and she didn't skid her tires on the blacktop before turning into the rocky lane, doing nothing to draw attention. Just a normal coming to see you kind of drive, blinkers and all. When she exited her vehicle, she moved to stand beside him—both staring at the house like it was some malevolent thing. He glanced at her. Even in her uniform, she had to be the best-looking sheriff in the state—and the maddest.

Her voice grated, like it had been unused for a while. Each word enunciated with precision. "I thought I told you not to be here."

"Good afternoon, Sheriff. I'm fine, thanks for asking." He held up his hands in surrender. "I'm only here until you clear the house. You shouldn't run solo until that's done. Then I'll get out of your hair."

"What do we have in there?" She folded her arms, staring through the open front door. "Do we need an ambulance, or coroner?"

He tried to put his hand on her arm, but she shrugged him off. Hands raised again, in a "don't shoot me" pose, he spoke softly. "There's no one here but us, Rita."

The icy stare he received set him back a step. "Fine. Have it your way."

He didn't mean for his voice to turn hard—couldn't help it. "You have five bodies inside. Maybe a sixth person dove from a window in the back. Lots of blood on the glass back there. I figure I know who it is. From their GOB tats, I'm going to take a leap and say they're all members of the Good Old Boys. My thinking is that two of them are rapists, and the other three are just collateral damage. They've all been used and abused with extreme prejudice. No need for an ambulance. You might want to have your people clear the rooms for sure, I just did a once-around from the outside."

"This isn't what I had in mind when—"

He raised a hand between them to cut her off. "Actually, I don't give a rat's ass what you had in mind. Not anymore.

Just for the record—I didn't do this, Rita. I'd have made them disappear. And, also for the record? Barnes and I are out. No more interference or trying to help. We're done."

Her flat gaze studied him. "I wish I could believe that. Look, I'm sorry. I can't seem to stop kicking your shins, can I?" Her intake of breath was sharp as she studied the house, marshaling her thoughts back to the matter at hand. "Wait...you mean...Jacy? I thought you...? She could do this? Murder? She's a medic, for God's sake."

"Yeah, and a good one, too. She's also 86W. You should remember what that is. That's a *combat* medic. I know rape is traumatic beyond description, men aren't supposed to be able to understand it. It might surprise you, but most of us already know that. But all women don't lock themselves in a dark room and seek counseling. How'd she seem to you yesterday?"

Rita thought a moment and nodded. "Angry. As much at herself as the perps. It still doesn't mean she shouldn't seek help."

"Agreed. I've already suggested it and hope she does. She's been to see her doctor already, so maybe he's moving her in that direction. Meanwhile, you won't be able to prove anything against her."

He waited until she met his gaze. "There's enough drugs in there to start your own side business. Your best bet is that it looks like another gang hit, maybe float the idea of a rival gang. No survivors. End of story."

"That's the way I need to see it? If it were gang related, wouldn't they have taken the drugs when they left?"

"Maybe, maybe not. These aren't smart people. I'd go with the simplest explanation. Occam's Razor." He ran his hand through his hair. "You won't find any evidence to the contrary. I'm sorry this has to drop on your shoulders."

"Alright. I'll go with it. There does seem to be a lot of gang activity going around lately. The GOBs appear to be killing themselves off. By my count, that's nine down." She stood a moment, looking around the deserted lot. The nearest neighbor was over a mile away. "No witnesses?"

"Who knows? I'm guessing people aren't too nosy in this neck of the woods."

"I hate this." Shoulders slumped, she sighed. "This is getting to be a damned bad habit, and I'm tired of covering your ass."

"What did you think would happen?"

She waved her hand at the house. "Not this. Not like this. I thought you'd rough them up, beat them senseless, drag their asses out of the county—not this."

"They raped her, Rita."

Her stare was intense before finally softening. "I don't know what else to do. Seems instead of solving murders, I'm always covering them up. So, go. You were never here. I got an anonymous tip. When you leave, I'll back up and pull in over your tire marks, although this gravel won't leave much of a trace. Then I'll start making calls. Now, get the hell out of here."

When he started to walk away, she stopped him. "Know this, Jim. You said you're through with stuff like this, and I hope you stick to that because I'm done. So far, we can sweep everything that's happened under the rug as gang related and people won't say much about it. Any more bodies and it will blow up in our faces. My job is important to me. I will not climb up on a cross and pay for your sins. I...will...not!"

He studied her for a moment. She was a good woman and a good sheriff. The question was...where did the woman go that he'd fallen in love with?

"You've made yourself clear, Rita. Even that you think I would murder people for no reason, or because someone asks me to. Thank you for that. It clears up a lot of things."

# TWENTY-TWO

JACY WAS WAITING when he returned home. She stood on the porch talking to Alina like they were best friends, visiting on a warm, laid-back summer's evening, both laughing as they watched him approach. He expected wide-brimmed, floral-trimmed hats and lemonade, maybe one of those umbrellas they could twirl over their shoulders as they conversed. A line from the movie *Last of The Mohicans* came to him, something about women being a breed apart and not to be understood. That was something he believed.

He tipped his hat, giving them a wary eye. "Ladies."

Jacy pointed to the shotgun leaning against the wall, her voice a soft drawl. "That's a sweet gun, not much kick to it at all, but I don't think hubby can use it. Especially hunting, although I'd love to have the extra rounds hunting boar. They've surely been tearing up my gardens. I didn't replace the shells since I didn't know what to buy to replace them. I can't picture myself walking into Walmart asking for zombie loads. And it probably needs a cleaning."

"A good cleaning with the right solvent will get the prints off." Jim pinned his gaze on her. On close inspection, her eyes were red-rimmed and tired, her movements listless. The wrinkles around her eyes seemed deep, but overall, she looked okay. Combat medics were tough, or they didn't survive.

"You jumped the gun, Jacy. I was supposed to be there for backup."

"Did I?" She winked at Alina as she stepped down the porch. "I have no idea what you're talking about. I've been checking cattle all day. Alina saw me drive by several times."

"I doubt Alina would be a good character witness. You two going into business together?" He nodded then, accepting the charade. "Enough said on that. But Jacy? You need to talk to someone. Maybe a counselor, but especially your husband. This will eat you up if you let it."

Shaking her head, she seemed to shrink a little. Body language would say she didn't trust him. "Hubby? No, he'd never understand something like that. I'll recover. Don't worry about me. Plus, Alina's a good listener."

"Yeah. I can imagine what kind of advice she'd give." That was scary. He'd never had much evidence of Alina having much empathy for anything. Another new leaf turned over?

She glanced between Jim and Alina. "Actually, she's surprisingly good. Dr. Bartelli says hi, by the way. It's funny, he made the same offer you did...damned near insisted on it."

Since the doctor was military, that didn't surprise him. People who serve seem to have a different outlook on life than most normal folk. "Well. You have friends,

Jacy. Never forget that. Sounds like you have everything under control." He paused. "Hey, can you show me your Beretta? I'm thinking about getting one and I'd like to see the modifications you've done."

Reaching under her shirt, she came up empty. Realization washed the color from her face as she stared back at him.

He held out the holstered pistol. "This is what backup does for you. You were lucky today. That's something you can't always count on. Or someone to pick up your empty shells that, however unlikely, might be traced to a certain firing pin on a borrowed shotgun. How many shots did you take?"

Like she was being berated by a drill sergeant, she came rigidly erect. "Twelve. I counted."

He'd figured on that. Good shooters always counted their shots. Knowing the number of rounds left in your gun's magazine was a matter of life or death.

"That's good because that's how many of your empties I picked up. That was sloppy and preventable. Don't ever turn your back on friends again."

"I'm...sorry. I hope there never is a next time, but I'll do better if there is." Jacy nodded to him, her lips quivering a little, still standing straight in rigid control.

Not knowing what else to do, he held out his arms. This time, she came willingly for a hug, trembled in it a moment, and then let him go.

"Anything you need, let us know. I know it's hard... well, actually can't imagine, but you know what I mean." He waited until her gaze met his. "Army strong, Sergeant. Go take care of your family."

For the first time, a hint of tears came to her eyes as

she stepped away, chin raised. It was a wonder she didn't salute. "All I can be."

When she was gone, Alina came toward him, eyes shining. "That was impressive. Can I get one of those hugs?"

He thought about it, considered it briefly, but fear of the consequences made him stop. The period of time they were together, before the era of Rita, was tumultuous and fevered. He wasn't sure he could handle that again, or turn it off once it started.

"Nice try. I'm not ready for that."

"I know. Not yet, anyway. You still have the ghost of Rita." She leaned against a porch post, rubbing her shoulder with a frown. "Jacy's in a hard place right now. She can't tell her husband, or he'd go tearing after someone, maybe anyone, and probably get himself killed. That girl believes in family, and her kids need a father. So, she must protect him from himself, even though she's the one who was violated. And the way she handled it? I'd say she's had the best closure possible. It's what you would have done. It's what I would have done."

"That may be, but I don't think polite society would approve."

Rita had put the word to it. Murder.

"You mean the sheep? The people who want to be surrounded by law enforcement so they never have to deal with anything unsavory? That polite society?" She shrugged and then watched him a moment. "We're not like them, Jim. And you know it. Circumstances have changed us, and for that matter, Jacy and the rest of your merry band. You and I are far more alike than you imagine. I know you don't want to think that, but it's the truth."

When he didn't answer, she continued. "And you've put Rita in a bad place, too."

His voice was sharp. "How about we leave Rita out of this?"

She shook her head. "Nope. Can't do it. She's trying to do a good job as sheriff, and believe it or not, I admire her for that. It's something she believes strongly about. She has a passion for the job. But you're a distraction. Legally and personally.

"Legally, she figures she should arrest both of us on general principles. We don't help her much with that. But she can't. At least, not yet. I hope she never feels she has cause.

"Personally? She wants to love you, probably thinks she should, but doesn't. She won't admit it, and it's doubtful if she understands why. For some women, there's only one love in their life, and I think her husband was it. Anything, or anyone past that, just gets all tangled up in her mind, and that doesn't end well. It's a position I've come to understand well."

Although not feeling like it, he grinned at her. "I'm not sure I agree about Rita. I always thought she was quite fond of me."

She chuckled. "Fond? Friend with benefits? Sure. But don't mistake sex for love. It's not the same animal."

When had she become this smart? Or was it just one woman knowing another? "Well, thank you, Dr. Ivanov. Send me a bill."

"Oh, you'll get a bill." She gave him a level stare. "We Russians are patient. And I'm enjoying the show. Being around you is like…"

He held up his hand. "I know. Like Jacy said. Watching a box of monkeys."

# TWENTY-THREE

AFTER ALINA WENT INSIDE, he picked up his phone. He needed information. The question was...from where? Listening to all the experts on TV and listening to the radio, was an exercise in futility. The CDC and WHO were politicized and had been caught in as many lies as the politicians standing around them. Even in a time of crisis, everyone has an agenda. He wondered if Google had a listing for Political Pandemic?

Before starting his book, Jim had done a little research. In mystery writing, there was usually a MacGuffin—whether the writer or audience knew it, or not. The MacGuffin was something that drives or triggers the plot. For years, a woman named Sally had been his MacGuffin.

They'd met on the concrete floor of an abandoned warehouse. He'd heard from his handler that a Shepherd had been captured. It was doubly bad that the Shepherd was a woman. It takes a special kind of courage for a woman to serve in the Mideast, considering what happens if they are captured. Death was preferable. His source also told him the powers-that-be were sitting on their collective asses, afraid that a rescue attempt would cause an international crisis.

Jim did what he was trained to do—high-risk rescue. He'd grabbed a known jihadi off the street, wrung him dry and found the place they were holding the woman was nearby. There was no time for subtlety. Breaching the warehouse, he'd fought his way to her, finally killing the last man trying to behead her. Hearing the shots and figuring a rescue was underway, the despondent woman found the energy to lunge from her attacker, receiving a wound to her face.

She'd survived, retiring to a desk job and ultimately became Jim's handler—at least, until he walked away from the Shepherds.

They'd become friends. She'd responded to his crisis last year and helped all she could, receiving a near-mortal wound in the process. He didn't know how high up the food chain she was now, but figured she could supply some information.

Her name was Sally. Given the humor and camaraderie of veterans, no matter what service they are in, she became known as Sally One-Eye.

Jim pressed five on his speed dial screen. It had been over a year, and it sounded like the same receptionist answered the call. "How did you get this number?"

He decided to play with her. "It's on my speed dial."

After several clicks later, she continued. "I'm sorry. We do not recognize this number."

The call dropped. Nope. No time for this. He dialed again. When the connection was made, he said. "I need Sally."

More silence, then breathy exhalation. "State your name."

"Jim Lane."

The voice perked up. "Shepherd Lane? *The* Shepherd Lane?"

Jesus take the wheel. It *was* the same woman. "Yes. Please connect me."

"She isn't here." Her voice had turned from all business to sugar. Now, she was playing with him.

"I know that. Your office is in a phone booth somewhere, or maybe in a moving van traveling the Midwest. You've never seen anyone you talk to. Most likely you develop amnesia after every conversation because they put that drug in your coffee."

A long, exasperated sigh culminated in a groan. "You're not being funny...and I don't drink coffee."

Jim chuckled. "Sorry. How do you get through the day? Just connect me. Please."

More clicks and he could imagine the call bouncing through trunk lines and towers all over the world. He would swear the last thing he heard was a splash. A voice he recognized finally answered. "Lane? Jim Lane? The actual Shepherd Lane?"

He couldn't keep the chuckle out of his voice. "Where are you, on a Boomer in the mid-Atlantic?"

She laughed. "Of course not, although the captain is pissed that he had to come up above the thermal layer."

It was his turn to give a polite laugh. "How ya doing, Sally?"

"I'm doing rather good, actually. Busy as usual. Now, since you haven't connected with us since I left the hospital over a year ago, I know you're not calling just to check on my day. What have you done and what will I have to fix?"

He liked her. They had a history, and she was always business. "I'm just looking for a threat assessment. World view. I've been bird-dogging the news and don't like what I'm hearing. Everyone has a different story, with different endings. I'm trying to decide if I should bunker up or break out the cyanide pills?"

"More likely iodine."

That got Jim's attention. Iodine was used to help with the effects of radiation sickness and was one scenario he hadn't considered. One of the oldest nuggets of wisdom stated that when you don't see your enemy...that's when you worry.

Alina came out the front door. He held his finger to his lips for her to be quiet and then pressed speaker before setting his phone on the table.

The sound of shuffling papers came loud over the phone before Sally spoke again. "I'm putting our threat level at seventy percent, maybe leaning toward eighty. That's a little better than the Doomsday Clock that's set at 11:59. In an abundance of caution, we've recalled all Shepherd operations. We don't want anyone stranded overseas. There's a lot of things going on and most of the action will be at home—sorry to say."

Eyes like saucers, Alina's hand was over her mouth.

"Okay, I understand. Sally, would you like to elaborate on those numbers?" He used her name so Alina would know who he was talking to. "What are we looking at?"

"Well, North Korea now has the capability to deliver an EMP strike on North America. Much as the current administration wants to deny it...but it's a fact. The scary thing is, they are willing to launch, just waiting for the right time. Unfortunately, we have no idea who is in charge over there. Their country is wildly unstable right now."

She cleared her throat, shuffling more paper. "Israel is done trying to appease the Muslim world. It's hard to negotiate with someone whose sole purpose in life is wanting you dead. The US is stepping back from the situation and that's about to go hot. If Israel gets the wind blowing in the right direction, away from the homeland, I expect them to turn a lot of sand into glass. That will make a radioactive buffer zone several miles wide. The surrounding countries will try to overwhelm the Israeli's Iron Dome defense system with massive numbers of rockets. If that happens, Israel will go hot again before they run out of munitions."

"Won't that trap them against their own radioactive wall if invaded from the sea?"

"Always the tactician, aren't you? But you're correct." The rustling of papers intensified.

His gaze locked on Alina's for a moment before staring out over the green valley. "That will not end well."

"You can wrap that in a fortune cookie," Sally continued. "Now, closer to home. The push from the people in charge is for the Shepherds to move from rescue to interdiction. We don't like it—but there it is. Terror cells have been flooding through the US borders for years. We can only assume they are ready to act. A lot of them have been in place, just waiting for the command to go ahead. We believe that scenario is at a critical stage as we speak. It's a good bet that our recalled Shepherds may be tasked to ferret those out if we have time. I'm sorry, but that includes retired hardheaded operatives. Anything else? I'm starting to get depressed, and my coffee is cold."

"What about this new coronavirus?"

"COVID-19? Scary as hell. With China on lockdown, it's hard to tell the mortality rate on that one. Given that it may have escaped from their Level-4 containment center in Wuhan, I'd say it's man-made and bad. They claim we gave it to them. We claim the opposite. We'll never know for sure. A big clue to how serious it was there would be the forty crematoriums they moved into Wuhan, each one operating twenty-four hours a day and seven days a week. They're doing the same thing in Beijing.

"There are rumors that they did it to their own people. A communist country, with more people than they can feed, might view that as acceptable collateral damage. Personally, I don't buy that. I'd rather think it's something that got away from them. For one thing, China's economy is at a standstill, and they don't want that.

"One other little factoid is troubling. About ninety percent of our antibiotics and antivirals are made in China. So if you're looking for something to stockpile..."

Jim was getting a cold knot in his stomach. "I didn't think COVID-19 was any worse than Type A or B flu?"

"It's not the flu. The common cold is a coronavirus and look how well we've done curing that. This little cutie works different and kills quicker if you're already immune compromised. Now, think of this—what happens if a scary new virus sweeps the country, and everyone is told to shelter in place for a few weeks so they don't spread it. The hospitals would be maxed out, clinics closed, businesses closed, nobody moving, except trucks delivering goods for the just-in-time inventories of food. Truck drivers get sick just like everyone else. Even if COVID-19 wasn't deadly, which it is, the fear of it can bring us to our knees. And then what happens, grasshopper?"

He shook his head, knowing she couldn't see it. His cold knot turned to nausea. "Given all the things you've mentioned? The opportunists, waiting for the perfect storm, will act."

"I always knew you were a good student. It's like a line of dominoes. The first has been pushed. It's teetering on edge right now. When it falls, if we can't pull a couple out down the line to stop the momentum, it all comes down."

When he didn't say anything, she continued. "Jim. Just so you know. We've moved command and control offshore." So, it was a splash, figuratively speaking. And that one item told him all he needed to know.

Alina broke the silence as she gasped, then held her hand over her mouth, because she got it, too. Her eyes turned big, expression begging for forgiveness.

"Is someone with you?" Sally's voice was sharp.

He couldn't keep from chuckling. "Oh, just Alina."

"Alina." He could almost hear her mind spinning. "As in Ivanov? Your Russian...whatever the hell she was? I can't wait to hear this story. Jesus. Wait a minute. What about Rita? Shots fired?"

"Long story." He sighed. "Rita is fine, but I'm out of options there. Whatever she and I had was falling apart before Alina arrived. We're not getting along." He gave her a hard glance. "Although she's not helping much."

Alina struck a pose for him that raised the ambient temperature ten degrees.

"Aw, dammit. I like Rita."

"Hey, I love you, too, Sally." Alina broke in with a musical lilt, whipping out her own cell as she retreated inside the door.

The momentary silence after the door slammed spoke volumes of her disapproval. "Jim, for God's sake, tell me you're not doing her."

His sigh was long and gentle. "Well, God left on the last train for the coast...but, if it makes a difference, I am not doing her, as you put it."

"Not yet..." Drifted out of the house.

"I heard that." Sally chuckled. "You're unbelievable. You can't stand things to be peaceful, can you? Would you put some cameras up around your place? We could link them to the internet and I could watch...kind of like a fly on the wall. I won't tell a soul. It'd be more fun than—"

"Please don't say a box of monkeys."

"Okay. I won't." She laughed. "But the visual is great. Look, I gotta go. I'm serious about those recalls of our people. I'll call you in a few days. If I don't...well, you'll be too busy to worry about me anyway. Have you talked to Barnes lately?"

How'd she know Barnes was in the picture? Something told him she was keeping better tabs of him than he knew. "Daily, but he's out for the next couple of days doing errands."

"Well, I've talked to him, so when he comes back, listen to what he says. He's just trying to help and it could be a solution for the short term."

More papers were shuffled, and the faint sound of a klaxon horn came through the phone. Maybe a surface ship? Probably a carrier group.

"When we talk again, I expect to hear you have a ham radio setup and be cognizant of Faraday cages. I may need to pull you back into service. On that same note and I can't believe I'm saying this, please approach your I'm-not-tapping-that roomie about becoming a team—just in case the whole terrorist cell thing gets out of hand and we need some hard solutions. She could be your backup."

He took a deep breath, seeing Alina peeking at him through the door. "Alright, Sally. I'll do that. I owe you and I'll pay my debts. I always do. Be safe...wherever you are."

After they signed off, Alina came out of the house. "Things are getting serious."

He gave a distracted answer, his mind on a dozen different things. "Sounds like it."

"I see it settling you down." She nodded as he gave her a startled glance. "All the things around here, important a while ago, become mere distractions. Now, I can see you distancing yourself. You're already figuring out how to disappear a few days to do a job, then blend back in like you've never been gone."

She had his full attention now. "You think you've got me all figured out?"

"No. That would be too easy. I keep peeling your onion, but there are too many layers. You're not an easy man to know. And to answer Sally's question, yes. If she needs me, I'll help. I am Russian American. This is my country, too. Although, teaming us up might be a mistake." At his surprised look, she shrugged. "You're a door-kicker like you accused the soldier of being. You see a problem and go right at it. I'm a bit sneakier. I like subtlety."

She nudged him with her hip. "Admit it. You're

already not so depressed about life, fighting with Rita, building your little kingdom here." Looking around the valley, she nodded. "Although, I approve. It's great." Her gaze was intense as it settled on him. "Makes me think about nesting."

He grinned at her. "Great. Alina, the psychobabble-ist. Besides, nesting is not a good idea."

"You made that word up, and you're wrong. It's Alina, the realist. Now, why the ham radio, and what was it? A Faraday cage?"

Jim studied her a moment, deciding to trust her. "They must be expecting the electrical grid to go down. The only thing that would do that would be an Electro Magnetic Pulse, or EMP, which would set us back to the pre-electricity 1800s. A Faraday cage is anything surrounded by tinfoil or something to block the damage. A strong EMP would fry all the electronics and computer chips. If the grid goes down, ham radios are about the only long-range communication we'd have, or short-range CBs—if they were protected."

She nodded, standing hip shot against the porch rail. "I called my father and gave him the news on the virus. He's buying a big-assed boat, one that can stay out to sea for months."

"I have no problem with that. It would have been nice to be able to see Sally's face after she realized you were there. I wouldn't have kept talking if I didn't want you to hear." He gave her a wry smile, shaking his head. "I can just see your father and Gregory on a boat all by them-selves for months."

"Oh, I don't know." She smiled, brushing off her jeans. "I'm pretty sure I heard giggles in the background while we talked. I'm sure they have a full crew with all the comforts. At least, I hope so. It's amazing what money can buy." She leaned in and pecked him on the cheek. "Right now, I'm going to visit Jacy, see if I can help with the munchkins. I don't think she's as tough as she puts on." She paused, watching him briefly. "Should I mention any of this to her? She's a friend. A new friend, but still…"

She hesitated a moment before continuing. "You know…"

He could see the wheels turning as she thought about something. "Every good team needs a medic."

"No. She has kids and we don't. It wouldn't be fair to ask her. Talking to her about all this is fine. From this point forward, the fewer people know about what we're doing, or what we have, the better off we'll be. It's okay to talk to her, but keep it private. Jacy is good people and needs to protect her kids. It's her hubby I'm not so sure about."

After a wave and smile, Alina drove away in her little Prius, kicking up dust on her way down the lane.

# TWENTY-FOUR

JIM SAT on his porch in pondering mode, something he'd done a lot of lately. The valley below was a beehive of activity. Pablo's new manufactured home, complete with faux-wood exterior, was erected, blocked, skirted, and ready to go. Three men with a flatbed truck were busy at the entrance to the valley, building a pipe-metal gate with fencing that extended from both sides into the limestone bluffs.

As he watched, an ATV launched from the activity and came up the hill with one man bouncing on the seat. A pickup with a utility bed followed on the drive. There was lettering on the side door of the truck that Jim would bet serious money had plumbing somewhere on it. The ATV skidded to a sideways stop amid a small cloud of dust.

Jim raised his hand. "Hey, Pablo. How's the world treating you? It looks like the work is going well?"

His foreman came up the steps. "Better than ever, Boss. Juanita is very happy and like you said, happy wife happy life." Pablo pointed a thumb over his shoulder at the other man approaching. "This is Gomez. He's a topnotch plumber and a friend."

Gomez extended his hand for a firm handshake. "Pleased to meet you."

"Likewise." Jim looked the man over. He could have been Pablo's brother. "I assume he's here to help. Credentials?"

Before the man could answer, Pablo interrupted. "I trust him. We served together."

"Seems to be a lot of vets around here." Jim shrugged and gave the man an appraising look. "Good enough for me, Pablo. You're the foreman. So, what do you need from me?"

"You mentioned something about ideas for water and electricity. Right now, my family has bottled water to drink and a generator. We carry water from the spring to flush the toilet and take baths in."

"Well, great as that sounds, I do have a better idea." The two men followed him around to the back of the house. "I have a well that pumps into the water tank to give me better water pressure and a ready supply in case the pump quits. Being so far downhill from this, I'm thinking you can tap into the pipe, it's about three feet deep, and run a line down to the house."

The plumber was nodding. "That's about a three-hundred-foot drop, so pressure should be good. What size is your pipe?"

"Two inch in the well drop, one inch on the lateral into the house."

"Good." He gazed around at the setup. "We can hook onto that and about halfway down the hill switch to three-quarter inch pipe to increase pressure. We'll need a shutoff and filter system at both ends for safety." He nodded with a smile. "I like it. This will work."

Pablo was nodding. "How about electricity? Should I get my own solar panels?"

Jim turned with the two men, and they looked at the new home at the bottom of the hill, shrouded in shade.

"Well, that would be okay in the winter, but summer might be a problem. My suggestion is to install your own but also hook up to mine. The biggest draw will be air conditioners in the summer, so you'd have additional power to run them. Sound good?"

The plumber looked skeptical. "So, we'd have to dig two trenches down the hill? It would take more time."

Jim laughed. "You see any inspectors around here? Use a heavy duty underground cable in the same trench. Your water line will be about three feet down. Put a foot of dirt over it, then lay your cable. I won't tell anyone. That should get Juanita fixed up in her new house in a short amount of time. I assume you have someone putting in a septic tank?"

"Already done, boss."

The men retired to the porch, and Jim brought out the beer. He didn't know how to approach the next subject without leaping in with both feet. Trust is often a two-part equation. First comes need. And then trust is earned. He didn't have time for that. All he could do was follow his instincts.

"Pablo, I've got some serious stuff to discuss." He gave Gomez a pointed look, waiting for confirmation from his foreman.

"Do not give it a moment's thought. Gomez is my friend and a good man." Pablo grinned as he looked at his friend, slapping him on the shoulder. "Mostly, he's a good man to have on your side."

"Good enough." He went on to tell them all he knew about the world situation and possible ramifications for them. It took an hour and another round of beer to get it done.

"So, you think this can happen here?" Pablo was watching him, waiting for the punch line of the joke.

"We are somewhat isolated." Jim nodded, glancing between the men. "But it's possible enough that we should prepare, at the least. The first punch will be this new coronavirus. People are already starting to panic with that. It hasn't affected us much here, but in the dense population centers, people are starting to act out on their fear. Countries, including the US, are starting to lock down. There's an end game afoot. Once the situation goes belly up with that, which it will, what better time to strike? I do know we're in the range of North Korea's missiles. Chances? My old boss put it at about seventy to eighty percent. She's usually very conservative with her predictions."

"The bottom line?" He shrugged and gave them a level gaze. "I want this place to be as self-sufficient as soon as possible. We may not have a lot of time."

Gomez was standing, hands on hips, staring into the distance. "How deep is your well?"

"Twelve hundred feet. The well and pump are inside the basement, so inaccessible from outside."

"Should be sweet water. Are your solar panels protected?"

Jim shook his head, grinning at the man. Once a marine...always thinking about how to blow shit up, or protect against getting blown up. "You can't see them unless you're flying and know where to look. It's a big array, though, and could be spotted with a drone."

"And the windmill?"

"It's not connected to water. The turbine charges more batteries."

Gomez glanced at him. "You've spent a lot of money. I'm envious. Our setup at home is adequate, but not so good as this."

Jim grinned at the man. "Wasn't my money, but I did spend it."

His foreman and the plumber were looking at each other like some form of hidden communication was happening. He could easily visualize these men surveying an enemy camp in hostile territory.

Gomez spoke, still gazing around the valley. "This is a defensible position. I have noticed the white rocks set about a hundred yards apart going down the hill. They look like decorations next to the road. You're not fooling anybody."

Jim nodded, watching as the two men turned to survey the valley again. After the fiasco of trying to defend an untenable position last year, he'd vowed to never be caught in that position again.

Pablo was pointing things out to his friend. "The only way in here by vehicle is through the gate. The rest of the valley is surrounded by limestone bluffs. Even the trees and brush surrounding this meadow have enough rocks and outcroppings to make foot travel difficult. It's a maze unless you know your way through."

"At first I was against a cattle guard at the gate," Pablo continued. "But I've changed my mind. It could be made to collapse on command and have spikes in the bottom. Even a big transport truck would have trouble getting through if we didn't want them to. Done this way, the first vehicle trying to get through the gate creates a roadblock."

"Supplies? Arms? Munitions?" Gomez was looking at him. "You have these?"

Jim grimaced before answering. "There is never enough, but what I have is adequate. What I'm short on is anti-viral meds, but I have an idea for that."

Pablo nodded, glancing at Gomez. "Jacy? I know she's a nurse, but…"

"She's 86 Whiskey. I'll be talking to her when I can."

The men stood with their mouths open, gazing at Jim. No one could believe that sweet, innocent-looking girl could have that kind of experience. It was a moment before Gomez continued. "For the short term, the virus may be the strongest threat. The media is stirring up panic at unprecedented levels. If all the hype is true and we survive, it may take care of the longer-term threat of a collapse."

Jim shook his head, wishing his new friend were right. But wishing isn't getting. Scared and unprepared people do stupid things out of desperation. That was a constant rule in the world.

"A big question is how long before it hits here. How do you think the locals will react when people from out of town flock in and try to buy up all the groceries? No, I think the panic will be worse than the sickness. The death rate is less than two percent, I think, but the media is painting it as if we're all gonna die. From what I've seen, the numbers reported don't make a lot of sense."

Gomez was pacing the deck. "I disagree, somewhat. We are all men of the world. Warriors, if my assessment is correct. We each see things in a different way, which is a good thing. I see the news and pay attention to things not said. In China, everyone is required to have a cell phone—that's how their masters keep track of them. Twenty-one million accounts were canceled. Some of those may be for normal reasons, but it's a staggering number. If they released this virus, they're paying a terrible price. Satellite photos show huge trenches being dug in the deserts of Iran. A trench you can see from space will hold a lot of bodies. Germany is stacking bodies on ice rinks because there is no place to keep them. So, I think this virus cannot be discounted. The results of it will be far-reaching."

Jim stared at the man but saw no sign of panic. Just grim determination. "Well, I can't disagree with all that. Here's an idea. What if it's coordinated? If people are sick, or sheltering in place, and businesses are closing, the economy will be in the tank. That's nail one in the coffin. At that point, the jihadis will think we're helpless and terrorize at will. Or the second nail. Say, we lose the grid, the jihadis pop up, and sickness strikes all within weeks of each other? Either of those scenarios can bring anarchy. At that point, a strong force of fighters could carve out a significant chunk of real estate in this country."

Gomez moved to the edge of the porch, looking across the valley. "If all this is coordinated, or even if they just take advantage of the situation, then I hope you have lots of paddles for our canoes, my friend. We are going to be up shit's creek. Way up."

As the men prepared to leave, Gomez spoke again. "I trust Pablo and he trusts you. That is enough for me. I will help any way I can and keep my mouth shut. The same courtesy will be expected in return. I have workers to help us for the right price and we can get all this done in a very few days. I understand money is available for all this?"

Jim gave him a grateful look. "Pablo has my card. He hasn't hit bottom yet."

"Good. Let's hope the banks don't go belly up before we can spend your money. I have one favor to ask. We have a place like this, not as large...but, close. My family is used to living off the grid. Poor people have this advantage. I think we'll be okay, but if things go bad...?"

Jim shook his hand again. "We'll be tight for room, but you have sanctuary whenever you need it. I'm thinking a time is coming when friends will need to stick together."

Watching them leave, he finished his beer. Might need to stock up on that. His family was growing. He'd just met Pablo and Gomez, but felt his assessment was correct. They were good men and he'd decided to trust them. Trust was something he hadn't done a lot of in the past.

Rita needed to be informed. She would respect Sally's information, more than his own. She and Sally had bonded in friendship the short time they were together. What Rita would do with the information was anybody's guess.

Activity caught his attention as he noticed men scattering at the entrance gate. Rita's vehicle, plus another patrol SUV, pulled into his drive—light bars flashing. A hard knot formed in his belly. He knew she was mad at him, but this...?

# TWENTY-FIVE

JIM WAITED, hands in pockets with studied casualness, while the patrol cars pulled to a stop. What the hell? Rita stepped out of her vehicle and stood watching while her deputy, PJ Rails, exited his. Surprisingly, Rails stood behind the door with his weapon drawn and aimed at Jim.

Jim moved to the front of the porch and leaned his left shoulder against the post. It was a little protection from PJ, but not much. Mind buzzing from his meeting with Pablo and Gomez, and ready for most problems that might crop up, this was not on his list. He wasn't in survival mode...yet. But having guns pointed at him made him do quirky things. Shooting at Rita was not an option, but the steroid junkie was another matter. Having any kind of altercation with law enforcement went against everything he believed in—unless they were outside the law. He knew that whatever her reasoning, Rita would not go rogue.

Hand resting near his pistol, he called to her. "What's

up, Rita? Having guns pointed at me isn't something I like much and especially from a friend."

She didn't speak for a moment. At the distance, he couldn't tell if it was anger or regret in her eyes. Her chest heaved as she took a deep breath before answering.

"Remember what I said about not paying for your sins? This is one of those times. You need to come into the office and give a statement."

Scenarios were running through his mind. What would cause this? Surely the GOB killings wouldn't garner this kind of response. "About what? The weather? World affairs? My view on COVID-19?"

She shook her head, coming around her door, hands on hips. "Dickie Johnson was murdered. After the trouble you've had with him, you're a person of interest."

"Dickie is dead?" A cold knot formed in his stomach. He shrugged and shook his head, still trying to make sense of the confrontation—and it was a confrontation. This was not a polite conversation. "No matter how he died, it couldn't be any more than justifiable homicide."

Dickie Johnson's death was no loss to humanity. Movement caught his eye behind the deputy. Where in the world she'd come from he didn't know, but Alina was standing in the deputy's place. Making eye contact, she nodded to his right. Both Pablo and Gomez had come out from behind the house and were standing to the side with weapons in ready-down position. Pablo had an AR-15, while Gomez held a tactical-looking pump shotgun. He almost smiled, not realizing he had a quick response team. Although, there was no way he could use them.

Rita glanced over at them. "You boys going hunting? I'm ordering you to back away from this situation, or we're going to have a real furball here."

When neither responded, she brought her attention back to Jim. "Is this the way it's going to be, Jim? Got yourself a little gang of your own? Gonna compete with the Good Old Boys? Is that why they seem to be disappearing? That's something I hadn't thought of before now. Maybe that's the real motive for everything that's been going on."

A little surprised at the turn of events, he turned his focus back to Rita. "Dickie Johnson must have a thousand enemies. His boss Roman Fielding? A thousand and one. Will I see them all at the station for a get-together? Or is it just me?"

"What did I tell you before?" She looked pointedly around his parking lot, shaking her head. Her sad gaze came back to him. "We have a small county, but we seem to have a remarkably high death rate. When someone dies a violent death, I look around and there you are, either in person or by name. You're a magnet for chaos. I can't in good conscience put up with it anymore. No matter the excuse, I can't look away."

"Well, it's nice to know I'm on your mind all the time." Magnet for chaos? That was a new one. Maybe he could use that in his book. "How was Little Dickie killed, if I might ask?"

"Like you don't know?" Shaking her head, she continued with a disgusted voice. "Seems he was cut up by an expert. He was stabbed several times in specific places—both kidneys, liver and once in the scrotum for maximum pain before having his femoral artery sliced."

He exchanged looks with the two men standing guard. They'd be thinking the same things. Stabs in the kidneys would incapacitate with pain, but knowing Dickie's strength, he'd still be standing. He might be able to lift his arms to defend himself, but that would be doubtful. Then come around front so he'd know who was doing the deed. A couple more quick, painful stabs in the liver to make his point. With legs like tree trunks, Dickie would be bleeding out, but still wouldn't go down. Next, a blade between his legs to make a point, then the edge of the knife turned sideways and up to slice the femoral artery. By that time Dickie would be too weak to scream. The assailant probably stood there staring into Dickie's eyes until the man finally toppled. That's the way he'd do it—in theory.

If he was investigating, the most important wound was the slice to the scrotum. Rita should know that. The weapon used was undoubtedly wicked sharp. A thought bloomed uninvited in his mind—something that could cut a half-inch rope in one slice. He thought about that and knew the answer at once. Dickie had disrespected a certain cowboy in front of his wife. Those things don't go unanswered. Maybe in the big city, but not in this part of the country. But what now?

He knew the longer he could stall, the less likely something bad would happen. "Where was he found?"

Body language and expression were all indicators that Rita's patience was running out. "Next to his car in front of the courthouse."

He smiled at her, noticing another small flurry of activity where Alina was standing. "No witnesses?"

"None. Now let's stop this"—she glanced at the two men—"Mexican standoff and get this over with."

Well, that was a wrinkle. In front of the courthouse? So, maybe not the cowboy? That was the same spot the farmer was dumped. Curious. Mrs. Hyatt didn't strike him as the type, but maybe a friend?

"What am I seeing in your eyes, Rita? Satisfaction? Indignation? What's there? Are you this mad at me, that you'll take the slightest excuse to embarrass me? You know damned good and well that I didn't do this. What is it?"

Her ponytail whipped to the side as she shook her head. "It's none of those. I'm doing my job. You used to know what that meant."

Jim slumped and then glanced at his friends. He didn't know how far Pablo and Gomez would go, figured it was just a show of support, but he knew Alina would go all the way—something he knew no one else would do for him, including Rita. In that moment, he realized he could always count on her. That wasn't always a good thing. Alina watched him, waiting for direction. He'd bet serious money her heartbeat wasn't above sixty. She was the real danger. Things could get out of control in a big hurry.

"Alina, stand down. Please. And that goes for you other two. I appreciate the support, but disengage. Nothing's going to happen here."

Rita gave him what he thought was a grateful look— maybe he was dreaming. "Step down here."

He walked down to ground level, keeping eye contact as he approached.

"Turn around." After snapping on her gloves, she reached to the back of her belt and retrieved the cuffs from their holder.

"Really? Gloves? Cuffs? Am I under arrest?"

"You can be. It's all SOP. No one rides in the back unless cuffed, or zip-tied. You know that. So, turn around. Be glad it's not zips." Once she handcuffed him, she did a thorough pat down for weapons. She handed his .45 and snub-nosed Rossi to a disgruntled Deputy Rails, who had walked up with grass stains on his knees, shirt pulled out, and a dent in the crown of his hat.

In a mild voice, Jim said. "I'll want a receipt for those."

Rita snorted. "Like you don't have extras? Don't worry, I'm not taking them. PJ, put his weapons on the porch." Pulling his tactical knife from his boot, she commented. "This is what we need to test for blood residue."

Pulling an evidence bag from her pocket, she dropped the knife in, careful not to cut a slice in the container.

"Don't lose that, I just got it." He smirked at her eye-roll. "Do you have a preliminary report? What kind of knife are you looking for? And be careful with that. It's sharp."

"I wouldn't expect anything else. You keep asking things that are none of your business. You've already got more information from me than you should. Maybe you need to take advantage of your right to remain silent."

He glanced over his shoulder. "No can do, Sheriff. It's my business if you're trying to haul me in for a murder charge. Don't do this."

She walked around and stood in front of him. "Level with me. I can help you. It doesn't have to be murder. Did you have another fight with him? Did he threaten you, attack you? A local jury wouldn't convict anyone for killing Dickie, you know that. Hell, you might get a medal."

He shook his head and closed his eyes for a moment with a big sigh. "Nice try."

Her hand moved softly over the knife, careful of the edge. "So, what's this button by the handle?"

"It releases a C02 charge directly into a wound. It's made for fighting off large animals."

Her eyes widened. "I've heard of these. Used by SEALs, or UDT teams for underwater work. Supposed to be bloodless so sharks aren't attracted. Sounds pretty farfetched to me. But this could blow someone's arm or leg off."

"No, just bust it open." Jim gave her a curious look, then turned away. "Pablo, you're in charge while I'm gone. Make sure the work goes as planned. This is just a bump in the road, so don't worry."

"We're not done here." She spoke softly, glancing over her shoulder. "What about Alina? Does she use a knife? She assaulted my deputy, so we need to address that."

Personally, he thought the deputy got off easy, considering who attacked him. "Come on, Rita. Why borrow more trouble? I doubt the steroid junkie wants anyone to know a little blond female took him down without a fight. Maybe your deputy stumbled and fell in performance of his duties. Sound about right?"

"Well." She stared at PJ. "It wouldn't be the first time he's tripped. There is some precedent for that. Especially, since the cow kicked him in the head."

"Now, that's a story I need to hear." Jim nodded his thanks to Rita, seeing a hint of humor in her eyes. "Alina, how about you go in the house? I'll be with Sheriff Morris and call you if I need a ride. If you would, please call Barnes and let him know what's happened, just in case I need a lawyer." He glanced at Rita. "Which I can't imagine. His number is on my contact list in the laptop."

"I have his number." She waved a hand at Rita. "You sure about all this? It's bogus and you know it...pure harassment. You don't have to cooperate."

He interrupted before Rita could respond and nodded toward the house. "Not now, Alina. Let it go. Please."

As she passed Deputy Rails, the man lunged at her from behind. A flurry of motion ended with him on the ground and Alina's knee in his groin. The barrel of her pistol was pressed on his forehead. His voice came out choked and high pitched from her knee placement. "Sheriff!"

"Stop it!" A small smile was showing as Rita spoke up, even as her thumb flipped the strap off her pistol. "Alina, he's young and inexperienced. You're assaulting a police officer. I realize he jumped you and I apologize. Let him go, please? As a favor? You're pushing the boundaries here, even for Limestone County."

"Like I owe you any favors?" She turned her attention back to PJ. "How about it, big man? Am I hurting you?" Alina pressed a little harder with her pistol for emphasis, got up and left the deputy with a red, round circle on his forehead.

"Thanks, Alina." Taking a long look around, Rita asked. "What is going on out here, anyway? It looks as if you are building a compound and adding people."

"Well," Jim said. "My business used to be your business. Not sure it is anymore. If you come back in a less official capacity sometime, I'll show you around." He changed direction. "Why did you come after me? None of this makes sense."

"You have a really short memory, don't you? Beating the crap out of Dickie—threatening his life if Dan Hyatt died? Past that? Someone saw you at his place. I'd like to clear you first and get you off the suspect list."

"Really? You have other suspects? Don't you mean he was at Roman Fielding's place? I was unaware Dickie had a place of his own. I assume Roman would be on your suspect list. Who made the report? Have you questioned the woman they shack up with? Bella? Or have you questioned your buddy Fielding?"

Her gaze slipped away and all he got was a shrug. Words can lead you astray, but body language never lies. He slumped in defeat. A bait box full of dead fish would smell better than this. She was right about one thing, though. The body count was rising.

———

THE RIDE to the sheriff's department building was uneventful, discounting the slow trip through town with the strobes on, highlighting the two-vehicle parade. It was Jim's first trip to the office since the town replaced the old double-wide manufactured home used for the sheriff's offices with a single-story, cement block building more fitting for a government entity. Ugly.

The only interesting thing was a black Escalade SUV sitting in the parking lot. Looking like an escapee from the President's protection detail, he hadn't seen one of those since last year. Was the mafia here? Or the FEEBS? Although on different sides of the law, sometimes their tactics weren't much different.

They did the embarrassing perp-walk through the building to arrive at Rita's office, enduring the stares of the covey of cubicle dwellers, mostly a few secretaries and then Deputy Frank Tucker. Watching the eyes of most of the inhabitants track him made Jim's ears burn more than it should. Entering the office, she kicked the door closed and tossed his hat on the desk. Coming around behind him, she removed the cuffs and indicated a chair in front of her desk.

The first thing he noticed was a lack of recent pictures. Her vanity wall behind the desk was adorned with awards and commendations from years past. Nearly every picture was of her and her deceased husband—some recent in sheriff's department khakis, most in military gear. A laptop computer sat on one side of her barren desk. One picture of her late husband sat on the other side. The room was a shrine and looking at it, he realized he'd just wasted the better part of a year trying to storm that particular bastion of sainthood. You can't compete with a dead man.

Still standing, rubbing his wrists and feeling defeated, he glared at her. "Do you want to tell me what that was all about?"

She went around her desk and sat, indicating that he should do the same. "Saving my job.".

Still giving her the stink eye, he clapped his hat back on his head. "So, all this was about taking me down a notch? A public show so people can see you're doing something? You know I didn't kill Dickie."

"You and I know it. But they"—her finger circled in the air—"they don't know it. Town council, county commissioners, White Rock PD—they are all on my case. In the court of public opinion, you were Facebooked, Tweeted and Instagrammed guilty in the first hour. So, now that people have seen you brought in, I can show that I have a weapon for analysis. I'll have your statement with an iron-clad alibi all tied up in a neat little package. You'll walk away with no repercussions and I'll go on with the investigation to try and find the hero who sliced up Dickie Johnson. That do it for you?"

He nodded, grudgingly. "You could have told me all that before we left. The handcuffs were a little bit too much. Your desk deputy gossips more than the ladies' quilting club."

She smiled. "Oh, no. It was perfect. We had to sell the show and you were pissed. Boy, were you pissed. Priceless!"

Pointing to the obvious video port in the ceiling behind and above her, camouflaged as a smoke alarm, she waited until he nodded that he understood. "Let's get to it. I'm interviewing Jim Lane in the matter of the murder of Dickie Johnson. Mr. Lane has shown he understands he's being recorded. He also waives the right to an attorney at this time. Where were you this morning?"

He decided to play it straight, although he thought she'd missed a few things in her promo—like, time and date, and a small matter of Miranda. "I was at my home. And you've already seen my witnesses."

"That would be Pablo, who is your...?" Eyebrows raised, she waited for an answer.

"Pablo Estevez is my new ranch manager."

Her eyebrows raised. "Ranch manager? I wasn't aware you'd turned the place into a ranch."

"Yep. Working on it. I even have a sign over the entrance gate, Lazy J."

She nodded, puzzlement apparent on her face. "And another man was present?"

He nodded. "Gomez. That could be his first, last, or both names. I don't know."

"And he is...?"

"He's doing plumbing and electrical work for us. Good man. Retired Marine."

"I see. Any other person that might vouch for you?"

"That *might* vouch for me? How many do you need?" He sighed, wondering if this whole charade was about this one question. "Alina Ivanov."

Her eyes were black, the pupils full-blown in anger, although it didn't show in her voice...just in the white-knuckled grip holding her hands together, the tendons in her forearms taut. "Hmmm. Sounds Russian. And her job description on your ranch is...?"

Jim grinned at her, not above poking the proverbial bear. "You know damned good and well who she is." His smile got wider. "She's an old acquaintance."

"Does she live with you, out on your...ranch?"

"Nope. She's staying with a friend of hers...for now." He thought she looked relieved, but probably imagined it and wondered why she'd care.

"Is that all the questions you have for me?" He knew Rita was smart, with a quick mind—and those two attributes weren't always held in the same personality. She hadn't missed his drawing out his answer about where Alina was living.

Unfolding her hands and leaning back in her chair, she said. "Pending the lab report on the knife we recovered, you should be in the clear. Thanks for your statement."

He saw her shift position and assumed she'd turned off the recorder. She came around the desk as he stood. When he tried to reach an arm around her back, she stepped back and glanced toward the interview mirror.

The door swung open and a tall, slim man strode into the room. His blond hair was high and tight with a buzz cut, black slacks over alligator-hide boots and a sport coat over a polo shirt. A gold shield was clipped to his belt, along with a pistol in a plastic tactical holster. Now, he understood the black Escalade SUV out front. Talk about a phallus symbol?

The man pointed at him. "Sit down, Lane. We're not through here."

Jim remained standing, wishing he had his Glock 22. Looking between Rita and this man was an education. He'd said we're not through, as in a joint effort. She wasn't mad—and should be, because he was out of line. So, a history between them? Puzzle pieces, previously scrambled, were starting to fall into place.

Rita spoke, careful not to get between the two men. "Jim Lane, this is Detective Trevon Miles from Springfield. He's looking into allegations of some shootings last year around Stockton Lake."

"Allegations? A year later? By someone out of their jurisdiction? By whom? Sorry, kids. I'm done here."

Miles took another step forward, swept back the tail of his coat, and put his hand on his pistol. "I said, sit down."

The gun was desert brown. A Keltec? Jim shook his head, giving the man the same smile he'd give a small child. "I don't think so. And you can stop with the posturing. You couldn't intimidate a twelve-year-old. And one more point of interest, Detective. Your hand is on your pistol. That's a threat. And you've made a fatal mistake. You're too close to me. If your thumb moves that safety strap, I will take you out."

"Stop this! Jim, Trevon is an old friend." She gave the man a pointed look. "Tone it down, please."

When Miles backed up, Jim took that as another point of education. The detective must still be wanting to curry her favor by not making her mad.

He grumbled, still watching Jim. "I still have questions."

Looking him up and down, Jim shook his head again. Head shaking was getting to be a habit in this office. "You're wasting my time. I have nothing for you. Get a warrant. I'll get a lawyer. We'll do this the old-fashioned way and you can talk to him."

The desk deputy broke the staring contest.

"Sheriff!" Deputy Tucker was standing in the doorway. "They got something going on at the grocery store."

"Price Cutter? What the hell...a robbery?" Rita was still holding her hand up between the two men.

"It's this COVID thing." Tucker stood with eyes wide. "People are fighting over toilet paper. The manager requested crowd control."

"Toilet paper?" She gave Jim an incredulous look and seemed surprised at his grim expression. "It's a respiratory virus. Toilet paper? What's going on?"

The deputy swallowed, wringing his hands. "The President just announced a national emergency. It's a world pandemic."

# TWENTY-SIX

RITA ACCELERATED out of the parking lot, tearing up loose asphalt and throwing gravel, herding her two-ton missile toward the grocery. She was looking daggers at Jim, who'd jumped into the passenger seat. On her way out of the building, she'd yelled at Deputy Tucker to alert White Rock PD and the other deputies.

He was wishing she'd watch the road as her finger was pointed at him. "You will stay out of this. Understand?" His only response was to tighten his grip on the panic bar above the side window and press his feet against the floorboard and imaginary brake pedal.

They rolled into a parking lot jammed full of people and vehicles. Maneuvering through the narrow lanes and dodging empty shopping carts, she slammed to a stop. Shoulders slumped, she expelled a giant sigh and rolled her neck to relieve tension. It didn't look like it was working.

"Well, you don't see that every day." Her voice was caustic as she viewed the scene, shaking her head and muttering to herself. She didn't seem in any hurry to intercede, and he didn't blame her. Situations between police and irate shoppers in parking lots tend to escalate in a hurry.

Just outside the front door of the grocery were two overturned carts, with bulk packs of toilet paper and twelve-packs of beer strewn on the asphalt. As they watched, a beer can ruptured, broke loose from the cardboard container, and scooted across the hot pavement, leaving a rooster-tail of foam.

Two over-nourished men in tee shirts riding up above their bellies, both with more hair on their forearms than their heads, were whaling away at each other. Two women duked it out just past them. Wives? Girlfriends? Who belonged to whom was anyone's guess, but this wasn't a scratchy, hair-pulling event. As they watched, one of the women threw a punch that splattered the other woman's nose in a shower of blood and knocked her on her back.

"Wow," Rita commented. "Talk about getting roached."

Jim nodded as he stepped out of the Interceptor. It was a good analogy since the woman was on her back with her arms and legs flailing in the air. He stopped at the front of the vehicle but didn't advance, so he could watch Rita's back. Although he wasn't feeling all that charitable toward her, it was a courtesy he'd give anyone, at least until her deputies arrived.

Rita finally left her vehicle, flicked her wrist to extend her ASP Talon to the full twenty-four inches and whipped it across the legs of one of the men. He went down like he was shot, screaming and holding the back of his thigh. The other man tried to back away, holding his hands out, but she flicked the tip of the ASP down on his shoulder, making him join his friend on the asphalt. Both were moaning and cussing while trying to kick each other. Short of being shot in the sternum with a large-caliber bullet, the ASP was as deadly and incapacitating as anything on her belt.

She was advancing on the women when Jim caught up. Her method of crowd control was being a one-woman wrecking ball. If she were alone, it would be the right response. She was not.

"Rita, stop. You've got a crowd." He stood in front of her until she settled down. "Don't use the ASP on the women. Just break them up."

Her breathing slowed, and sanity returned to her eyes. His wary gaze watched her as she grabbed both women and separated them. What was that all about? It was a level of anger he'd not seen before.

Seeing one of the men struggling to stand up, he walked over and kicked the legs out from under him. "Stay put."

Rita had the wannabe cage fighters sitting on the ground and was talking to the store manager. "Were these items paid for?"

The manager shrugged. "Yeah, the one couple came in and bought me out of toilet paper and loaded up on beer. The other folks wanted them to share. That's when the fight started. I never seen the like." He stood, hands on hips, shaking his head. "Sheriff. None of these people are local. This craziness started early this morning, soon as we opened. If this keeps up, there won't be anything left for the town. We only get deliveries once a week—twice for perishables."

"I'm not sure what we can do about that unless things turn violent like this. It's still a free country."

Jim cleared his throat, and Rita gave him a puzzled glance. He mouthed, "Civil emergency."

"I don't think..." She thought for a moment, gaze never leaving him, nodded, and grabbed the manager by the shoulder. "Get all this picked up and back on the shelves, and be sure to refund their money."

Jim followed her inside the crowded store as she walked to the checkout and told the girl to put her on the Public Address System. "Attention shoppers. This is Sheriff Rita Morris of Limestone County. In accordance with local ordinance"—she gave Jim a quick look—"we are declaring a civil emergency, pursuant to the state emergency due to COVID-19. Your ID will be viewed before you can check out. If you don't have a local or county address, you cannot take anything out of here. You are advised to go home. Thank you for cooperating."

A florid-faced, portly man was next to be checked out. He smirked at a woman behind him before lashing out. "You got no right to do this. This is America, and we can shop where we want."

Jim was starting to intervene, but Rita got in the man's face. "Where are you from?"

"If it's any of your business, Kansas City."

"Well, mister. I have every right in the world to do this. There are a lot of stores between here and Kansas City. I know for a fact that KC has thousands of stores. I suggest you take your ass out of here and hit the road, or you'll be sampling the food in our holding cell."

He tried to stare down the sheriff, but was an amateur facing a pro. Wheeling away, he grabbed a woman and ushered her out—throwing curses over his shoulder at them and life in general.

While the manager stood thanking her, Jim noticed

about half the shoppers in the store abandoned carts as they left, casting dirty looks at Rita as they passed.

Deputy Rails arrived, and she brought him up to speed, posting him at the door to check people as they arrived. Jim smiled as he looked around. While not strictly legal, this one act would cement her popularity with the people and save a lot of hassle. They walked outside to see the parking lot only half full, and the toilet paper hoarders were long gone.

Rita turned to look at him. "This is nuts. What are these people thinking?"

"They're scared. The other stores in town should be warned, so they can come up with limits on quantity. The way things are sounding on the news, we'll be under lockdown soon. People are not prepared. It's like panic buying before a hurricane. Except this could be months."

"Months?"

He gave her a long look. "Don't you watch the news? Social media? Facebook? Anything like that? The media is making it sound like Armageddon. You don't read science fiction, do you?"

She shook her head, gazing around the parking lot. "You know I don't. I've no time for that. Not anymore."

"Well, you'll be up to your pretty neck in it real soon. You'd better crack a news outlet and get up to speed. If I were you, I'd call some of your fellow sheriffs and let them know what you've done—what might be coming their way, if it hasn't already. Then get with your county commissioners and the grocers to ensure the supply chain for your county."

He shrugged, realizing he'd overstepped, and gave her an apologetic shrug. "Well, that's what I'd do."

Her phone chirped, and she held up one finger,

asking him to wait. As he watched, her normal dark complexion went several shades lighter. She nodded, then seemed to realize the other person couldn't see that and replied. "I understand. Thank you."

She stared into the distance for a moment before turning her attention to Jim. "That was the head of our county emergency management office. The Regional Office of Homeland Security just reached out to her." Her gaze took in the parking lot, as she slowly shook her head. "They've shut us down. Shelter in place, except for essential businesses, like places that sell food and the pharmacy. I never dreamed…?"

"Seems sudden to me, too." He knew it would take something like the virus to panic people. It's always the fear of the unknown that makes the masses unreasonable. They could be moving into dangerous times.

Rita seemed to snap out of her daze, giving him a grim smile. "Thanks for the advice on this, Jim. You were ahead of the curve, as usual. I need to go back to the office and come up with a plan, contact some people. I can't keep my deputies at all the stores. Oh, and thanks for keeping me from whacking those women that were fighting. That would have been a bad image."

Her voice was all business, gaze cool and impersonal. Looking at her, he might as well have been a coworker with no previous history with her at all. They were no closer than before. He was still pissed at her for bringing him in for a talk. It was all for show, and he didn't understand it—didn't accept her explanation.

"Glad to help. You're going to need a lot of bodies, so don't forget your citizen Sheriff's Posse. I'm sure they'll volunteer. And one other thing. Call Sally One-Eye. If you need her number…?"

Not sure she heard him or was paying attention, he tried to touch her arm, but she was already heading for her vehicle. "That's alright, Rita. Don't worry about me. I'll get a ride somewhere."

He looked around the parking lot half full of vehicles, heat waves rising from the asphalt. "Maybe."

———

AFTER A SHORT PHONE CALL, he had about a half-hour wait before his ride showed up. People were scurrying around, unloading shopping carts into cars and trucks. Most of them had tight expressions, not greeting anyone, or making eye contact. Fear traveled faster than any virus outbreak, but only half as fast as stupidity.

"Thanks for the ride, Barnes." He reached over and cranked up the air conditioner.

His friend glanced at him with a serious expression. "You got a fever?"

He didn't know where Barnes had been, but that seemed addled. "What?"

"Anyone with symptoms has to quarantine themselves. Everyone else is supposed to shelter in place. No meetings, non-essential businesses closing, restaurants closing except for drive-throughs—you ain't heard any of that? It's all over the news."

"Yeah, I've heard it. Have we been attacked yet?"

"Nah. As far as I know, it's only that Wuhan, man. The coronavirus. All the knee-jerk reactions are a sight to see. It ain't pretty." He took his gaze off the road for a moment. "You think we will be? Attacked, I mean?"

"Dunno, who can say? It'd be a great opportunity, wouldn't it?" He felt a little better prepared than Rita, but not by much. The speed of escalation was amazing. Listening to the radio on the way to the ranch, he thought of it as a ranch now, it sounded like the world, in general and the CDC and WHO in particular, were caught with their collective pants down.

Jim knew it would be thousands of times worse in the dense population centers than in their rural county and was thankful for that. They wouldn't have to worry about the virus as much as panicked people fleeing the city. People would take the order to shelter in place as a directive to go somewhere else, preferably away from crowds.

He filled Barnes in on the fight at the grocery store. "The chaos and craziness, we'll call it C squared, has already started. Rita and her deputies are going to be run ragged keeping up with this. So far, the lower Midwest has very few cases, but once that escalates, EMS will be the first to be overwhelmed."

Lost in their thoughts, they traveled in silence, until Barnes commented on the unusual amount of traffic. "Where in the world are these people going?"

"Who knows? Just away from where they were." Jim's phone chirped, and he answered without looking. "Lane."

"This is Sally." Her tone of voice was dead serious. "I need to call you later. Say, seven p.m. your time? It's about that little side project I spoke of. Anyone you want involved should be there. All hands on deck. Clear?"

"Crystal."

She'd disconnected before his answer was fully finished. And side project? Was he ready for that? He'd been dormant for two years. Not inactive, unfortunately. But it was a different mindset. The problem was his head.

Was that ready? What kind of attitude adjustment would it take to get his head ready?

"Barnes, we have some things to talk over."

His friend gave him a quick look. "Oh, you have no idea."

Slowing down to pull through the gate, Barnes pointed to the wrought iron emblem over the entrance. "What's that?"

Jim looked up. "That's the new ranch brand. We're the Lazy J. I even have a business card."

Tilting his head sideways, Barnes commented. "Looks like a fishhook."

Jim glared at him as they rumbled across the cattle guard into the lane leading up to the house. When it came into view, he noticed two large travel trailers parked on either side of his house—need to be pulled by large diesel trucks. People were scurrying around dragging hoses and electric cords for temporary hookups. Both were fancy enough to have electric levelers for the uneven ground.

He glanced at Barnes. "How long have I been gone? I distinctly remember those not being here when I was shanghaied this morning."

"Well, things are moving fast. Since everything is going to shit, I've got the wife sheltering in place for safety. When things clear up, she'll be coming down here. We'll need a place to stay until things get sorted out." He gave a quizzical look. "I assume that's acceptable?"

"You know it is, although I kinda figured you'd live on the pontoon boat." Jim waved his hand toward the windshield. "And the other trailer?"

Barnes grinned. "I'm guessing that belongs to your

resident assassin. She said you kicked her out of the house, so..."

"Well, that's just—" He stared out the window of the pickup. "I don't know what that is."

Barnes snickered at him. "Your love life is getting a little bit tangled. If things were better, I'd be filming some kind of reality show out here."

The pickup rolled to a stop and Jim reached for the door handle, glancing at his friend. "For one thing, I don't have a love life. I haven't been laid since Moses was a pup. Things are getting way too complicated for my simple mind. I'm seriously thinking of running away from home."

Barnes grunted and then gave him a serious look. "You got an even bigger problem."

He gave an exasperated sigh. "Which is?"

"All the women buzzing around you carry guns. One of them has anger issues and a badge."

———

AS THEY WALKED up the steps to the porch, Alina came from the trailer on the north. "Alina, we need to get people together tonight. Sally One-Eye wants to call at seven p.m. for a meeting. Can you do that for me?"

He watched as she typed into her phone. "All done."

"Just like that?"

Next to him, a phone beeped and Barnes glanced at it, nodding to Alina.

"See? I'm very useful and eager to please."

"Oh god." Barnes snorted as he walked away to his trailer on the south. "I've got things to do. Watch the gun, man."

Alina was looking at each of them. "What's that supposed to mean?"

"Hey, Barnes." He stood, looking at the trailers. "This place is looking like a bruise."

His friend stopped, giving a condescending glance over his shoulder. "What?"

"Your trailer is black, Alina's is blue. Black and blue. You know, like a bruise."

"You're losing it, Jim. Get a grip, or get help." Barnes nodded to Alina as he moved toward his own trailer.

Jim chose his favorite chair on the porch while Alina dragged another close to sit beside him. She asked, "What did he mean by that?"

"He thinks I'm too tense, because I don't have a love life."

"I agree." Her hand rested lightly on his arm. "Whenever you're ready."

Giving her a startled glance, he didn't pretend to not know what she meant. "I'm not sure that's a good idea."

She laughed, nodding with a wide smile. "There was a time when you'd have shouted, hell no. Now, you're not sure. I am making progress. You should know that we Russians are a pragmatic people."

"Hardheaded."

"Perhaps." Inclining her head, she shrugged. "Maybe. But I can tell you, once we give someone loyalty, it never changes. What we had before was me walking off a party boat into your bed and staying the summer. It was a wild time. As you Americans say, it was lightning in a bottle."

He sighed, surprised he couldn't bring up any anger. "There was also a small matter of betrayal."

"In a way, I suppose. But I have apologized for that. We had no commitments, no promises. Expectations?

Yes, and I'm sorry about that. There aren't enough adverbs in your language to express how terribly sorry I am. I was in a bad place and didn't handle it well. All I ask is a chance to show you that I've changed. For your information, and this may interest you, I've been celibate since our little blow-up and I'm getting fidgety—that's another country word I'm learning."

"Fidgety." He was mesmerized, lost in those ice-blue eyes. "So, what's the bottom line?"

"In the world of business, legal or illegal, to win a contract, you must offer something no one else can. That's basic economics. So the bottom line, as you put it, is something your lady sheriff doesn't seem to be able to offer. I'll be your friend. Your friend with benefits, your partner, or your whore. Only for you. That's my promise, and it's a promise that can only be broken by blood. Just like the blood debt. To be clear, I love you. I want to be near you. Wait, that's wrong. I *need* to be near you. Please don't throw me away." She stood and moved against him. Her kiss was soft and full of promise. "I'll be inside if you want me."

Want her? That was never the problem. Could he do it? Had they both reached a place of reconciliation? Did he have the same deal with Rita? No commitment, but expectations? He glanced at his watch. It wasn't even noon. The meeting was at seven.

His brain seemed to be arguing with itself as he walked toward the door. Once inside, he could hear her singing over the splashing of the shower. Unbuttoning his shirt, his last rational thought was—why the hell not?

———

IT WAS NEARING four in the afternoon when Jim sat on the edge of his bed, the cool air from a nearby vent drying his body. Alina, naked, lay supine with her face turned toward him. Raising on one elbow, she reached and ran a finger down his back. "That was worth the wait...better than I remembered."

His gaze traversed her body until he locked on her eyes. "It was. Not that it solves all our issues."

"Of course not." She lay back down with a smirk. "But it's a damned good start, don't you think?"

After a shower, he walked out on the porch and was startled to see Barnes sitting in a rocker, watching blackbirds invade the garden. It was slim pickings, because the rabbits and raccoons had been there the night before.

Barnes grinned and shook his head. "Well, that was a noisy interlude."

"Damned pervert. What are you doing here?" He settled in his chair by the desk. "Sorry. She's a bit of a screamer."

"Really? I thought that was you. Sure sounded like it." He waved at the field around them. "I'm riding point for you. Someone needs to run things while you're lollygagging around. Your contractor that installed the gate and fence came by with a bill. Pablo and Gomez came by, thought someone was getting killed. Gomez mentioned a squirrel must have got its nuts caught on a tree limb. I tried to cover for you and told them you were watching a movie with the sound turned way up. Probably cause hearing loss." He smirked at Jim. "I gave that bill to Pablo."

"Did you remind them about the meeting? I think Alina sent everyone a text."

"They'll be here and will tell Jacy. That should complete our band of merry men and women."

"What do you think about including Rita?"

Barnes stared at him a moment, shaking his head. "That's your call, although I wouldn't recommend it. She has too many irons in the fire right now." He paused as Alina came out with wet hair, fresh from the shower and wearing a tee shirt. She dragged her hand across Jim's shoulder as she exited the porch on the way to her trailer, leaving wet tracks with her flip-flops.

"I'm afraid," Barnes continued, watching her walk away. "The dynamics of certain personnel, should they get together, might be more than we can bear."

Jim shuddered, thinking of that conflict. "You're probably right, but I think she needs to know the world situation."

"Well, the local situation is that woman just hauled your ass in for questioning as a person of interest in a murder case. Just for show and knowing you didn't do it. I'm thinking she's losing her damned mind. Send her a memo and get clear of that whole situation."

Jim glanced at his friend and then grinned.

"What?" Barnes barked at him.

"I think the shoe is on the other foot now."

"Meaning...?"

"I hope your wife gets here in a hurry. You're getting cranky."

———

EVERYONE HAD JUST ARRIVED when the call from Sally came. He'd put his phone on speaker when she requested they set up a video conference.

Jim looked around with his eyebrows raised. "I don't know how to do that."

"You're hopeless." Alina jumped forward and grabbed his laptop. Taking Jim's phone and getting some information from Sally, she soon had things going.

Sally glanced off screen, nodded to someone, and then continued. "Let's get started. Jim, why don't you introduce your group?"

"Sure. Folks, we're talking to Sally, my contact within the Shepherd's group. Let's just say you won't find the Shepherds in any directory or on anyone's payroll.

"Sally, you already know Alina from her previous incarnation." He paused as Sally smirked and shook her head. "You also know Josh Barnes, our ex-highway patrolman and general flub-up. I think you two have been talking lately. Next is Jacy Mane. She's our nurse and medic. My foreman, Pablo Estevez. We also have an additional friend who's helping with some of our hurry-up installations who's given his name as Gomez, no first name, no middle initial." Jim grinned at the man. "We'll call him Gomez Gomez. I have a sneaking suspicion he's off the books. Estevez, Mane, and Gomez are vets."

He looked at the people sitting around him. "We are all veterans of something, in one way or another. There is a lot of experience around this table."

"So," he continued. "That's my team of concerned citizens. What's the situation?"

"What about Rita?" Sally's image was trying to look around corners through the camera lens of the laptop.

He shrugged. "She's got her own problems and is not part of this." He emphasized the word not.

"Well, okay. I do want you to brief her when this meeting is over. Agreed?" She grinned at the screen. "So, what you have there is an assassin, a medic, ex-patrol-man, and two guys who like to break things and blow shit up. Is that about right?"

He shook his head, holding up a hand. "Let's not get ahead of ourselves. We do not have an agreement, and to be honest, I haven't talked any of this over with them. I was waiting to hear about the situation from you. You should know that any work for the Shepherds would be done by Alina and myself. All the rest are support for maintaining our home base as a secure location."

"Understood. Do we have a name for your group? I need something to put in my reports."

He thought a moment, glancing at the others. "I don't want anything put in writing that leads back to us. While one agency may approve, others may not. That also includes phone records and calls. You may refer to us as X."

"X?"

"We're all ex-something-or-other here."

Sally waved her hand in dismissal. "So, X-Group. Understood. Kinda catchy. They'll all be on the payroll… as long as there is a payroll."

After that little bomb dropped, there was a minute of silence as everyone absorbed that nugget of information.

"Barnes," she continued. "Hand out the hardware."

Reaching into a large envelope, Barnes pulled out three leather billfolds holding a badge and photo ID. He handed one each to Jim and Alina, keeping the last one for himself.

"Okay. The three of you are now federal agents. Anyone checking on these will be routed through to a federal prosecutor in DC and then to me. I'll be sending one to each of the others. Gomez can call me later. I'll need more than a couple of last names. Congratulations to all of you."

Alina couldn't stop her chuckle and then laughed outright as she looked at her ID. "Where did you get my picture? Sally, you realize my family may put a hit on me for this? How in the world...?"

"You know the old saying," Sally said with a grim expression. "Strange bedfellows..."

Jim tossed his badge holder on the table. "I'm not sure I like where this is going."

"Well, don't let this go to your head," Sally said. "All these are good for is, maybe, a get-out-of-jail-free card with the locals—just in case things go south."

"I still..." He glanced at his friends, who were looking impatient. "Let's leave this for now. What's up in the world, Sally? News accounts are less than reliable."

"First up? COVID-19, or SARS-Co-2, or 2019-nCoV, or commonly known as OH SHIT. This virus is about three to ten times more virulent than influenza—depends who you talk to. Adverse effects range from hardly a blip on your health radar to needing a respirator to breathe. If that happens, your chances are not good. The best defense is, if you deal with the public, or are in public, wash your hands and use sanitizer a lot and don't rub your eyes, pick your nose, or chew your fingernails. Jacy should be able to fill you in on that."

She paused. "Which brings me to another thing. Jacy, do you have children?"

Jacy's gaze jerked to the monitor screen. "I do."

"You need to isolate and minimize their exposure. Keep them home or someplace safe. I'm sure you know, kids are a petri dish for everything in the world anyway. They're not in much danger from this, but can pick it up and spread it. You know the drill. Enjoy the great outdoors."

"I do," Jacy replied. "Pablo has a family, too, but they live on this ranch now. Unfortunately, my place is more public."

"I have a suggestion," Alina spoke quickly. "We have an extra travel trailer. Jacy can move into it, at least for the short term, until we see how this plays out. It's summer, so the children will mostly be outside anyway." She turned to look at Jim. "This valley is a great place for kids."

All eyes were on Jim's startled look. "We have an extra trailer?"

Alina perfected the cat ate the canary smile. "I'll move in with you."

"Okay," Sally interrupted a snicker from Barnes. "I'll let you people work that out. Isolate, practice good hygiene, and all should be well. Jacy, do you have access to hydroxychloroquine?"

"The malaria medicine?"

"Yep. Combined with a Z-pack, it has shown some good results. Check on it first, I'm not sure about using it with kids. Just between us, I'm not sure it works at all. Treatment is a fluid situation and is being highly politicized. Doing nothing might be better than doing the wrong thing."

"Also," Sally continued. "If you have a doctor friend, try and get Remdesivir. That's showing promise. And again, we're still in the realm of the unknown. As far as we know, a voodoo witch doctor may be as much help."

"I'm on it." Jacy was busy tapping on her smartphone.

"Sorry for the information dump, but there's a lot going on. For whatever reason, the media is driving this pandemic beyond any recognizable reasoning, and people are scared. Scared people do stupid things. Large population centers are looking at civil unrest that may bleed out into the country. My advice is to buckle up and hunker down to ride it out."

Jim nodded. "We've seen some of that already. Rita is supposed to be working with county officials to come up with a plan."

"Yeah, well. Plans never work past the first shot. You, of all people, should know that." She paused, looking at some papers. "You might have noticed I'm on a ship, what with all the banging and clanging going on. I cannot understand how people sleep on these rust buckets."

"I noticed you're wearing the latest computer-generated camo." Jim grinned at her. "Shouldn't camo on a ship be gray, with pictures of rusted bolts on it?"

Sally stared at him a moment. "Are you through?" At his nod, she continued speaking. "Russia and OPEC are trying to drive down the prices of oil, hoping to wreck our economy. For unknown reasons, we are helping them by shutting down our own economy with shelter-at-home orders and closing businesses. North Korea is still practicing with their long-range missiles. We have intercepted a few of those. They apologized and said the missiles got away from them. So far, our government is treating them like school kids playing with fireworks. I don't have to tell you what happens if one of those gets through to detonate in our atmosphere."

"Hence, being on an EMP-hardened boat," Jim said flatly.

"Correct. Folks, it's getting real. Now, here's where the rubber meets the road. We have jihadi cells scattered around the country. Right now, we are tracking and erad-icating them as soon as they are found. We've hacked into the FBI database for the information. Since they'd rather watch them to see what they will do, the FEEBS are always a step behind. We've finally stopped that idiocy. We're not waiting and are taking a proactive stance. A recent little group was busted up, and we captured one brave soul alive. He put on a show of acting tough. I think it took our guys about five minutes to break him. Tough Guy gave up a few names, with a couple of them being in your area. These names are for people who funded them through the drug trade. Do the names of Roman Fielding and someone named Dickie ring a bell?"

Jim held up his hand to silence his group. "It does. You can take Dickie off your list." His gaze fell on Jacy. "He got sliced and diced in front of the courthouse recently. We all know Roman Fielding."

Sally gazed at him from the screen. "You vouch for all of your people?"

He met the quizzical stares surrounding him with a small smile. "I do."

"Roman needs to go away. With prejudice, as the saying goes."

"That could be a problem." Jim's voice was harsh. "Rita seems to think he's a model citizen."

Sally nodded. "I'm sorry, but these money connec-tions for bad operators need to go away. The order is for him only. No one else."

Alina snorted and shook her head. "Sally, he's always surrounded by his gang of redneck drug dealers. You endanger us by limiting the scope of collateral damage. None of those druggies are worth saving."

"Well," Sally said sarcastically. "It's always nice to

hear from a professional."

"Stop," Jim interjected, keeping his focus on Alina. "She's right, Sally. We need more latitude."

"Not going to happen. We have no authority for that."

He picked up his shield and tossed it toward the monitor, bouncing it on the keyboard. "Then I can't accept this. All you're going to do is get the wrong people killed."

"Dammit, Jim." Sally's voice was rough. "I don't have time to argue the point with you. The gloves have come off with how we're handling anyone who's a threat. Don't put yourself on that list."

"What?" Alina launched from her chair and leaned into the laptop's camera, startling everyone with her clipped Russian accent. "Sally, you know me. You know my family. Is correct?"

All they could do was listen. The view to the screen and Sally's image was blocked.

"I do," Sally replied in a calm voice.

"Then I will give one warning. Do not threaten. We have a very long reach."

"I thought you were retired." Sally's voice bordered on a chuckle. She was not intimidated.

Alina snorted before she straightened and returned to her overturned chair. "I am. I have other interests now. Something more domestic. But my father is very bored and looking for something to do. I'm sure we have several contacts on every ship at sea."

All eyes were on Sally as she sat staring back at them with a grim expression. "All right, Jim. Call off your attack dog. I hope you understand that you have an extremely dangerous bedfellow. Be careful she doesn't turn on you."

"I am fuzzy little pussy cat for Jim," Alina replied in her best Russian-southern drawl.

Sally laughed. "God, that's the most frightening thing I've ever heard. Well, do what you gotta do. But know this. If you make a huge mess and it all blows up on you, I can't always protect you. There are limits."

Jim nodded, giving Alina a worried glance. "Understood. Should I contact you when it's done?"

"Not directly. Just send a text or drop a message. He's small potatoes. We just want him off the table, so he doesn't help anyone else." She was interrupted again as someone handed her a piece of paper. Her shoulders slumped as she scanned it.

She glanced up at them. "Well, the hits just keep on coming. The fleet has been recalled. All military personnel have been ordered to return home, supposedly to help fight the pandemic." She shook her head. "There's something going on, the numbers don't add up. Oh, and China just set off a nuclear test—I'm guessing as a warning because we're laying the responsibility for the virus on their shoulders."

"So, there you have it." Her voice became crisp and hurried. "Russia and the OPEC members trying to bankrupt us because we're no longer dependent on them for oil, China possibly unleashing a virus worldwide to disrupt the economies of the western world, terrorists and anarchists in our own country ramping up operations, and North Korea lobbing missiles our way, threatening an EMP. If you can get a good night's sleep after this, you're better than me. I'll call if anything else happens that's major and might affect you. Good luck to you all. I'm out."

# TWENTY-SEVEN

THE GROUP WAS silent while trying to digest everything Sally had said. Jim's gaze caught them all as he smiled, lowering the lid on the laptop. It paid to be careful where Sally was concerned, and he didn't want her listening in. On second thought, he carried the laptop inside and left it on the kitchen counter before returning to the group.

"Alright, folks. Sally doesn't mess around, does she? That was a lot to take in. I just want you to know one thing. Sally's interests, or the Shepherds for that matter, are not necessarily ours, at least in the long term." He glanced around at them. "I trust everything said here will be in confidence. That's not a gag order. If you trust someone outside our circle, let them know about the world situation. Keep in mind, it may all come to nothing, and we live happily ever after. That's why we can't make too many waves locally. We don't want to mess in our own nest."

"Gomez," he continued. "We consider you a good friend. If there's something you need at your place to ensure survival if things go bad, don't hesitate to spend my money. We'll use it as long as it lasts. Pablo can help with that." He grinned at his foreman. "He's getting really good at that."

"Jacy, Pablo, Gomez, all of you have families. Other than being aware of what's going on, I don't want you involved in anything other than taking care of the home place. In my opinion, that's the most important part. Our long-term survival is important. What Sally didn't say is the most worrisome. The fact that she's moved her flag to a warship speaks volumes. All this may blow over. I hope so. But we must be prepared for the worst. Comments? Jacy, you first."

"Since I'm your medic, I'll keep my focus on that." Jacy cleared her throat and glanced around the group. "I've been following reports on this COVID-19, wondering why there's such a panic. And Sally is correct. The numbers do not add up with the response. In my estimation, the virus has mutated three times and will change many more times. The present attrition, or mortality rate, is around three percent. Right now, the biggest fatalities are with the old, obese, and those who already have life-threatening conditions. What I'm afraid of and what I think world governments are afraid of is a mutation that is more lethal—possibly a near-extinction event. With something like this, the more infections there are, the more chances of mutation. That may be the answer to the over-the-top response and why they're not sharing their concerns—to try and stop it before it gets worse. So, isolate when you can. Wash your hands religiously. If anyone is sick, let me know. We may need another trailer to use for quarantine or even a sick bay."

"I don't like this, or think it's fair," Gomez interjected. "Most of us have taken an oath to protect and defend this country. Far as I know, it hasn't been rescinded. If there are terrorist cells around, we want to help."

"Well, so far, it's just an enabler. I suspect Roman Fielding funneled money to the terrorist cell in return for product, which in turn netted him a lot more money." Jim shrugged. "But I know how you feel. If push comes to shove, I'll ask for help. But for now, play defense. We need to stay under the radar, both from the gangs and law enforcement. If things go bad, none of that will matter. We must take care of ourselves first and play the long game. That's the priority, as I see it."

"I have a question." Pablo was watching Jim with wary eyes. "Who are you? If this Sally person is legit and all this information is from top levels in government, what does that make you?"

Jim shook his head with a wry smile. "It makes me a plain old Joe with a certain skill set. They'd call me an asset. An expendable asset. Although, I'm flirting with being a liability. Other than that, I'm nobody."

"He's a cowboy," Jacy said, meeting the gaze of the two ex-soldiers. "And I don't mean boots and saddles."

Giving her an odd look and anxious to change the subject, Jim clapped his hands. "So, it's way past suppertime. Let's get with it and start fresh tomorrow."

Jacy stayed behind, watching everyone leave. Barnes walked away, talking to Alina.

He knew she wanted to say something, but preempted her. "I have a knife just like the one your husband has, same handle and everything. If you wish, you can take it as a replacement. His old one needs to be thrown far, far away."

"Why?" She gave him a long look. "You think he killed Dickie?"

"Given the nature of the wounds, that was my guess. And he had good reason."

She shook her head. "He didn't. I would know if he did. Donny Ray has changed a lot in the last few years and more so lately, but not that much."

He stared at the fescue fields surrounding them, the honeysuckle wind making the tops move like waves in the ocean. It was more calming than his next thought. If not Jacy's husband—who? Dickie wouldn't have any lack of enemies, but the killing seemed more like a hit—cold, not in anger. Unbidden, he remembered another set of cold, blue eyes. Someone grieving, but who seemed just a little...off. The nature of the wounds, debilitating, precise, targeted for the most pain, the efficiency. Revenge is the oldest motive in the world. The applicator of that cold dish could come from all sizes. Could they have another operator in their midst?

"Something has startled you, and you don't like it. It looked like an internal alarm just got tripped. What is it?"

When he didn't answer, she continued. "Well, at least be careful."

Jacy's voice was soft as her gaze searched his. "I feel dust and sand all around you. You're running hot and cold; I see it in your expression—monsters are stirring."

"I'm fighting it." He gave her a small smile, meeting her gaze before his attention turned to Alina walking toward them. "But I may need my monsters."

———

THE NEXT MORNING dawned cool with a foggy mist rolling through the fields. Thunder grumbled to the west, signaling heavier rain on the way. Jim had been up for a couple of hours with too many thoughts running around his head to allow sleep. His first task was to go and bring Rita up to speed on all the news from Sally. He had no idea how she'd react. Once he let her know, his obligation was ended. She could call Sally for confirmation.

Her single-story ranch-style home was nestled in a tree-lined and quiet street just north of the square in White Rock. When he parked on the street, he noticed the oversized Cadillac Escalade parked behind Rita's SUV. Morning meeting?

A light was on inside, so he knocked softly, not wanting to disturb the neighborhood. When she didn't come to the door, he tried a little louder. Finally, the sound of a dead bolt disengaging signaled her arrival. Rita opened the door dressed in a terry cloth robe, hair wet from her shower.

"Jim? What are you doing here?"

"Sorry to come so early, but it's going to be a busy day. I heard from Sally and she asked me to share some things with you."

Trying to close the door a little more, she glanced over her shoulder. "Now's not a good time. Can't you come by the office?"

He used his foot for leverage against the door. Since she was using one hand to hold her robe closed, she couldn't stop the door from opening. Her home had an open floor plan, so he could see Detective Miles sitting at her breakfast table in T-shirt and boxers, spoonful of cereal poised halfway to his lips.

And that said it all. A quickie one-nighter would have had the man scrambling for clothes discarded in haste, eager to leave before being seen by the neighbors. In that instant snapshot of life, he saw only a relaxed and somewhat surprised atmosphere.

Their little vignette paused for a couple of breaths. They'd always been able to read each other, and his thoughts must have raced across his face like watching a movie, his expressions crossing, one after another. He knew this was coming. All the signs were there. His friends had told him. He supposed he didn't want to admit he'd failed. But abstract possibilities were easy to ignore, and he'd done so. The vision of the competition for your woman, sitting in his shorts at her kitchen table, was game, set, and match.

"Jim, I..."

He held up his hand, allowing the door to close from her pressure, hiding the good detective. "Save it. It's not necessary. Sorry to intrude."

"Why are you here? What's this about news from Sally?"

He shrugged, matching her gaze. "There are some locals in your county running a drug operation to fund some jihadi wannabes. Things are going to shit nationwide, and Sally wants this particular problem cleaned up. As for the rest of it?" His voice became a muted growl. "Pull up your big-girl panties..." He stared at her a moment. "If you're wearing any, and figure it out yourself. You're the sheriff. I'm out, so you get your wish. Have a good life, Rita."

He wished for a standard transmission, so he could chirp the tires as he left roaring down the street, but his truck just wasn't that macho. Instead, he crept away at a steady twenty miles an hour because it was a residential neighborhood full of people who had no expectation of being disturbed by his troubles.

RITA CLOSED the door with a soft thud and click and then leaned her head against it. That didn't go the way she wanted. A muted conversation was happening behind her, so she glanced over her shoulder at Trevon Miles, talking on his cell. She closed her eyes. No use beating herself up now.

That situation didn't go as expected either. Miles had stayed by her side yesterday, and while not official, had offered some good advice on handling the situation. She'd met with everyone she could think of, from emergency management to the Chamber of Commerce, to get ahead of the shelter in place orders. She thought they'd made good progress. They'd relied on common sense, instead of the political tripe coming down the pipeline.

Few of those guidelines made sense. People could go to the grocery store, but not to the lake and fish, or swim, or anything else. The one thing that was decided. They were a small county and would make up their own rules —trying to follow the health department and local doctor's advice as much as possible.

And then last night happened. Stress and alcohol did a number on her brain, and she woke this morning lying next to Detective Miles. She hoped that brief interlude was nice because she didn't remember much. Although possible, date rape drugs probably weren't on the table. Just stupidity and morning-after embarrassment when Jim came to her door. Her first order of business would be to send Trevon packing and try to forget what little she remembered. She could deal with Jim Lane later.

When she turned and started to walk toward the breakfast nook, Miles palmed his pistol. She froze, wondering where he'd hidden a pistol in his boxers. The last part of his conversation barely registered. Something about Trader Jack and not wanting to do something?

For a fleeting moment, her mind raced with jumbled thoughts—run toward a gun—run away from a knife—no place to run to, no time. Forcing a calm she didn't feel, she nodded toward the gun. "Did you save that weapon? I don't like—"

He interrupted and gave her an apologetic shrug. "Sorry, Rita. Last night was spectacular, it really was, but things are going sideways. Roman says you have to go."

She eyed the pistol, thinking to stall him. If she could get to the bedroom, her pistol was on the dresser. "Roman. Roman Fielding? Why are you talking to him?"

"Sorry. When you're trying to pad your retirement, you can't always be choosy with who you deal with. For now, he's calling the shots and wants you gone."

Inching toward him, that stopped her a moment. "Gone? Wha—"

The pain punching her gut was no more surprising than the reports from his pistol. She backed toward the door, stumbled and fell. Curled into a fetal ball, she gripped her stomach, tears of pain streaming down her cheeks. Her thoughts were jumbled, trying to speak past the pain and the icy coldness spreading throughout her body.

"Why?"

Miles leaned over her, pulling one of her hands away from the wounds. "Yeah, you'll bleed out. Tough luck. I didn't want to do this. You're good people, but you trust too much." He paused. "Why? Because Roman told me to. We have to move our operation, but he wants to clean the slate on the way out."

Fighting through the pain, she was aware of footsteps going away and the front door closing. She fumbled her cell phone from the pocket of her robe. With slippery fingers, she keyed the SOS function before dropping it. Protocol stated that upon receiving the call and it didn't terminate quickly, the closest 911 operator would be notified. Pressing her hands to her stomach again, she thanked God the detective used a wimp-assed nine mil. Her second prayer was that she would live long enough to tell Jim Lane who shot her. She recognized the lethargy and dizziness setting in from blood loss—fought against the closing blackness. Maybe she had a chance. She wished...

# TWENTY-EIGHT

JIM CLIMBED the steps and sat in his usual chair on the porch. Closing his eyes, he rubbed his face. Sleep was hit and miss the night before. Coupled with the scene at Rita's house, he felt drained of energy. When he opened his eyes, Alina was placing orange juice and an omelet on the table in front of him. He still wasn't sure how to take a domesticated mafia hit woman, but was grateful for the energy food. Just what he needed.

"Where'd you go so early? I was going to make you a nice breakfast. Now, all you get is a cold drink and a microwaved omelet." She sat next to him, toying with a spoon in a cup of coffee.

He'd never seen her wear a robe and was glad he wouldn't have to make that comparison between the two women. A T-shirt and optional panties were her usual fare, depending on company. She was beautiful in the morning light and a woman who could get by with using little or no makeup. He met her gaze and knew those clear blue eyes would be relentless unless he told her the story.

"I went to see Rita." The expected jealous explosion didn't come. Instead, she gave him a "well?" gesture, waiting for the rest of the story.

He gave it to her in few words with no embellishment. There was no point in confusing the issue with his own feelings.

Alina nodded when he finished and shrugged expressively. "That wasn't unexpected. You felt something was going on, and although it was inadvertent, got confirmation of your suspicions. Besides that, you'd already moved away from her, or yesterday would never have happened. Correct?"

"Of course, you're right. But it's not that simple." He speared a piece of the omelet, savoring the bacon, cheese, and peppers mixed with the eggs. "I kept getting mixed signals from her. It was hard to know what to do about it. Mentally I'd already moved on. But still…"

"Sometimes I think people should have an outside source evaluate their relationships. Especially men. Kind of like doctors shouldn't treat themselves. In my opinion, biased as it may be, it was quite simple. You were the one mixing up the signals."

She finished her coffee, sucked on the spoon a moment, and continued. "Life doesn't have to be complicated, even for people like us. We already have the blueprint by watching what people do, not what they say or want us to believe."

He watched her with interest, not sure he could take such a simplistic approach. "Well, in light of all this, you should be jumping up and down. You've won."

"To say I've won is to assume I'm your only other choice. Am I?" She watched him closely, waiting for his answer.

"You know damned good and well I'm not smart enough to juggle two women." He shook his head at her. "Now who's making things complicated?"

"Not me." She grinned, watching him a moment before continuing. "Life is simple. Circumstances are simple. You are not. You, I must show every day that your life is better with me than without. I'll make mistakes, and it will take a very, very long time. That's my goal."

"I never knew you to be so smart." He took another bite of the omelet. "Or such a good cook."

"Well." She smirked at him. "That's not entirely fair. If you recall, when we were together before, we never did too much talking. And we did a different kind of cooking."

———

WHEN HIS CELL PHONE BUZZED, he was surprised to see Allison Crewes on the caller ID. With a puzzled glance at Alina, he accepted the call on speaker. "Deputy Crewes, what can I do for you?"

"Sheriff Rita always told us that if anything bad happened to her, to call you." Amid the background noise of wind and a car door slamming, her voice was rushed. "We just airlifted Rita to Mercy Hospital in Springfield. She took two shots to the stomach early this morning. She managed to get an SOS call through before she lost consciousness. PJ rolled on it and called for EMS. That's all I know. I'm headed to her house right now."

He didn't expect the cold rush running through him, didn't know if it was fear or adrenaline. Usually, he would be able to compartmentalize, set emotion aside.

Not this time. It took him a moment to reply. "She's alive?"

Her voice was faint over the sound of her Charger winding up. "As far as I know, she is. But barely. The medics said she was hanging on."

"Any idea what happened or who the shooter is?"

"None. She was found just inside the front door, but it was closed. A cereal bowl was on the table. Maybe hers, I don't know. Someone could have come to the door, interrupted her breakfast. They may have hit her right then. Jim, to be honest here...we're kinda chasing our tails. I don't have enough experience, and PJ is useless. With everything else going on, I'm afraid of making mistakes we'll pay for later—"

"Okay," he interrupted. Rita's county was small and run loose, but there were still procedures. "Here's what you need to do. Make sure Deputy Tucker is looking for your Black Book. It'll have emergency management— who to call, what to do, and everything else. Let him handle that end of it. That'll get him started on something positive, and he'll be your mouthpiece to the public. So far, you have an unknown shooter. Other counties must be notified. There's protocol to follow."

Taking a deep breath and squeezing Alina's hand that was gripping his arm, he continued. "Listen. You know the drill—you've had the training. Cordon off the house. Get DNA and prints from everything you can, and I mean everything in the house from doorknobs to the flusher on the toilet. Call Springfield PD and get protection for Rita as soon as that chopper lands. This could be something personal we don't know about."

He paused, gathering his thoughts. "I know I'm not part of your team, but I'll get you some help in the short term. I'm sure State will step in once they hear of the shooting of a sheriff. Got all that?"

"Got it." He heard her catch a sob and turn it into a cough. "You don't think we should go to the hospital?"

He wished they could, but now wasn't the time. The last he'd heard, the hospitals were on lockdown. People were dying with no family around, no one to care—other than the doctors and nurses. He knew they cared, but it wasn't the same. "Look, I know you're close to her. But you can't go. Not now. That's all under control. We can't help her and I'm sure she wouldn't want us to waste the time. Bad as it sounds, she either makes it, or she doesn't. It's out of our hands. What *is* up to us is getting the shooter. Agreed?"

Her voice was starting to pick up steam. Maybe she was hitting her stride and had put away the fear and concern for Rita, at least for the moment.

"Hopefully, she can tell us who the shooter is." She was close to yelling into the phone.

He took a deep breath, hoping his feelings didn't come out in his voice. "We can't assume that. Two to the belly? That's not good. She may not recover. You need to focus on your job right now."

"Yeah. I got it. Thanks, Jim. I appreciate it."

Trying to get her mind off Rita and on business, he asked. "How are things in town?"

He'd seen a crowd of people, for White Rock that was about twenty, walking toward the courthouse early that morning—probably to beat the heat. There's nothing like excessive heat, or rain if it ever happens, to break up a protest.

"Not bad. We had a mini protest in progress. A couple of kids started throwing rocks at the courthouse, but I rounded the little shits up. They're in the back of the cruiser now."

His laugh turned into a strangled cough. "Turn them loose. You got bigger worries."

"I don't know. They're loving the ride."

Jim ended the call and glanced at Alina. "We need to go."

She stood and hugged him. "No. You've already said it. She'll be taken care of. We're not relatives. Because of the virus protocols, they won't let us in. All we could do is pace the halls, even if we got in. We'll have to wait. I like Rita. I respect her, but we shouldn't go."

Her expression was grim as tears appeared in her eyes. "One thing we do need to think about. Once they find out you were there this morning, let's pray the shooter didn't use a .40 cal. I know you wouldn't hurt her, but others do not. We may have to grab our bags and hit the ground running."

He shook his head. Not happening. Snatching up his cell, he made another call. "Barnes. Where are you?"

"Coming out of the Hot Spot with a box of jelly rolls. Why?"

"Rita has been shot. They've airlifted her to Mercy in Springfield. There's a crime scene at her house. Josh, I was there early this morning. People will have seen me." He gave him the address. "Deputy Crewes will need help to sew that place up tight. I want you to play this straight up, no matter what. Can you help?"

Engine noise competed with his answer. "On my way. Sorry, man. Hope she pulls through. Any ideas on the shooter?"

"Oh, I got a real good idea. That detective from Springfield, Trevon Miles, was sitting at her breakfast table eating cereal this morning." An idea came to him that made him slump in his chair. "Shit. He's dirty, and I got her shot. I mentioned to Rita about a local drug operation funding jihadis, and I'll bet he heard me. She must have taken the hit right after I left."

"Okay, buddy." Barnes was all business. "I'll use my brand-new federal agent badge as my authority to help, at least until State shows up, and I know most of them. I'm on it."

"Thanks, Josh. When I looked in the door, that damned Miles was eating cereal. Make damned sure the cereal bowl and spoon get wrapped up nice and tight."

"What's the point? If he's the shooter, are we going to arrest him? If he's tied to Fielding...?"

"I'm not worried about an arrest." He paused. "Everything has to look normal, Josh. Outsiders have to see that the department is doing their job. They'll be crawling all over this. Sew things up tight, legally. We'll take care of the rest."

"Understood. I don't need to know anything more. And Jim? Be cool on this."

Jim disconnected the call and noticed Alina returning her cell to the table. "I called Jacy. Since she's a nurse in the Mercy system, she can waltz right in there and keep tabs on Rita. That's the best we can do. Right now, you need to relax and not have a stroke."

He took a deep breath. "Easier said than done."

"Yeah, I know. Let's focus on other things for a moment. If Miles is dirty, he'll be connecting with Fielding. Any idea where they might be? We could wrap this up in a hurry."

"Fielding has a place north of town, but I can't imagine

they'd be stupid enough to meet there—not after shooting a sheriff and all the other things that have happened out there. I can't imagine him going back to The Gallows. I'm thinking they'll want to disappear." He shook his head. "There's a ton of places to do that. All they'd need is a four-wheeler."

"Okay." Alina was rubbing his neck and shoulders. "Let's do the next best thing until we have more information to work with."

"Now? I don't think I could..."

"Not that, stupid. I'm thinking a weapons check. Once we figure out where they are, we'll be leaving in a hurry. Of course, if you're thinking of something else, I'm game."

"Weapons check it is."

————

IT WAS straight up noon when Jacy called. They were in the kitchen, and he put his phone on speaker. "Hi Jacy, what can you tell us?"

"She made it. It was a three-hour surgery, touch and go for a while. Blood loss was bad. But she got lucky. The nine mils were jacketed and didn't hit bone, so they went straight through. They didn't hit her spine. Nicked the liver, punctured her stomach, some bowel resection—it was tedious and took some time. She's strong, so I think she'll be fine unless peritonitis sets in, or something weird happens."

Jacy paused. "She was pretty loopy from the anesthetic, but she kept saying two words. Miles and jack or jacks. I don't know what it means, maybe nothing. Maybe she has miles to go...? The morphine was knocking her out by then. It will probably be tomorrow before she can talk."

"I know what it means. Trader Jack's. He's into about everything shady around here and tried to set me up for an ambush. The other is Trevon Miles. We already figured him for the shooting. That's where we'll go."

"Maybe we should give those names to law enforcement. There were some mighty pissed-off sheriffs and deputies roaming the halls. They'd love to take these guys down."

"Won't work, Jacy. Until Rita can positively ID Miles, there are no witnesses or proof. By the time law enforcement reacts, the people responsible will be gone. Better we take care of our own—in-house, so to speak."

"I figured that. Sounds like a plan. Look, I'm heading to you. The kids are at my folks' and I'm coming to help." She hesitated a moment, and all they could hear was road noise. "Jim, do not let the monsters loose. You hear me? Not until you have a team for backup. Alina, you hearing me? Don't let him go off half-cocked."

"I hear you," Alina said. "I've already put out the call. We assemble in one hour. Drive safe."

"I will and thank you. Keep that mutton head under control."

He stood after punching *End* on the cell's screen. His hands were clenched, and he felt himself trembling. Taking a deep breath, he glanced at Alina while pacing up and down the veranda. "I have a team?"

She intercepted him and linked her arm with his. "Yes, you do. Be patient. We'll get this done with a minimum of danger on our side. Remember? We have long-range plans."

"You think we should let this go, give it to Barnes and the sheriff's department?"

"I didn't say that." Leading him through the door, her voice was firm. "Come with me. You need to wind down and get your head together."

His relief was a physical letdown after hearing Rita would make it. The adrenaline high had cratered, leaving him tired. She was right. He needed to rest. Maybe ten minutes off his feet. His mind was already working on gaining entry to Trader Jack's, how to get past the guards. "I don't think I can sleep."

"Of course you can. I'll help." She pushed him backward on the bed.

———

FIFTY MINUTES LATER, Jacy walked in, finding Jim and Alina drinking coffee at the kitchen table. Glancing at them while she retrieved a cup and filled it, she gave a curious smile. "Well, you look...calm, given the circumstances."

"We are." He gave Alina a look. "I think we're ready to go."

Before he could say anymore, a truck skidded on gravel. Gomez and Pablo strode through the door. Without a word, they filled their cups from the large pot on the stove.

Gomez grimaced as he took a sip. "You call this coffee? It's like colored water."

Pablo was more to the point. "I hear Sheriff Rita took a hit. What's the situation on that?"

Jacy took over at that point, giving them an idea of

her wounds and recovery time. "She'll pull through, I'm confident of that."

"Good. The entertainment level is a lot higher when she's around." Pablo smirked and stroked the ends of his mustache. "What's the plan?"

Jim tried to give him a stern look. "You need to get serious. The plan is for me to drive to Trader Jack's, find Trevon Miles and put him down. If Roman Fielding is there, that's just icing on the cake."

"Just like that, by yourself? You're taking a lot on your own shoulders. What about us?" Gomez did a little circle with his finger to include everyone at the table. "What's our job?"

"Stay here. It's not your fight."

That gained him a hard stare from everyone. Gomez snorted and shook his head. "No can do. Not happening. I know where Trader Jack's is, I've done business there. If you give us an hour, we can come in from behind and take care of his play soldiers in their fancy camouflage suits. Rules of engagement? Everyone needs ROE."

Jim thought a moment, realizing he couldn't stop them from helping. He nodded his assent. "I appreciate the help. No killing unless threatened. If you perceive a threat, consider it a free-fire zone. These are not good people. Also, the last time I was there, Jack told me they have drones for surveillance. With the storm coming in, that may not be an issue. Get into place and then wait until we get to the gate. That way, if the drone is up, the operator will be focused on me, and you can move in."

"Intel? From what you said, you've been there the most recent. What have you seen there?"

He glanced at his people. His people. That sounded odd to him. "There was a guard at the entrance gate. He wore a plate carrier but no plates. That might indicate their level of preparedness. We all know how heavy those are, so their hired hands may not want to wear them in the heat. Just be aware of that for shot placement. There were sentries around the business entrance, and they didn't make any effort at concealment. There is one hidden guard in a corner of the main room of the trading post. Jack seemed proud of that one. That's all I know."

He glanced around the table. "We go in at three p.m. That gives you a little over an hour to get into position. Time enough?"

Gomez and Pablo were nodding. "We'll use the four-wheelers to get close. That's all open range over there, so fences won't slow us down. Then we'll move up on them. Ample time."

"Good." Jim nodded. "If anything goes south and we get rolled up by any law enforcement unit, our cover is that we're moving on a jihadi camp looking for Roman Fielding, as per Sally's orders. You're under direction of federal agents. Don't hesitate to play that card."

"I don't know. Does this seem odd to anyone?" Jacy was shaking her head, staring out the window. "Here we are in the middle of peaceful America, ignoring law enforcement and planning a precision hit on a target. It seems a little surreal."

Gomez answered for all of them. "If you think it's peaceful, you ain't watching the news. Between the pandemic fiasco and the riots in the cities, this country is about to go to DEFCON ONE. The National Guard has been mobilized and there's talk of activating the regular Army to help restore order. The bad thing is the Army is trained to break things and kill people, so that is not going to end well. Sorry. I understand your concern, but we'll be the least of law enforcement's trouble." He slapped Pablo on the shoulder. "Let's go, brother."

"Wait a minute," he called after them. "I have body armor laid out in the bedroom."

Pablo waved. "Nah. We got our own."

After the duo left, Jacy remained. "What about me?"

"I don't want you in danger. That's nonnegotiable. Follow us to the entrance and park just inside. Keep your head on a swivel in case we miss someone. When we go through the gate, call Gomez so they can start their run. As soon as it's over, we'll call and let you know the situation. Don't come in early. Once this blows up, Alina and I will consider everyone we see as the enemy."

Jacy stood, eyeing them with a thoughtful expression. "If this Sally person is so powerful, why not call in a Predator and level the place? Problem solved."

It was a good question. "I'd actually prefer that. The problem is the supplies. There's a huge stockpile there and we may need them if things in the world continue their present course. Plus, and although I doubt it, there may be innocents involved. We don't want collateral damage if we can help it."

She stood, hands on hips, staring at them until she finally nodded. "Good enough. I just need some justification to go off the rails. Suddenly, I've gone from being a rancher and student to being on a strike team for...who are we again?"

"We're nobody."

"Yeah, I was afraid of that. Be careful, you two."

Alina gave her a half-wave. "We'll do our best to stay healthy. What about the ghost armor?"

Jacy shrugged. "Like them. Got my own."

As they watched Jacy leave, Alina spoke to him. "So, about a thirty-minute drive to get there?"

When he nodded, she continued. "That gives us about a half hour to wait."

"We're not gonna..."

"No, just hold me. We've lost our edge, Jim. This won't be easy. I'm worried."

Before he could answer, his cell phone buzzed. Sally.

Putting the phone on speaker, he answered. "This can't be good."

"It's not. The shit has absolutely hit the fan. Have you watched the news?"

Did she think they sat around watching the news all day? "We're a little busy right now. I have less than twenty minutes until kickoff."

"You're aware of the rioting in most large cities?"

"We're aware."

"Well, the President has authorized military force, including the standing Army, to put down the insurrection. I know where he's coming from and agree with his sentiments, but that's going to blow things wide open. Law enforcement is walking off the job. Can't say as I blame them. People will flee the cities. You folks need to hunker down and be ready to repel boarders."

"You mentioned a kickoff. I doubt you're playing football." Sally paused. "Is everyone okay? I assume I'm on speaker since I hear birds in the background?"

He glanced at Alina. "You are on speaker with Alina and me. We've no secrets here. We can't hunker down, as you say. Rita has been shot. She's currently in Mercy, Springfield. My medic says she'll pull through, barring complications. We're getting ready to roll on the shooter and possibly Roman Fielding. I've got my door-kickers out as we speak. Barnes is assisting the sheriff's department in Rita's place, at least until State takes over the investigation."

"Dammit! How did it happen?"

"Details are unknown. Rita isn't talking yet. I went to her house earlier to give her a situation report and found she had an overnight guest. She was shot shortly after I left. My working assumption is that the man she was with, posing as a Springfield detective, is part of the local drug ring with Roman Fielding. We have reason to believe they're holed up at a place called Trader Jack's. We'll find out in about an hour."

Sally was silent for a moment. "I'll take care of Rita. Given the situation, I'll have her moved somewhere safe." Another pause. "Jim, the national situation could blow over or be the start of something really bad. The riots are not spontaneous and are spreading. They're just too well-scripted to be an accident. Some are already calling it a coup attempt; others are pointing to foreign involvement. No matter what, take care of yourselves. Let me know when you have resolution. Godspeed."

Alina's hand squeezed his as he answered. "Thanks, Sally. We'll be in touch."

He stared out the window. "Shit."

"Well said."

"Body armor?"

"Gives me heat rash." Alina looked at her watch and gave him a quick peck on the lips. "We gotta roll, cowboy."

# TWENTY-NINE

THE GATE to Trader Jack's stood open, with no guard that Jim could see. That was odd enough to make him wonder if everyone was gone. He could see Fielding or Miles fleeing, but not Jack. There was too much for the trader to leave behind.

He keyed Jacy's speed dial number. "Change of plans. The entrance gate is wide open with no guard that I can see. Come up, pull inside, and block the drive with your vehicle. We don't want anyone coming in behind us. Don't stay in the truck."

"Got it. I'll hide out with the skeeters and chiggers, maybe across the highway. I'll call Gomez to start his run as soon as we disconnect."

It was a short drive through a waving sea of fescue and shady patches under trees to arrive at the store. Alina commented that it was odd to have all this pasture but not an animal in sight.

"I expect on a day like this any cow critter with a lick of sense will be down in the valleys under shade—probably belly deep in a creek."

The windows in the truck were down, and engine noise barely competed with the meadowlarks and wind hissing through the grass during their slow approach. Thunder rumbled again in the west. The front was slow moving and would dump a lot of water if it ever arrived.

Alina laid her hand on his leg, rubbing a little. "I'm not used to this whole showdown at high noon in broad daylight thing. I've always preferred a subtler approach. You know, candlelight, maybe a glass of wine?"

He patted her hand. "I don't like it either, but we can't give them time to get away."

Rolling to a stop, he blocked the footbridge over the spring. "Stay sharp. This could go south in a hurry. We'll try to sell it to them like we're coming in as customers. They don't know what we know. The last time I was here, I had Jack holding some ammo for me. We'll use that as an excuse. Maybe he'll remember that. As far as I know, they don't know we're after them."

"On the other hand." Talking softly, he continued. "I don't like the fact that they let us waltz in here so easily. Before any of this started, I got stopped in here, and I'm sure they watched me all the way in and all the way out. Something is not right. Watch the windows once we're inside. They're wide open and they weren't before. I'm betting they're open so once we're inside, his men can come up and shoot through. Pablo and Gomez better be as good as they think they are."

He paused. "I don't think we'll surprise anyone. They can see and hear us. I need you to watch my back. I'll take care of everything else." No arguments, no comments. She was ready to go. He liked that about her.

Alina stopped as they crossed the bridge and commented in a too-loud voice. "Look, Jim. They have those orange and white koi, just like you used to. We should get some of those."

He paused with her. "Dunno. Our water might be too warm. The koi pond I had on the lake was spring fed with cool water. We'll have to ask inside about them."

The solid plank flooring of the front deck echoed their approach in measured cadence, like a customer would march right up to the door. Moving inside, he felt Alina sliding in close behind him, dragging her fingers across his back and then moving to his left toward the corner lookout post, examining a table full of pants and shirts in hunter green. A quick look around didn't show anyone in the store but Jack. Looks could be deceiving, and there were a lot of places to hide. He put a friendly smile on his face as he approached the clearly nervous proprietor. One look, and he knew they were expected. It was too easy.

Jack leaned with both hands on the glass counter, right next to the sign that read—*don't lean on the counter.* "Hey, Jim. How's it going?" His greeting was gruff and seemed to be forced.

He watched sweat drop from Jack's nose onto the counter—his small eyes darted around the store and couldn't seem to find anything to land on.

"You seem a little anxious, Jack. What's up?"

Those eyes finally settled on him. "Nothing much." One hand came up to wipe his forehead. "Seems a mite warm in here."

"Maybe you should open the door to the cave some more. That would cool things off." The door behind Jack was open just a little. Convenient. Before he could reply, Alina strode slowly up to them. Silently she pointed toward a cleaning rag sitting on the counter. From the oil on it, he supposed it was used to clean firearms. When Jack handed it to her, she brought up a slim dagger and casually cleaned blood off the stainless steel blade, staring at Jack with no expression.

Still watching the door behind the counter and thinking it'd opened a fraction more, he asked her. "That's a subtle approach?"

"Seemed appropriate. The man tried to pull a gun on me—makes me do odd things."

"Tell you what, Jack." Most of his attention was now on the door. "Why don't you tell whoever is hiding behind that door to come out? There's no point in you getting involved."

Alina drifted off to the left, and as soon as Jim spoke, he moved to his right. The door popped open, and a shotgun blast cut the air where they'd been standing. Screaming and holding his right shoulder, Jack dropped behind the glass display case. Alina started to move forward when Jim held up his hand to stop her. She backed a few more steps.

"That was stupid. You shot your helper. So, here's what is going to happen. Anyone behind that door comes out with empty hands, or we start shooting through all this sheetrock to see how many ricochets we can make happen. You got nothing but rock walls all around you. Or you can come out shooting. It's your choice."

"Coming out." Trevon Miles must have been hiding to the side of the door. He stuck both hands out and then moved out of the room.

While Miles stood with his hands up, Jim walked around the counter and nudged the blubbering Jack with his foot. "We're looking for Fielding. Anyone else back there, Jack?"

Jack sat up, holding his shoulder. His wound looked more painful than serious, having taken a few pellets from the shotgun blast. "No. No one else."

Jim nudged him again. "You real sure?"

He nodded in bobblehead fashion. "Positive."

"Good. Miles, you walk around to the front of the counter. Slow."

"I'll have you arrested, Lane. You and your skinny blond friend are looking at hard time." Miles stopped moving and looked at both. "Unless you let me go right now. If you do that, we'll forget about this."

Alina spoke softly. "Why did you shoot Rita?"

He shrugged, smirking at them. "I don't know what you're talking about."

Jim shook his head. "She's not dead, and she named you. I'd say it's open and shut."

His innocent look morphed into surprise and then desperation. "Please. I have money. A lot of money. And drugs. Whatever you want, I'll get for you. What will it take to make this go away?"

Suppressed bullets are not silent, but Alina's .22 was damned close. His mouth formed a near-perfect circle as he gave her an astonished look, and then Miles lowered his hands to clutch his stomach. The two wounds were nearly identical to Rita's, but unlike the larger caliber, didn't exit his body. He leaned against the countertop, leaving a bloody handprint, before sliding to the floor. Alina walked up to him.

Interrupting her, Jim said mildly. "He wasn't armed."

She glanced at him as she kneeled by the grimacing man and patted him down for weapons, finding a small, nine-millimeter pistol tucked behind his back. She tossed it on the floor at Jim's feet.

"Well, there you go. He was going for a gun. It was clearly self-defense."

Miles groaned before sitting up straight. "Those wimp-assed .22's won't kill me. That's not even a real gun. Call an ambulance. You've had your revenge. This is enough."

Alina snorted as she glanced at him. "On the contrary. I just put two hollow points into your gut. You're bleeding and crapping all over your insides. It'll take a few minutes, but you're dead, shithead. You may as well enjoy the trip."

Footsteps coming in from outside interrupted them. Jacy was first through the door, shouldering her med pack, followed by Pablo and Gomez. She went directly to Miles, seeing he was wounded, but Alina stopped her. "He's the one who shot Rita."

Jacy stood, staring at the man for a moment. "He's dead anyway. One of your rounds must have clipped an artery. Anyone else?"

Jim pointed behind the counter. "Jack could use some attention."

He glanced that way and froze. Jack was holding a shotgun on them, and Jim felt like an idiot. Of course, he'd have a gun hidden behind the counter. A quick glance showed all the team had their guns pointed down. There was no chance of Jack not getting a shot off before they could intervene. It was a rookie mistake and a second glance at his team showed that they all knew it.

"You sure this is how you want to play this out, Jack?"

"I'm sure. You assholes shouldn't have busted into my post. Guards will be here any minute. Then we'll dump your bodies." He nodded at Alina. "Except, maybe her. She's skinny, but I like 'em that way."

Gomez spoke up in a calm voice. "I'm afraid you paid too much for your guards. It's hard to get good help these days. They won't be coming to help you."

Looking at Jack, he knew the man was going to play it out to the end, thinking he had an advantage. "C'mon, Jack. Think about it. It doesn't have to go down this way. You sent me into an ambush, or tried to. I don't appreciate that. But maybe you were forced to do it. I'll never know. Either way, it doesn't have to end in a killing."

"You're lying. And I have some good men out there. There's no point in stalling."

Western writers had laid it all out before. Jack's shotgun was already in his hand, but he still practiced trigger control, his finger was not on the trigger. How long does it take to draw and fire? Back in the day, with four-pound Dragoon Colts, or even the shorter barreled Colt .45s that came later? Way too long. But today? With well-schooled shooters? One-quarter of a second. Sugar guns. He'd seen it done. Barnes practiced it for Cowboy Action contests. It would have to be a headshot. Anything else would allow Jack to fire. A headshot would cut his strings like a puppet. All he needed was a distraction. It was spooky how Alina read his mind.

"Jack?" Alina was wearing a white blouse. A strange choice of color, given their activities would likely lead to blood spatter. It already had a few red streaks on it. "You like the way I'm put together?" Slowly, she brought her left hand up to undo the top two buttons. "Maybe we can make a deal. You like to trade, and I don't want anyone else dying today."

He gave her a quick glance. "You can't talk your way out of this. What I want...I take."

"Of course you do. That's why you're so interesting.

And Jack?" Her voice was soft, gaze penetrating. "Tell me about those koi?"

"Those..." The incongruous comment threw him. "What?"

When Jack's gaze moved to Alina, Jim shot him. All things considered, his headshot was lucky. Alina's shot wasn't luck and followed a split second later.

Jack collapsed straight down, shotgun banging on the counter and making them all flinch.

Gomez broke the few seconds of tremulous silence that followed the pop from Jim's pistol. Alina's suppressed round was never heard. "Pablo, watch outside."

Shaking his head, Gomez strolled up to the counter, looking at the bodies. He turned to Jim. "That was damned good shooting, but you shouldn't have had to do it. I won't make that kind of mistake again, boss."

He put his hand on the man's shoulder. "It was my screw-up, too."

"Anyway," Gomez continued. "We got three KIA outside, two in here..."

Alina held up three fingers, pointing toward the corner of the room.

"Okay, three. You know those idiots had a couple of claymores rigged up? One was pointed the wrong way. I've never seen such sloppy amateurs. How they didn't blow themselves up I'll never know. I'll have some of my people come and comb these woods just to make sure nothing is left out there. They've got the equipment to do it. And if you don't mind, we'll secure this place. It's a gold mine for supplies."

"Anyway, Pablo and I will take care of disposal. We

saw a passel of feral hogs over between a couple of hills. The big red one must weigh over a thousand pounds."

Jim glanced around the room, remembering Big Red. Alina stood in a relaxed pose, but that was deceptive. She hardly blinked, staring at him, still maxed on adrenaline and waiting for his next move. Gomez was talking to Pablo outside on the porch. The smell of cordite and blood was thick in the air, along with the smell of death. A man lay dead at their feet who didn't need to die, killed by some innate stubbornness that wouldn't let him quit. And Roman Fielding was in the wind.

This was not the way he wanted his world to be.

# THIRTY

THEY'D BEEN KEYED up on rushing adrenaline at Trader Jack's. Now, Jim and Alina were let down, knowing the one they wanted, or the Shepherds wanted, was gone. Law enforcement couldn't be called for a BOLO, or be on the lookout, because there were no charges. All anyone could do was sit back and wait for him to show up somewhere. The best guess would be the Springfield area. It was a good bet he had contacts there and would be able to continue his drug trade.

A possible link would be if they could find friends of Trevon Miles. They might lead them to Roman, but it was a long shot. That would be a job better suited for Sally's minions.

Cruising well under the speed limit, lost in thought on the way back to the Lazy J, his cell startled them as it rang with an unknown number. Curious, he accepted the call on speaker and put the cell in a cup holder.

"Hello?"

The voice came through soft and fast. "Hi. You don't

know me...well, maybe. This is Marsha, the girl you talked to at The Gallows? The bartender?"

Alina gave him a raised eyebrow look and crooked smile.

"Hey, Marsha. What's up?"

"I think we're about to get fired and I could use some walking around money to tide me over. Do you think that might happen?"

On a certain level, he was glad this girl was innocent enough to not be a skilled negotiator. He already knew what she was going to say.

"I think I can help you with that. Do you have news for me?"

The ambient sounds muted, like she'd just cupped her hand over a receiver. "He's here."

"Thanks, Marsha. I assume you mean Fielding. We're on our way. Do me a favor. If he leaves before we get there, try and see which way he goes. It'll be a big help."

He floored the gas pedal as Alina grabbed the panic bar.

"I didn't get all that. Fielding?"

He glanced at her. "He's at The Gallows. A little bird told me."

"Yeah, well. That better be all you've done with your little bird. I've seen the girls that work there."

He tried to gauge her temper, failed, and laughed. "You're jealous? My god, she's like twelve."

Alina snorted. "And working in that bar? You know she had to turn at least one trick just to get that job."

It made him uncomfortable, knowing she was right. He gave her a tight grin before concentrating on the twisting road. She was jealous. That was a new...dangerous...wrinkle.

TWENTY MINUTES later found them at The Gallows. The parking lot was empty, except for Fielding's deep-red Dodge Challenger with the scoop hood and a couple of older vehicles he assumed belonged to staff.

"Alina, there's one side door on the east. That's the only back door I know about. You come in that way and I'll come in the front. The office is in the back, so let's try and move any extra people outside."

"Are we going to take him down? We only have Sally's word that he's dirty."

"That's always been good enough for me, but we'll let him call it. If he surrenders, I can have one of Sally's minions here by nightfall to take him off our hands."

Her glance was skeptical. "What will they do with him?"

"They'll probably pick him up in a chopper. Bounce up to about a thousand feet and see if he can fly." He shrugged. "Or they'll take him somewhere and squeeze him to see what he knows about terror groups or cells. Maybe a capture would be a good thing...considering."

She started to walk away when he grabbed her arm. "Please be careful. There's no telling what we'll find in there. A big shootout will get unnecessary people hurt. Understand?"

Her palm cupped his cheek. "You're telling me to be careful? How sweet."

"Do you want my extra Glock? It's got more bang than your Ruger."

Shaking her head, she smiled. "Nah. This is what I'm used to. Don't get all maudlin on me now, cowboy. We have a job to do. Let's get it done."

He watched her walk toward the side of the building and wished he felt as confident.

———

JIM STOOD inside the door of The Gallows, his Glock in one hand, held by his side, waiting for his eyes to adjust to the gloom. Marsha was behind the bar and started to say something, but he held a finger to his lips. The room seemed deserted, chairs upside down on tables, the odor of disinfectant heavy in the air. She started to speak again, and he shook his head.

The side door creaked open, and Alina moved quietly into the room, nose wrinkling at the heavy smell. There was a door to a back room that he assumed was the office and a staircase going to a second floor. He turned to Marsha as he got close to her and spoke softly.

"Where is Roman?"

She looked at his pistol a moment with impossibly round eyes, took a shuddering breath, and then pointed toward the door in the back.

"Is he alone?"

She swallowed a couple of times. "Yeah, I think so. Some blond chick was here for a few minutes, but she left already. I could have told her she wouldn't get a job. Too old. Good looking, though."

He nodded. "Anyone else here that we should know about?"

To punctuate the question, a thin shriek came from upstairs and then the sound of a slap.

His shoulders slumped. Nothing was ever simple. "Who is up there?"

Marsha was shaking, hardly able to speak, still staring at his pistol.

Alina leaned over the bar and placed her hand on the girl's arm. "What's going on?"

"MaryAnn...the day waitress. One of Roman's men came in, grabbed her, and took her upstairs. They've been up there a couple of minutes." She shuddered again, her voice pleading. "Can I go now? I'm gonna pee my pants."

He placed a hundred-dollar bill next to her hand and tapped it with his finger. "Thanks for your help, Marsha. Don't stop here, go across the street."

The girl scurried out the door, and he caught Alina's gaze, pointing upstairs. He'd have to trust her to handle whatever she found. She nodded and walked to the stairs. From the angry voices coming from the upper room, stealth would not be needed.

Moving to the office door, he gently turned the knob and pulled it open. One glance was all it took. The room wasn't large, just a desk and chair with a file cabinet in a corner. A large safe stood against the wall and behind the desk, with the door open. A huge man sat in the chair facing the safe, he assumed it was Roman. He also assumed the man would hear the door open, but he didn't move. The way he was slumped in the chair made Jim think he'd have to refer to it as a body. Even while sleeping, you have muscle control. This body was too...settled.

Keeping his pistol pointing at the man, Jim moved around the desk. The front of Roman Fielding was covered in blood, a good part of which was pooled around his feet. It looked like stab wounds under his sternum and then in the groin. He'd bet every penny in his bank account that there would be wounds to both kidneys from the back.

His best guess would be that someone knocked on the door. Roman probably walked to the door, opened it, and not seeing anyone threatening, turned to walk back to his desk. It was his fatal mistake. Although, if his guess was correct, it might not have made any difference.

He left the office, careful not to leave footprints, and was surprised to meet Barnes barging through the door. Helpful Marge must have called 911. Maybe he should get his money back.

Both men had raised their pistols but holstered them when they saw each other.

Barnes tried to see past Jim. "What happened?"

"Roman is dead." He watched his friend closely, knowing what he'd think. Barnes had heard Sally's assignment along with all the others.

He looked disgusted. "Couldn't you find a better...?"

Jim shrugged. "I didn't do it."

Before Barnes could reply, a body came tumbling down the stairs in a loose roll, followed by Alina. She dragged the unconscious man away from the bottom step by his heels and then held her hand out. "Zip ties?"

Handing a couple of them over, Barnes's gaze was swiveling between them. "What the hell?"

She looked at Jim. "You said no shooting, so I didn't."

"Barnes?" She paused, catching her breath. "This fine upstanding citizen dragged a waitress upstairs and was getting ready to impress her with his charm—at the point of a gun, I might add. I kicked it under the bed."

Hearing a siren approaching and the high-low warble of an ambulance, Barnes glanced outside before asking. "Is she alright?"

"She damned near got raped." Alina gave him an annoyed look. "So, no. She's not alright."

Tires skidding on gravel drew their attention to the front door. As she came bouncing in, Officer Crewes was directed upstairs. "There's a girl on the second floor who was"—he glanced at Alina who shrugged in return—"possibly raped. Take care of her and secure a firearm that was kicked under the bed. We can match it up with the clown that accidentally fell down the steps. Then get PJ to come drag this asshole back to a cell. If he ever comes to, read him his rights."

Barnes turned to Jim. "Wanna show me Roman?"

"Not really." Jim shrugged, pointed at the office, and then sat at the bar. "I've seen him already."

Alina went around the end of the bar to an upright cooler and brought back three beers. They sat without talking until Barnes came out of the office, closing the door behind him.

Standing in front of them, he said. "Show me your hands, both of you."

When they complied, he remarked. "No blood on your hands, and that was messy in there. Alina, I assume the blood on your blouse isn't from here?"

Jim spoke up. "We had a bit of an altercation out at Trader Jack's. It's taken care of."

"You can tell me about that later if I ask. So far, I haven't heard anything about it." He glanced at them. "So, if you didn't kill Fielding." Barnes took the third beer, contemplated it a moment before taking a huge swallow, and then asked the obvious question. "Who did?"

Jim glanced at Alina before he replied. "We seem to be making a lot of assumptions today, but I do have a theory. Marsha, the bartender with the small bladder, said some blond chick left just before we got here. After we came in, Alina went straight upstairs and I went to the office. He was already dead."

Barnes nodded, taking another drink. "From what I've heard and seen, Roman's manner of death looks suspiciously like the way Dickie died."

"I'd say you're right. Dickie beat that farmer into a coma, and I'm sure Roman told him to do it—he probably helped. We'll never know about that for sure."

Barnes was examining his beer bottle. "Thinking of the community as a whole, it looks to me like this random act of violence was self-limiting and has reached its logical conclusion. I also have it on good authority that the local judges are social distancing in their homes and don't want to be disturbed."

Jim gave a relieved glance to Alina and then at Barnes. "Oh, it wasn't random. But I agree, there's no danger to society."

Barnes drained his bottle and placed it on the bar. "This person we're trying not to mention...male or female?"

"Definitely female. A widow."

"What's your take on her?"

Jim thought a moment, glancing at them both. Alina seemed highly interested in his answer. "Unknown. I've only spoken to her one time, and she was grieving with her daughter. All I know is it'd be safer with her on our side rather than being a loose cannon—especially not knowing what kind of cannon she is." He paused. "As it is, her pastor told me she has relatives in KC and may move there. This may be the last we hear of her."

Barnes grinned at them. "Well, good. We'll leave it at

that. The underbelly of this county is starting to thin out. With all that's gone on, it does send a message. Limestone County is a tough place for a drug dealer to make a living. Or, in general, a tough place to break the law."

"That being said." His level stare took in both. "If my position is made official, we're going to have a serious conversation."

# THIRTY-ONE

JOSH BARNES MADE a dust trail up the drive in a sheriff's Interceptor SUV, nearly going airborne over some of the dips and potholes. Skidding to a stop, he exited the vehicle and stomped up the steps to the porch. Without saying a word, he grabbed an empty glass. Holding it up to look for dirt in the bottom, blowing into it, and inspecting it again, he opened the cooler to fill the glass with ice. Adding tea to the process, he set his Stetson on the table and settled into a chair with a deep sigh.

Jim glanced at his friend. "Rita did it better. You came in on four wheels and missed most of the potholes. I can only give you a seven on style points. Best I can do."

Barnes gave him a pained expression. "She had more practice. Besides, I just don't have that kind of anger in me."

Nodding, Jim put his feet up on an extra chair. "So, how's the world outside the Lazy J? Congratulations on taking the new position of sheriff, by the way."

Barnes saluted with his tea glass. "Thanks, but it's a

temporary appointment and has a definite expiration date. Leaving that aside, life outside the Fishhook is going reasonably well. Rita will make a full recovery and be back on the job in a few months. I might stick around as a deputy after she gets back for safety reasons. Being your friend is too dangerous, I might resign from that position."

"Wifey?" He gave Barnes a concerned look.

"She finally came home when I promised to strangle you in your sleep with a pillow. I don't know why that particular method appeals to her. Kinda makes me want to throw away my own fluffies. Anyway, I've got her shacked up in a new house. A contractor had just built it on speculation, and then the market fell through. I bought it cheap. The downside is... she loves the kitchen and I'm gaining weight. I think she figures that if she can't stop me, she can slow me down."

"Sweet. Pillows, huh?" He shook his head, smiling at his friend. "And the world?"

Giving a monstrous sigh, Barnes frowned. "Well, now that our wonderful population is rioting in all the major cities, the panic over the virus has all but disappeared—which is bad because it's the real thing and shouldn't be ignored. Other than that, it's about what you'd expect. The food shortages did not go away. The government idiots are trying to figure out how to ration gas, which is ridiculous because so many truck drivers are staying home and already limiting supply."

"This is really good tea." He paused for another drink. "The electrical grid is going down over parts of the country, mostly from neglect—linemen and workers are staying home. I don't think there was any kind of EMP event, but even if there was, nobody is telling anyone anything. We could be in the middle of World War Three, and no one would know it. All we poor citizens know is that prices are up, food is scarce, and jobs seem to be walking away. Money's not worth a damn anyway. It's the perfect definition of snafu."

A looming civil war might be more accurate, but he didn't correct the man. The new mantra from groups in the country opposing the violence and looting in big cities was 'shoot transformers, not people.' Without power, it would be like medieval times—an army of discontent laying siege on a starving castle. There was time enough to discuss that with him and the added result of no electric power in the cities.

"So, with your new love nest in town, you don't need your trailer?"

"What?" Barnes cast him a sharp look. "God, I hope not. Not now. We can't travel anyway. Why? Want to buy it?"

Jim pointed down the valley at the four-wheeler making a dust trail toward them, sounding like a muted bumblebee. "I'm thinking we're about to have another boarder at the Lazy J Ranch."

"I think you're trying to start some sort of commune." Barnes looked at his friend. "Lazy J? Sorry, it still looks like a fishhook. Everyone thinks so. That's the new name, you may as well get used to it."

"You started that rumor."

Barnes snorted into his second glass of tea. "I call it like I see it."

As the four-wheeler drew close, Barnes slapped on his hat and glanced at Jim. "I called Sally for you and scratched that name off her list. She was pleased. I also told her I would take a dim view of any more shenanigans in my county."

"Shen...what?"

Barnes closed his eyes for a moment and then sighed. "Dammit, Jim. You've stacked bodies way too high. You can't sweep that many under a rug without making a mountain of problems."

"In all fairness, it wasn't all my doing." He gave his friend a sad gaze and shook his head. "And it couldn't be helped. You know that."

"Well, some couldn't. I'll have to take your word for the rest. I guess Sally was right. No plan or operation survives the first shot."

"You can take that one to the bank."

"Still." Barnes slapped the table. "Retire, dammit. That's an order. Tell Sally One-Eye and the Shepherds to take a hike. I'm out of here." As he walked to his vehicle, he tipped his hat to Jacy. "Ma'am."

She gave the departing sheriff's vehicle a curious glance as she settled into the newly vacated chair, dropping her medical bag on the floor.

He felt like he was giving interviews. Her face was blank, giving no hint of her mood.

"What's up, Jacy?"

"Things are godawful in town. I went in for bread and milk, came home with a box of week-old doughnuts I picked up off the floor. Some fat guy in cutoff overalls and no underwear tried to take them from me. He must have had a serious sugar addiction. I had to pull my pistol to get him to back off. How long will this crisis last?"

He shrugged. "You heard Sally's epistle. A week? A month? Depends on what happens. You've seen the news, what there is of it. Some places are shutting down.

Police are walking off the job in major cities, and who can blame them? The streets are out of control with no one patrolling. Hospitals have gone bankrupt after gearing up for a pandemic that didn't happen. Ironically, now it may happen. That's sad. The dominoes are falling. The economy is crashing and the vultures from overseas are lining up for a meal. The effects could last for years."

"Gee. You're just full of good news." Jacy stood in front of him, full of nervous energy, tears glistening in her eyes. "It's not any better at my house. I've been stupid. I put off shopping until this morning—I hate shopping. Now it's too late. We won't find much at the stores now, will we? Even out of town?"

It hurt him to see her in this shape. The loss of direction and hope is a bastard that sneaks up on you and lays waste to everything you hold dear. "Probably not. Especially if you tried to make it to the city. That would be worse, and I wouldn't recommend it."

She stared at him, tears finally escaping and rolling down her cheeks. "I'm at the end of my string. You don't know it, but on top of everything else going bad, hubby took a flyer. I tried to tell him about the rape—big mistake. He blamed me and took off. No one has seen or heard from him, not even his folks. I can't believe he'd leave his kids." Shaking her head, she sighed. "He's changed. I've been blind to that, too."

Pausing a moment, she continued. "You know? We've never made a garden, didn't have time. We don't row crop, so that's out. I guess me and the kids can eat hay with the horses and then butcher them for food. I don't know how long we can...? My boys..."

It was time to show her how he'd prepared for the coming storm. A little at a time, for as long as he'd been here, he'd go to a wholesale grocery and buy in bulk. At times it seemed like a useless endeavor.

"Check it out." He tossed her a set of keys and pointed toward the outside door to his basement. "Light's on a glow-in-the-dark pull chain."

She looked exasperated. "What? Why do I need...?"

He held his hand up to stop her. "Just humor me. Please."

The basement door creaked open as he watched a flock of turkeys pecking around in the field below, along with a couple of deer. They often used each other as sentinels. He'd need to set the scope on his rifle for that distance. Fresh meat would save using his stores and he'd been reading up on making jerky and preserving meat. They needed to get started on that soon, or others would beat them to it and deer would be hard to find.

A huge gobbler spread his magnificent tail and strutted around for a moment as the hens ignored him. He could relate.

Coming up the stairs from the basement, Jacy carefully closed the door and set the padlock. Settling beside him, elbows on knees, her sigh was long and drawn out. "You have enough supplies down there to feed a small city. I may have stolen some Spam and crackers."

His gaze sharpened as a yellow, feral cat came out of the tree line, stalking one of the smaller turkeys. Of all the things turkeys were afraid of—domestic cats were not on the list. Now, a bobcat... This would be fun to watch.

He glanced at her. "Just enough for me and a few friends to last a good while. But we need to keep adding to it."

She nodded, watching him closely. "And who will that be? Your friends, I mean."

"The team, of course. Josh Barnes and Wifey if they need to come. Pablo's family, although they're better prepared than me. That misbegotten and shot-up hellcat working in the garden—"

"I heard that!"

Jim turned to look at Jacy. "We'll need a medic, I'm sure—kids and all."

Her shoulders slumped, and then she straightened. "Thank you, I appreciate it. Probably can't come right away. Lotta decisions." She glanced around. "There are too many hens in the kitchen around here, anyway. Doubt if I want to add to the circus."

He shrugged. "I doubt the hens, as you put it, would have the same job. I don't see that as a problem." This was about the only thing he'd anticipated that worked out. "Before he left, Barnes bequeathed you his trailer. It has more room than you think. And don't worry about when to come. You'll know. We'll be here. Just call if you need us."

"One thing, Jacy." She was watching him intently. "Any medical supplies you can find, we need to stockpile, especially antibiotics for gunshot wounds, cuts, and the like. Maybe some more of those quick-clot thingies, just in case."

"Thingies?" Her look was sad, and then she nodded with a smile. "I can do that. People probably haven't bought out the veterinarians yet, and I'm sure that Trader Jack's will be a gold mine for stuff we need if Gomez will let go of it." She grinned. "I assume he's still holding that?"

He chuckled. "You assume correctly. We've done some discrete inquiries and can't find any relatives for Jack. Looks like ownership belongs to whoever can hold it. Gomez has a few of his cousins taking care of that. There's at least a pallet of MREs—meals ready to eat—if anyone gets desperately hungry. Since we have a working relationship, I don't see any problem with access."

"Alina told me she saw a pallet of N-95 masks. Why a trading post had those, I'll never know. I'm thinking the hospital can use those. I'm hearing about shortages already."

She was moving slowly toward him as he spoke.

"How about this? You're our medic, so that puts you in charge. Figure how many masks our group might have a need for, say in the next year. I can't imagine that would be much. Also, keep Barnes and the department in mind. Then if there's anything left, take them to the clinic. Any help we give, I'd prefer it to be local."

As he finished speaking, Jacy stepped into him, her kiss slow and gentle, tender with no hint of passion or promise—lasting over a minute as her tears salted their lips.

"You've given us hope on so many levels—prepared when we did not. For my children and for me...thank you." Stepping back, her voice was low and husky. "Don't tell killer I did that."

He cleared his throat before he could speak. "It's probably too late, but I'll try it if you want. She hears things I didn't know existed. I'm thinking she's part bat."

Jacy took a deep breath and called through the screen door. "Alina. Do I need to look at your shoulder?"

"Nah. I'm good, thanks. And I'm not a bat. Is your lip lock over?"

"Yeah. He's all yours." A soft touch on his cheek and Jacy dropped her medical pack in the basket on the four-wheeler, the embossed red cross faded, worn, and bloodstained. With a wave, she rode slowly down the valley. Maybe it was his imagination, but her back seemed a little straighter.

He felt movement behind him, turned, and watched as Alina moved toward him. Her thin blouse was wet with sweat, and she had a towel around her neck. Her wet hair was up off her neck in a topknot.

"This gardening crap is hot work."

He drew her into his lap. "It is. Know what? You're domesticating well. I'm proud of you."

She tightened her hold on him. "When people look at you, they don't realize how controlling you are."

"I'm controlling? I haven't had any say in much since you got here."

Her smile was serene. "That doesn't matter. So, are all the pieces in place to go forward? Barnes has the county under control? Your friends are taken care of?"

Gazing down the valley, the turkeys chased the yellow cat around the clearing. The tom blocked its entrance to the protection of the woods. He didn't know what a laughing turkey sounded like, but imagined they were doing it. Jim remained silent until she stirred impatiently on his lap.

She tried again. "Barnes said Rita will recover. She's doing alright?"

He nodded. "Sounds like it. It'll take some rehab. She's really going to hurt for a while." He knew that wouldn't be enough for her, knew she'd keep probing.

Her voice was still soft, her tone understanding—not what he expected. "You love her, don't you?"

He gave her an uncomfortable glance. "I suppose I always will to some degree. You can't switch something like that off, it takes time. But the feeling is not like before. It's hard to explain. Wish I could do it better."

Turning in his lap, she locked in on his eyes. "She doesn't love you."

For the first time, he was able to think about Rita rationally. Alina was right. They both thought they should have a relationship, but the spark wasn't there anymore. It was like they'd come together in war, had won it, but couldn't maintain the peace. "I know. Now."

"What about me?" Her voice had taken on a little girl quality. With her, he'd never know if it was fake or the real thing. He couldn't imagine her worried or anxious.

He gave her a long look. "I'm thinking that's more of a love-hate relationship."

"Well, then. Doesn't sound like boredom will be an issue." She moved into his arms, making room for herself, snuggling into a hug. "I'll take it."

————

A COOL BREEZE blew through the valley, bringing a mixture of honeysuckle, cedar, and fresh-mown hay from over the hill. As shadows extended behind them, Alina came out and nodded across the valley. Lights were coming on in his foreman's house. "I'm feeling left out."

He started as if someone poked him in the ribs. If there were such a thing as Spidey-sense, it was crawling up his back. It was nearly dark under the veranda as he gave her a guarded look.

"How so?"

"Juanita and Pablo have a house full of kids down there. They're so happy. I can hear them laughing from here. I'm thinking Jacy will be moving here soon. She has children."

He really, really needed to see her eyes to judge her expression. "I'm aware of that."

Her smooth hand caressed his face, fingers lingering as she pulled away. "Are you really? You do remember I'm quite a bit younger than you? There are other clocks at work here, not just the Doomsday Clock you worry so much about."

He stared at her a moment, thinking his mirror image must resemble a fish out of water, gasping for air. "Alina. This world is getting more dangerous by the day. We have no idea what tomorrow will bring. That is not a good idea."

"Dangerous? Yes, it is. But so are we. Think of all the things we could teach our children." She gave him a direct stare and then smiled and patted him on the leg as she went inside. "Supper's ready. I made your favorite. Apple pie is in the oven."

"Pablo has kids, so does Jacy. We can teach them." His voice sounded plaintive in his own ears, lost in the closing of the screen door and her laughter.

Fried chicken, mashed potatoes and gravy. Green beans. He checked his belt to ensure it was still at the same notch. He'd have to be careful, or his waistline would be expanding. He and Barnes were having similar issues. Were the knights of old kept home in this manner —when they couldn't fit into their armor or find a horse large enough to carry them?

He gazed at the door as warm light beckoned through the windows. Dishes clinked as they were set on the table. Had his life turned into a cliché? Could they hold on long enough to make happiness commonplace? This woman was an enigma inside an enigma. She was deadly as any soldier he'd ever met, yet talked of nesting—yearned for it, loved to garden and cook. And possibly the most dangerous trait of all? She was aware of her biological clock—and nesting.

One thing was true. Before turning over a new leaf, one should first look under it. Resisting the fight-or-flight adrenaline rush that coursed through his veins, he turned and walked through the door.

# A LOOK AT BOOK THREE:
## BROKEN ARROW

**A POST-APOCALYPTIC THRILLER FULL OF CONFLICT, HEARTBREAK, AND FAST-PACED ACTION.**

Jim Lane doesn't like the direction the world is headed. Everyone he knows—including his resident-assassin girlfriend—is telling him to withdraw from conflict. He's too jaded, too prone to violence, they say.

But everywhere Jim looks people are angry and afraid. And they're starting to take it out on one another with frightening regularity. With world conflicts breaking out, terrorists streaming through borders, prices going up, and fuel and food shortages growing by the day...things aren't looking promising.

Finally retreating to his secluded ranch near Stockton Lake to take care of his own, Jim is hellbent on finding peace. But when he's caught off guard by a rabid motorcycle gang who wants the area for their own, Jim begins to wonder if good exists anymore.

How can this shepherd rest when predators are constantly running rampant?

***AVAILABLE MAY 2023***

# ABOUT THE AUTHOR

Darrel Sparkman is an award-winning author of novels, novellas, and short stories. He's been included in three western anthologies, worked as a feature writer for *Saddlebag Dispatches* and blogged a short time for *Sundown Press*. His ideas come from a diverse past of serving as a combat search and rescue helicopter crewman in Vietnam and volunteer Emergency Medical Technician First Responder. He has worked as a professional photographer, computer repair tech, and was once part-owner of a commercial greenhouse operation and flower shop.

Darrel is enjoying semi-retirement and finally has that job that wakes him up every day—with a smile on his face.